Nicholas Royle was bo
of five novels, includir
and *The Director's Cu*
story', he has written n.
in a variety of anthologies and magazines. He has edited twelve
anthologies, including *A Book of Two Halves* and *The Time Out
Book of New York Short Stories*. He lives in Manchester with his
wife and two children, and works as a lecturer in creative writing
at Manchester Metropolitan University.

'An assiduous champion of the short story' — Laurence Phelan,
Independent on Sunday

'Royle is well known for his excellent short fiction' — *Starburst*

'Royle's… cool, steady prose sets a tone between Pinter and Derek
Raymond' — Christopher Fowler, *Time Out*

'Nicholas Royle writes at the very edge of genre, both at the
cutting edge and at the border with something that is rather
different' — Roz Kaveney, *TLS*

'He's the only writer I'd happily describe as a cross between Iain
Sinclair and Ian Rankin' — Stewart Home, *Big Issue in the North*

'His books are a tonic for our jaded palates' — Jonathan Coe

MORTALITY

short stories by

Nicholas Royle

A complete catalogue record for this book can
be obtained from the British Library on request

First published in 2006 by Serpent's Tail,
4 Blackstock Mews, London N4 2BT
website: www.serpentstail.com

ISBN: 1 85242 476 1
ISBN-13: 978 185242 476 3

Typeset at Neuadd Bwll, Llanwrtyd Wells

Printed in Great Britain by Mackays of Chatham, plc

10 9 8 7 6 5 4 3 2 1

CONTENTS

The Rainbow / 1

Dotted Line / 9

The Cast / 17

Christmas Bonus / 33

The Inland Waterways Association / 39

The Space–Time Discontinuum / 53

Flying into Naples / 61

The Churring / 77

Negatives / 99

The Madwoman / 111

Kingyo no fun / 123

Nine Years / 145

The Comfort of Stranglers / 149

Buxton, Texas / 161

City of Fusion / 177

Avenue E / 187

Skin Deep / 193

Auteur / 211

Trussed / 225

The Performance / 235

Acknowledgements / 245

For the Chisellers

mortal *adj.* 1. (of living beings, esp. human beings) subject to death. 2. of or involving life or the world.

mortality *n.* the condition of being mortal.

THE RAINBOW

In the days before the rainbow came and stayed, no one really understood what rainbows were or how they were formed. People knew enough so that when rain fell and the sun shone they would look out of the window or go outside. But once there, they didn't know which way to look. Towards the sun or away from it? It didn't seem to matter how many rainbows they saw, they always forgot which way to look the next time. It was as if it were the least significant detail. As soon as their random gaze fastened on the arc of the spectrum, all other considerations melted away and they became children again, lost to wonder.

The Rainbow of the Buttes Chaumont changed all that.

There was nothing unusual about the rainbow when it appeared to the residents of the 19th and 20th *arrondissements* on a sunny, squally afternoon in early June. Or there was nothing about it that appeared unusual. It did in fact turn out to be the most unusual rainbow there had ever been, because when the rain stopped and the sun continued to shine it didn't go away. It wasn't immediately returned to whichever great warehouse rainbows get stored in when not in use.

The rain stopped around 5 p.m. and a few of those people who were out and about expressed mild surprise when the rainbow failed to fade. Half an hour later, with the sun glittering in the puddles scattered around the many paths of the parc des Buttes Chaumont – and for that matter the streets of the *quartier*, cobbled thoroughfares and paved walkways alike – and glancing brightly off the surface of the ornamental lake, the rainbow still had not faded. People, more people than usual, made their way to the top of the artificial hill and the grand pagoda that crouched there with its views of Montmartre and the Sacré-Coeur and the north-east suburbs of Paris – and now the rainbow. Its mid-point seemed to be almost directly overhead. It occurred to some that it was the first time they had been able to stand underneath a rainbow rather than have no choice but to view it from afar.

Naturally, I joined those people making their way to the park. I first noticed the rainbow as I was leaving a *boulangerie* on the avenue Secrétan with a demi-baguette that I had purchased to have with my dinner that night. At this point it had already stopped raining, but I was aware that rainbows can sometimes linger while rain is continuing to fall in invisible showers. My apartment lay between the *boulangerie* and the rainbow in any case, opposite the library of the 19th arrondissement, so I walked in that direction. A demi-baguette was all I needed since I would be eating alone.

I approached my building with my key in my hand and stopped when I reached the street door. I looked up at the rainbow shimmering through the trees and, instead of unlocking the door, carried on walking towards the park. Why bother sticking to a schedule when you're the only one who will be affected by its being altered? I no longer had to worry about Gilles expecting me back. I could do exactly as I pleased. We neither of us had to worry about the other any more. Those days were over. Now I could please myself. I crossed the road and entered the park. All around me, neck muscles strained to allow people to look up at the rainbow. The ambient level of conversation was higher and more excited than normal. Strangers smiled at each other, even exchanged remarks. *Why hasn't the rainbow faded? What's going on?* Along with everyone else, I made my way up to the pagoda on top of the hill. I had to queue when I got near the top, but for once nobody seemed to mind waiting. Instead they chatted freely with one another. Having got over their awe and astonishment in a surprisingly short time, people became very relaxed with the idea of a rainbow that wasn't going away.

I stood at the top for ten minutes or so and no one jostled me to make me give up my place. Being that much closer to the rainbow, although still some distance away, altered the perspective. Now it was a little like standing underneath the Tour

Eiffel and following the curving perspectives with a giddy eye. It was quite a big rainbow, starting close to Notre-Dame des Buttes-Chaumont on rue de Meaux and finishing somewhere near place des Fêtes. Eventually, feeling lighter than I had on my way up the hill, I made my way back down the path in order to head home and cook dinner. Witnessing a miracle may be a moving experience, but it doesn't preclude eating. Or drinking. Without making any special effort I would probably have got through a bottle of Beaujolais.

Halfway down the hill, just before my path turned to the right, on the stone bridge ahead of me, I saw Gilles. He was standing alone, looking up at the underside of the rainbow. My breathing became shallow and my mouth turned into a desert as I thought about going over to him and seeing whether he would acknowledge me, but I knew that it would finally shatter my fragile heart if, among all these strangers who were swapping confidences and even touching each other on the arm as if to verify they were still alive, he turned away – as he had every right to do.

I walked away before he could look down and see me, and returned home.

The apartment had been cramped when the two of us had shared it, but it was a sad, abandoned place without him. The fridge had always been too full of his little bottles of German beer, but now my dried-up bits of cheese rattled around in it. With his CDs by Michel Petrucciani and Erroll Garner constantly playing, there had never been a moment of true peace, but now the endless silence threatened to drive me mad.

I tore bits off my demi-baguette and chewed them as I stirred a white sauce for my pasta. I opened a bottle of Beaujolais and drank half of it before I had even sat down.

The rainbow was all over the TV news. The politicians spluttered and made pompous pronouncements that should have been cut to spare them their blushes. The Church made much out of the fact that the northern end of the rainbow dangled tantalisingly above their outlet on rue de Meaux. Local residents and businesses had turned the place des Fêtes into a street party, presided over by the colourful shadow of the rainbow's southern end.

The science correspondents searched in vain for rational explanations, the meteorologists had their heads in the clouds. Best of all, as ever, were the vox pops. *It's just beautiful, it makes me so happy*, sighed a young girl with rainbow hair, dancing away from the reporter's microphone.

I slept badly that night, although there was nothing new in that. I had slept badly every night since Gilles had gone. It wasn't that the bed was too big without him, but that it was too cold and the wrong shape. I woke up thinking it must be morning, but it was dark outside and when I checked my watch I saw it was only 1a.m. Rather than spend an hour or two trying to get back to sleep, I decided to get up and put on some clothes.

The night air was surprisingly warm, like an angora cardigan draped about my bare shoulders. The traffic was light, enabling one to hear the gentle percussions of a thousand footfalls as more and more people flocked to the parc des Buttes Chaumont. I fell in step with them. No one spoke, but their silence was inclusive rather than alienating. Everyone belonged. In the night sky the colours of the rainbow were different. The shades were subtly altered and considerably muted. Standing beneath it, you imagined you felt its microscopic moulting pixels falling on your upturned face like a shower of glitter, but it was just a light breeze feathering the tiny stiffened hairs on the back of your neck. I went back to the apartment and slept like a baby for the first time in a week.

The next morning it was almost impossible to move from the apartment into the street for the outside-broadcast vans, their huge wheels up on the kerbstones, a rainbow-hued gallimaufry of cables snaking across the pavement. Short-bearded men in fleecy tops and baseball caps muttered busily into mobile phones as they strove to forge order out of chaos. Other men stooped under the weight of broadcast-standard video cameras. Still others hefted bright lights and fluffy mikes. A hundred reporters rattled off their pieces to a hundred cameras, all of them standing with their backs to the rainbow. Rank upon rank of photographers sought out the best angle, their tripods an aluminium forest. Inevitably, a handful of photographers started snapping the snappers, their picture editors having told them to come back with something different for once.

Policemen stood about, hands on hips, clearly unsure what role to play, content for the time being just to gawp at the rainbow. Overhead, helicopters weaved in and out of the great arc itself, their buzzing a constant drone that became almost unnoticeable. But then, from one of the aircraft, dangled a man on a thin wire. Lowered to the rainbow, he could be seen from the ground actually to touch it. A collective gasp went up from down below. He turned and waved at the crowd, then returned to his close inspection of the rainbow. Signalling to his pilot, who maintained his stationary position, he carefully moved to straddle the rainbow. Then, taking something from a tool-belt around his waist, he appeared to cut into the rainbow and remove a small section, no bigger than an ice-cream wafer. Giving a further signal to the hovering machine, he was winched clear. The crowd burst into applause. A thousand camera lenses glinted in the sunshine.

Need I mention that not a drop of rain had fallen since the night before?

I somehow managed to worm my way through the crowds to the gates and so into the park. In tiny pockets between the massed spectators, jugglers juggled and unicyclists unicycled. Fire-eaters ate fire, but they did it more or less for fire-eating's sake, since everyone around them was looking up at the sky with fixed, beatific smiles upon their faces.

I waded through to a slightly less crowded corner of the park, where a few enterprising characters had set up little stalls selling rainbow-coloured fruit lollies, rainbow-dyed T-shirts, rainbow-patterned yo-yos and rainbow stickers, transfers and temporary tattoos. Since I had not had any breakfast, I handed over ten francs for a rainbow lollipop and headed for one of the gates on the south side of the park. Glancing up at the lambent hues visible through the trees, I meandered vaguely in the direction of place des Fêtes, which I ultimately approached, with a wry smile, by way of rue des Solitaires.

Place des Fêtes had been turned into an open-air trade fair. The square was a riot of candy-striped awnings and trestle tables, individual covered booths and open-plan consultation platforms representing everything from merchants selling genuine broken-off pieces of rainbow to New Age gurus promoting their own ten-step plan to transforming your life with the rainbow's help. A handful of white youths in black bomber jackets glared sullenly at a stall set up by the Rainbow Alliance, which described itself as a broad-based, non-party-political group formed with the sole purpose of crushing the National Front once and for all. I added my signature to a long list of names scrawled on rainbow-printed paper, then thought about wandering over to the commercial stalls on the far side of the square.

Some people you recognise from a split-second's blurred view from behind, others you can stare at for half a minute and still not be quite sure. Gilles belonged to the former group. I spotted his back, moving through the crowd in front of me. The tiny whorl of hair on the back of his neck confirmed his identity when I got closer, but really I hadn't needed that confirmation – I would know him anywhere, even now. Perhaps especially now.

Once I had accommodated the sudden lump in my throat, I decided to follow him. He slipped easily through the crowd, pausing occasionally to look up at the end of the rainbow, which glowed and shimmered like a mellow firework. Fittingly, a fire engine stood near by, its ladder extension reaching up to the underside of a patch of orange. A fireman stood guard on the appliance itself at the bottom of the ladder. A couple of very tall cranes had been erected, like the ones used to get bird's-eye views of football stadia. From the relative safety of the pod at the top of each crane, officially sanctioned research scientists and rainbow data collectors worked at the colourface itself.

I looked down at Gilles and felt my heart loosen. He had been gone a week, no more. I had spoken to no one about it. There was, after all, no one who could console me. Nor could anyone bring him back to me. Somehow it felt longer than a week and yet at the same time I couldn't believe that seven days had passed since he had last been by my side. I had thought I had loved other men until I met Gilles and I realised I had never even looked beneath the surface of being with another person.

He hadn't changed. There was still that irritating tuft of hair that stood up from his crown – irritating to him, rather than to me. If he'd gone off with someone else, there would perhaps have been pressure to get a haircut. I got close enough to see that there was a stain on the sleeve of his shirt that had been there before. Tomato juice from the last Bloody Mary he had made for me after our last night getting drunk together. If he were still alive, he would no doubt have visited a launderette in the meantime.

I followed him to the stalls across the square, where his gaze ranged over the various gaudy chunks of rainbow. I watched his hand move from one to the other, hesitating then moving on. He withdrew his hand for a moment and I thought he was going to turn around and see me, but then he reached out and picked up a piece that graduated from indigo to violet.

A curious thing happened. As I watched over his shoulder, the piece of rainbow in his hand became less distinct. It seemed to dissolve. I began to feel light headed and had to look away.

I became aware of a general murmur around me. A murmur of consternation and, increasingly, dismay.

I looked up. The rainbow was fading. Its subtle dismantling had begun.

When I looked back to where Gilles had been, he had disappeared into the crowd.

DOTTED LINE

When my psychotherapist suggested I stop reading the obituaries, I laughed. I mean, he wasn't serious, was he? Apparently he was. Then cut down, he advised. Read them every other day. Still, it was one of the few actual pieces of advice he offered. I should have been grateful for it. Mostly he just nodded his head and agreed that I was in a bad way.

You're surrounded by it, aren't you?

What?

Cancer. Your father died of it five years ago. Your friend died of it more recently. Your partner's an oncologist. You're constantly fund-raising for cancer research.

I do a 10K run once a year.

It must seem like there's no escape from it. Like it's only a matter of time. Not a matter of if but when.

I looked at the baggy knees of his trousers. His polo-neck sweater could have done with a wash.

Precisely. Which is why I'm here. More than anything I want to stop obsessing over it. I want to stop thinking about it every minute of the day. I want to stop examining every bump and swollen gland and worrying myself sick. Perhaps literally. I want to stop bothering my GP with false alarms.

Mmm. Yes. Of course.

How much was I paying this guy? If all I wanted was someone to talk to, who would agree with everything I said, a phone call to the Samaritans would be a lot cheaper. Or I could stand in front of the mirror and talk to myself.

To be fair to the old bugger, he'd helped me isolate the reason why I was the way I was. Learnt behaviour, essentially. My father had spent his adult life fretting over pains and sprains. He had cancer just about everywhere it's possible to have it. Or thought he did. And then he went and got it in the only place it had never occurred to him to check. He was one of the 250 men a year who are diagnosed with breast cancer. And one of the eighty or so who die of it.

If I'd ever stopped to think about it, I'd perhaps have appreciated the foolishness of following in his anxious footsteps. But you don't. You absorb behaviour patterns. The abused become abusers. The children of chronic hypochondriacs end up mithering their GPs.

You're not your father. You're a different person. You don't have to behave the way he used to behave.

This was more like it. But while I can see the logic in that, I don't know how to stop what I'm doing. I need to get my head in a different place and I don't know how.

Thanks. Have forty quid.

When is your ENT referral?

Three weeks' time.

They used to call it going to see a specialist. My father was always going to see a specialist. We go and see the consultant.

The GP had referred me. Out of desperation, I suspected. It would be my second referral in two years, since moving to the area. The first had been prompted by a change in bowel habits.

Doctor, Doctor, I've got the shits. Like every morning.

There can be any number of reasons for a change in bowel habits.

I know, that's what worries me.

Cancer is by no means the most likely.

Could still be cancer, though? Could still be?

My better half thought the ordeal of an endoscopy might put me off seeking further referrals for imaginary cancers. Not that I have a problem with anal penetration, as he well knows. He was thinking more of three-day starvation followed by twelve hours of serious laxatives. Opening your bowels became unnecessary. They were permanently open. Stay near a toilet. Imagine you're walking through the Mersey Tunnel and you look up and see a trapdoor. You open it and sixteen tons of filthy water come cascading out. It was like that. Then hospital. The indignity of the rear-fastening gown. That doesn't fasten. The consent form. Sign on the dotted line. The sedative. Count backwards from ten. Ten, nine, eight…The remaining awake but not knowing about it. Not remembering. Amnesiac sedative. Date rape drug. The coming round. The all-clear. The euphoria.

I'd take the euphoria again, but leave the rest.

Perhaps you need that euphoria, my better half suggested. Sometimes I wondered how well we understood each other. He seemed wilfully to misunderstand my need for reassurance as if it were general, whereas it could not have been more specific, and he was the oncologist, after all.

I can't be your doctor as well as your lover.

You keep that beard, I can't see you being either for much longer.

The euphoria lasted. The changed bowel habits didn't go away. ISQ. But now I knew it was IBS, rather than RIP, I wasn't bothered. I remained vigilant. I always had a look. When I found myself fishing out a slimy fistful and delving into it with my ungloved fingers, astonished at how hot it was, because I'd seen some red in it, I knew I'd reached a low point.

It wasn't blood.

I would have to stop eating beetroot.

I stood in front of the mirrored cabinet door and stared at my reflection as I scrubbed my hands in the sink. I dried my hands, then opened the cabinet. There wasn't much in it. A tub of moisturising cream. Complimentary miniature shampoos. My father's ivory-handled cut-throat razor, which I took out and studied under the halogen light, then put back.

When my ear got blocked I went back to the GP.

He had a look down it.

There's nothing to see.

It's not constant. Sometimes it's right behind the ear. Sometimes under the jaw.

Dysfunctional Eustachian tube. Nothing to worry about. It will resolve itself spontaneously.

It didn't.

It went on for months and months. A year.

It didn't hurt, but it could be uncomfortable. And I thought it might be caused by a tumour, whether in the brain, the lymphatic system or wherever. Some days I wouldn't feel anything, then one day it would be back. I would wake up with it right behind my ear and the day would be fucked. Everything I did, everywhere I went, the sensation of the blocked ear nagged at me. You've got cancer, you've got cancer, you've got cancer.

Aware that it wasn't fair to subject my better half to a barrage of questions, I suggested we go out for a drink. He said I was drinking too fast. I could hardly wait to get it down me, he said. It wasn't a good way to handle the situation, he said. So then I went drinking on my own. I drank locally, but recognised too many faces, and there was only one thing I felt qualified to talk to them about, so I started going into town. I covered the Northern Quarter, from ice-cool style bars to boozers with flock wallpaper, and ended up walking down the middle of Thomas Street trying to focus on road signs, the names of shops, anything. On the side of a building was an enormous advertisement for a tattoo parlour located around the corner. Right underneath it was another ad, in a similar style, for a tattoo removal service at the same address. I found this hysterically funny, so funny that I crouched down in the middle of the road laughing at it, then threw my head back and fell off my heels, hitting the tarmac with a hard enough knock to open my scalp. Still I laughed. Small groups of people slowed down to stare and I tried to explain to them what was so funny, but I'm not sure they got it.

Later, walking back up Thomas Street, I realised the blockage had gone for the time being, so I started waiting for it to come back, ever vigilant. That was the thing, as I told the psychotherapist during my next session, I had to be vigilant.

If you catch it early enough you might be able to do something about it. Usually, by the time it lets you know it's there, it's too late. So I keep watch.

But you want to change this behaviour? That's why you've come to see me?

It's taking over my life. It's affecting my ability to get on with everyday life. But I also worry that if the psychotherapy has the desired effect, it'll mean I'll let my guard down.

Mmm. Yes. Have you had something done to your neck?

He shifted position, trying to get a better look.

I got a tattoo.

His polo-neck sweater still hadn't had a wash. How could I take advice from a guy who always wore the same clothes and never seemed to wash them?

What is it? Your tattoo.

I didn't answer.

You don't have to tell me if you don't want, but perhaps it would help to talk about it.

It's a dotted line.

A dotted line?

A dotted line.

Do you mind showing it to me?

I unzipped my top.

Does it go all the way round?

I turned round to show him.

Why did you have that done?

Isn't our time up?

If you want to stay longer and talk more, we can.

No, that's OK.

We all have to die at some point, but you mustn't let this stop you living your life to the full before your time comes.

Yes.

Good luck on Tuesday.

Tuesday was my referral to ENT.

I arrived at ten and sat waiting for an hour before being called for a hearing test with an attractive young South African audiologist. As he leant across me to place the headphones on my ears, his shirt eased away from his neck and I noticed the dotted line across his throat. It was faint, but it was there.

He gave me a device with a cable at one end and a button on the top, the sort of thing weather forecasters use when they want to change the picture.

Every time you hear a noise I want you to press the button.

OK.

I did well in the test, the consultant told me later. He showed me the graph. I had perfect hearing. Like that was some sort of consolation.

The consultant was very smartly dressed, unlike my psychotherapist. Shirt and tie. He shook my hand and asked me to sit down. It was a strangely high-backed chair, raised off the ground, something like a dentist's chair. Two women, one young enough to be a medical student, the other of indeterminate age, but with little trace of intelligence in her dulled eyes, sat in simple chairs against the side wall to my right. The consultant sat in front of me, but side on to me with his legs partly under a desk.

Please tell me what the problem is.

I told him. I told him everything. He listened patiently and was sympathetic. I liked him. He said he was going to have a look in my ears and up my nose. He did this. There was nothing to see. I noticed him looking at the dotted line around my neck. When he saw that I had seen him looking at it, he looked away.

I'm going to give you a local anaesthetic on the back of your throat, then thread a telescope up your nose to have a look at the Eustachian tubes and see what's going on.

He put a piece of equipment on his head like a hat with a bright light attached that made him look like an angler fish. It was quite a tight fit. He undid the top button of his shirt and loosened his tie. I saw the grey dashes of a dotted line around his neck.

He started to thread the telescope up my left nostril. It felt as if a tiny snake were entering my head. I looked at the consultant's desk and saw a pair of orange-handled scissors lying next to two sharpened pencils. I closed my eyes. The back of my throat had gone numb. It was difficult to swallow. I was reminded of the time I had taken too much cocaine and had started to panic. I told myself I wouldn't panic this time.

Swallow for me. And count to five.

I tried not to think about the shining worm working its flexible way around the inside of my head.

Swallow again. And sniff. Excellent. Very good. Now I'm just going to have a look on the other side. I won't have to go all the way this time.

I pictured the two women sitting against the side wall.

Excellent. OK.

I felt the device worm its way out of my right nostril and

opened my eyes. The consultant sat down and looked at his notes, then looked up at me.

I saw no evidence of malignancy whatsoever. I had a very clear view of both Eustachian tubes and there's no sign of pathology. So you can stop worrying.

OK.

Do you smoke?

No.

Drink.

Moderately.

Is your weight constant?

Yes.

I looked at the dotted line still visible inside his loosened collar. He fastened the top button and tightened his tie.

If you think about the sensation – about any sensation or pain – it will become more noticeable. Maybe now you will be able to ignore it? Dysfunctional Eustachian tubes can, in exceptional cases, be caused by a tumour, but those really are the exception. There's nothing to worry about.

As he stood up and offered me his hand, his collar shifted and I saw the edge of the dotted line again.

As I cycled home I replayed what he'd said over and over again and before I had even reached the end of Curry Mile I'd alighted on the comment he'd made about tumours causing dysfunctional Eustachian tubes in exceptional cases. He'd said he'd seen no evidence of malignancy, but what if the dysfunction in my case were caused by a tumour and there was simply nothing to see? What if the tumour was somewhere else, not immediately adjacent to the Eustachian tubes? Farther round, farther back, but still having an effect, still pressing on the tubes? I mean, I wasn't a doctor, I didn't know what was possible and what wasn't. What if the type of tumour he'd been talking about was not the same as the type he'd been looking for with the telescope? Saying there was no sign of malignancy was not the same as saying there was no tumour.

There was something else. When he'd asked me if my weight was constant I had answered automatically, but in fact I didn't know what my weight was because I hadn't weighed myself in months, because I was scared to. The last time I had weighed myself I had lost a couple of pounds. What if I weighed myself again and found I had lost more weight? What then?

I stopped at a red light and a black car pulled alongside with spinning chrome hub caps and thumping music spilling out of the open windows. An Asian guy in a baseball cap with a curled brim stared at me from the passenger side. He was wearing an unzipped tracksuit top with a white singlet and a gold chain. There was a dotted line around his neck.

When I got home it was lunchtime, but I wasn't hungry. I went up to the bathroom and weighed myself.

I had lost two or three more pounds. I knew what my better half would say, that I ate less these days, which was true, and that I took more exercise and ran around everywhere and never gave myself a break, which was also true. Nevertheless, I was losing weight. I was losing weight and I knew what that could mean.

I gripped the edges of the washbasin and stared hard into the mirrored cabinet door. I stuck my neck out and looked at the dotted line running around it. I felt the blood-flow to my head increase. A pulse throbbed in my neck, at my temple. I felt a faint sensation just below my left ear. The Eustachian tube. My jaw clenched. I remembered what the psychotherapist had said about how we all had to die some time and I fingered the dotted line on my neck. I watched as my hand went to the side of the mirror and opened the cabinet door.

THE CAST

Zsa had been coming to the weekly games for a while, so she was there when it happened. Possibly her presence had something to do with it, because I would have been trying even harder in order to impress her. But still, the point is you've got to be careful not to want something too much.

It was coming up to the end of the football season. Soon the authorities from whom we rented the pitch would be returning it to summer use by taking down the goalposts and corner flags. It was minor-league stuff, you see. We played in the park on Sunday mornings. But we were no less competitive than if we were were playing in front of the Kippax or the Stretford End.

I was better in goal than any other position but that's not to say there was no room for improvement in my game. In fact, that was true for the whole team, even my mate Docs, who played at left-back. I would rather have called him by his real name, which was Dave, but everyone else called him Docs and I didn't want to appear different. That's important in a football team.

The average age was about twenty-five and the other teams we played in the local league tended to be a bit older, but we gave our best, always competing strongly for the ball. We were still bottom and because there were teams waiting to enter the league there was the threat of relegation. This game was important: if we lost we would almost certainly go down. If we drew we would still be in with a chance. But that's the lot of a goalkeeper in every match he plays: you can't win the game, only try to stop your team losing. So it was vital I kept the ball out of the net. It was up to the rest of them to score goals at the other end and, given that we hadn't scored a single goal in the league all season, the pressure was on me to keep a clean sheet.

It was a bright cold day, winter sunlight sparkling in a few remaining frost patches, and our breath froze in front of our faces. Zsa had picked me up in her car and we arrived about the same time as Docs and a couple of the others. We exchanged hellos and I introduced Zsa to Brian and Stud. She already knew Docs; the three of us had been out for a drink once or twice. I fell into step with him, talking about work and what a pain in the arse it was to work so hard you just felt like falling asleep when you got home, and Zsa walked with Stud and Brian. Stud didn't get his name for nothing. I found myself keeping an eye on them at the same time as trying to talk to Docs.

'We've got to win today,' he was saying, but it hardly registered because I was watching Zsa.

I know what you're thinking: I'm one of those jealous, possessive types who watches his girlfriend whenever she talks to another man. I'm not actually, but you see the thing is I knew she was having an affair. Well, let's say I believed she was. I was sure of it. But I wouldn't have beaten her up or anything. I just wanted to know, so that I knew. That's fair, isn't it? I just wanted to know what was going on.

There are all sorts of signs. She stops listening halfway through what you're saying. Her gaze wanders. She tells obvious lies for no apparent reason and you can tell when you know someone that well. You see it in their eyes, that subtle glaze. Sometimes she smelt different. She took to eating mints.

But the thing was, I loved her. I really did. When I could see she was lying it hurt me. I was glad she'd come to watch the game because I knew she wasn't actually that keen on football. It meant something to me that she would be standing there.

Zsa had to wait outside while we went in to get changed. 'I'll walk around,' she said, leaning slightly towards me and not sure whether to kiss me or not. I felt a bit awkward in front of the lads and said, 'OK. See you in a few minutes. We're on the top pitch.' I ducked unnecessarily through the doorway.

The changing room was half full. Voices bounced off the walls. Taunts about professional football teams and the weekend's fixtures were tossed from man to man, across the bags and boots and shirts sitting in the middle of the floor. 'Hi, Cat,' someone said. My nickname, after Peter Bonetti. 'All right?' I answered, dumping my bag and squeezing between two bodies to get my arse on the bench. In the corner a discussion was going on. The subject was girls and what you would do if you found out someone was cheating on you, and as always in the changing room the exchanges were made at full volume.

'I'd give her an extremely hard time then find out who he was and go and twat him,' said Tim, a stocky Geordie who could outplay most of the opposition but always kept the ball too long and ended up losing it.

'I'd be so angry I wouldn't know what to do.' This was Tommo, a gangling centre-forward who looked impressive and nimble on the ball despite his height but invariably hooked his shots way over the bar. Not that I was in any position to criticise: the goal difference always reflected my own lack of natural goalkeeping ability. I was mostly enthusiasm, part instinctive lunge and no real talent.

'What about you, Cat?'

I'd always thought I'd be sad rather than angry. I'd let go of the girl and have no interest in getting at the other man. What's the point? If someone wants to go, you let them, and if they've gone off with someone else you have to conclude they want to go. There's no point being angry. It's not as if you'd want to make them stay, because they've betrayed your trust. I don't know, maybe you can't buy this. Perhaps I was just too together to be true, but that's how I felt.

I shrugged. 'I was thinking about the game,' I said lamely.

'Where are my shin pads?' Docs asked. 'Why do I lose everything? I've lost my shin pads.'

It was true. He was always losing things. Someone threw him a spare pair.

I really had got myself quite worked up about this game. It was more or less up to me to save the team from relegation. I love goalkeeping. There's something about the particular responsibility you feel as the last man. The thrill and the satisfaction of making a spectacular save far outweigh the excitement of scoring. Every keeper has a favourite type of save and although of course they should prefer the opposition never to have a shot on goal they secretly long for an opportunity to try to make their favourite save. But they must achieve success in this or they'll be left crumpled in a heap in the six-yard box like last week's washing. Like every other keeper, I have a favourite. Or more to the point, a save that I had never quite made and had always wanted to make.

We were beginning to move out. The passageway out of the changing rooms was dark and echoing with the clatter of studs. Outside the sudden sunlight blinded me and I had to squint up the hill towards the pitches. We left behind the booming camaraderie of the changing rooms and broke into a trot. Voices got lost more easily out here in the tense cold air. I couldn't see Zsa anywhere but it shouldn't have mattered: I was with the others and soon we'd be playing, melded into a perfect group working together to one end. What better way to spend a Sunday?

'What will we do in the summer?' I asked Docs.

'Baseball,' he replied promptly. 'Or softball. I've even bought a bat. We've got to do something.'

He was right again. We had to keep the team together for the autumn, provided we managed to stay in the league.

We kicked around for a while and I did what I always do, using up all my good saves and dives in the warm-up. It was a perfect day and I couldn't wait to get started. Docs volleyed a long shot in towards the goal which I dived for and pushed past the post. 'Nice one, Cat,' I heard him say. Sometimes I thought he used the nickname ironically but he was pretty much my best friend so that was OK. I returned the ball to him and then noticed Zsa entering my field of vision. She walked down from the top of the hill, sunlight making her a blurred silhouette, but I could spot her at any distance. She didn't look all that different from any other woman wrapped up warm in a thick coat, furry hat and jeans, but when you know someone as well as I knew her, you know they're coming even before you've seen them.

She was standing just behind the touchline a few feet from the goal as we kicked off. I took my eye off the game to smile at her. She smiled back but there was something not quite right about it. Like a mask that was slightly crooked. I watched the game. Docs was chasing an attacker into my third of the field. 'Played, Docs,' I shouted as he dispossessed the attacker with a sliding tackle. I looked round at Zsa. She was clapping. There was a throw that went to Stud and he passed it back to me. I collected with my feet and took the ball to the edge of the area, then picked it up and gave it a good kick up the park.

Zsa was still smiling as I walked back to the goal line. Still smiling or smiling again. These days she was a bit like someone playing a part instead of the real person. She had all the gestures and knew what to say but there was something that left me unconvinced. I don't know what it was that started me off thinking she was seeing someone else. Probably just a stray glance she wasn't expecting me to catch. Or an over-elaborate excuse for turning up late. Something like that.

Soon I was distracted from these morbid thoughts by the game. It had turned into a real contest, with lots of midfield tussles and attacks that generally fizzled out before they reached me. 'Docs is having a great game,' I said to Zsa.

'Is he?' she replied. 'They all look the same to me in those shirts.'

'Nice one, Docs,' I shouted as he intercepted another cross. 'Come on, Blues.' But Docs lost the ball and as red shirts bore down on my goal he hared after them, eager to make up for his error. There was a tough scramble in which I slid at the feet of two attackers and narrowly missed grabbing the ball. Docs fielded it safely back to me and I hit him on the back, panting for breath. 'Great stuff,' I said and rolled the ball out to Mike, who took it up the wing.

We swapped ends at half-time with the score standing at nil–nil, almost unprecedented for us, and we congratulated ourselves. In the team talk we said things like 'We've got to push up more and get some good crosses in for Tommo' and 'We need to run with it more and hit more first-time balls'. I pointed out that whenever I took a goal kick the only people moving for it were in red shirts. 'You mustn't expect the ball always to come to you,' I said. They nodded. I knew it would make no difference but you had to say these things: it was a sort of convention that made us feel like a football team.

Usually immediately after half-time you find out that one of the teams has raised the pitch of their game as if their oranges had been stuffed with steroids, and when we're playing, it's always the other team. Only this time it was us who picked our game up and took it to the opposition. We fought and we pushed forward, we didn't give up when we lost the ball. On the break they got in a couple of decent shots, which I stopped easily. We looked like a team who knew what they were doing and I think we all felt that it would bear fruit if we kept it up. We communicated, we passed into space, we started runs from deep positions and with about a quarter of an hour to go we scored.

What can I say? Think of the excitement when Geoff Hurst scored the winning goal at Wembley in 1966. We were euphoric. Never before had we gone ahead from nil–nil. We shouted praise and exhortations to each other not to lose the advantage. I even saw Zsa jumping up and down on the touchline. 'Who scored?' she wanted to know.

'Docs,' I said. Yes, it was Docs. He'd gone up for a corner and when the ball curled out he slotted it home with great panache.

The pressure was really on me now. There was a danger that we would become complacent, unaccustomed as we were to being a goal ahead. Within minutes they slipped a long ball through our defence and I had to punch a good cross away and concede a corner. They took a short one and their centre-forward tried a shot that again I could only deflect, but this time Docs was on hand to tidy up.

About five minutes from time they were crowding round my penalty area looking to get a cross in, keeping possession whenever our defenders tried to take them on. They looked better than they had all game. One of them made a short pass to a tall blond guy who earlier in the game had failed to get on the end of a couple of crosses and suddenly I knew what he was going to do. Out on the edge of the area he had a quick look round. There was no one free of a marker. Even as he swung his leg back to take the shot I imagined the trajectory of the ball, a gentle curve into the top corner of the net, and me lying in a sorry heap in the mud.

He struck the ball and I knew this was my opportunity. The ball could only have been in the air a second, two at the most, but from where I was standing time stretched. This was it. I might never again have the same chance to make my favourite save. I'd been waiting for this as long as I'd been playing football, ever since rainy school afternoons when I ran up and down the wing just dreaming of being in goal.

I longed to leap up towards the top corner of the net and meet the incoming ball with my outstretched fingers inches beneath the crossbar, tipping it over for a corner when every single person on the pitch had expected to see the ball sail into the back of the net. My boots would be at least two feet off the ground, I would be practically flying, making the subtlest, most vital contact with the ball to keep my team in the game. Afterwards they would gather round me, clapping me on the back and saying, 'Blinding save, Cat' and 'Great save, keeps.' That would be nice and I would enjoy it but it was the save that I had been waiting for, the acrobatic leap into space, the perfect timing and the ball tipped over.

The ball left the blond forward's foot and I leapt. My stomach lurched. I could see my hand stretching to meet the ball and the intersection of post and crossbar growing huge out of the corner of my eye. It was as if I were drawn there, as if it had been written that I would make the save. It was perfect. I felt the contact with the ball and for a final sweet moment the wind on my face and I knew the ball was safely over the bar.

Then I froze.

I suppose I just wasn't expecting it. You've heard about it happening to other people but you don't think it'll ever happen to you. Well, believe me, it just might.

One or two of the players stood open mouthed but most of them had either seen this happen to other people or they'd heard about it and they just hung around looking a bit pissed off that the game had been interrupted. Hey, well, I'm sorry, guys. You know, I didn't mean to do it. It's just something that happens if you want something badly enough and then you get it. Obviously the conditions have got to be just right, or just wrong, depending on how you look at it. There's got to be that fusion of complete satisfaction and ecstasy and I don't know how many different emotions. You can't plan it. You can just hope it never happens to you.

I had frozen solid, to all intents and purposes turned to stone, and yet I remained suspended in the air, my head about twelve inches beneath the bar, my arm outstretched towards the corner of the goal where I had tipped the ball over the top in what had obviously been a perfect save. This wouldn't have happened otherwise. My legs were tucked up beneath my body. I'd seen some of the great goalkeepers do that when making this kind of save and clearly I had managed to match my idea of what they could do.

Docs approached close enough to touch and tapped his knuckles on my leg. It would have felt harder than his own. Not exactly solid, the sound was more resonant, as if the leg were hollow. As if my body had become a cast of itself. Zsa came round the goalpost and gazed up at me, her eyes huge. Perhaps this was new to her. I hoped not because I needed someone who knew me as well as she did to help get me down in one piece. Or rather two pieces.

I heard some desultory discussion about the game and how it might be concluded. One of their forwards suggested simply playing on for the remaining few minutes, leaving me where I was. 'Don't be a dick,' said Tommo, for which I was grateful. 'What if you take a shot and hit him? You know what'd happen.' This subdued the other player and he looked round for the ball, just for something to do. He seemed to be embarrassed by my predicament, as if I had burst into tears in front of a packed assembly or dropped my trousers in a lift.

It should go without saying that I felt a degree of cool detachment from what was going on beneath me. There was nothing I could do to influence events. I couldn't speak or communicate in any way. I was a statue, a brittle cast of myself as I had been in that single moment of goal-saving. I thought I ought to be experiencing some anxiety but in fact I felt quite calm. I was reminded of the time when my car went out of control on the motorway and spun round and round. I had just sat there, aware that there was nothing I could do, everything would just go on with or without me. It could only have spun round for three seconds yet it had seemed like an eternity before it smacked against the crash barrier and I was knocked back to my senses.

The difference now was that the sense of eternity was stronger. My survival was in the hands of twenty-one men in football shirts – and Zsa.

'Can't we just move him and finish the game?' asked Stud. 'And then carry him back to the changing room or something?'

'It's not that simple.' I was pleased to hear Zsa's voice entering the debate. She was standing right underneath me so that I couldn't see her. My field of vision was that of the cast's. 'You have to break something off,' she continued. I was so glad she knew what to do. I resolved not to think bad things about her in future. If she had wanted me out of the picture it would have been so easy to keep quiet and see whether anyone else knew how to get me down. 'It has to be something he won't miss, like a bootlace or something.'

'Why can't we just pull him down?' someone asked.

'Try,' she said. She knew they wouldn't be able to.

A number of the biggest men gripped hold of my cast, however, and tugged. There was no give and they backed off, faintly disturbed or perhaps just irritated by the delay.

'The laces aren't free,' said Docs. 'There's nothing to get a hold on. Can't we just snap his foot off? It's just a cast, after all. It's not really him any more.'

I became frightened for the first time.

'Don't!' said Zsa sharply. She knew. She knew. 'Don't do anything. There's got to be something we can get at.'

Docs spoke again. 'Bob. Bob, can you hear me?'

It was the first time someone had talked to me rather than about me. But I couldn't respond.

'I'm sure it's all right to break a bit of anything off,' someone else chipped in, one of their players eager to get on with the game. 'It's not as if that's him. I saw a thing about it once. You snap something, anything, and that frees the cast. Then you take it to the bloke's flat and leave it there alone for a few days. And he's as right as rain. I've seen it. Don't ask me to explain it but that's what happens.'

'Don't come near him,' Zsa commanded. Thank you, Zsa. Thank you.

'Look, love,' the same fellow said. 'I don't expect you to

understand but we've got a game to finish here. We get him out of the way and finish the game. There's only a couple of minutes to play. Then we'll help you carry him home.'

'Hang on.' I recognised Brian's voice. 'We're without our goalie now. We can't play on without him.' This both pleased me and sparked my anxiety.

''Course you fucking can,' the other man said. 'One of you lot goes in goal. That's what you'd have to do if he was injured or something.'

'Shut up! Shut up, all of you!' Zsa shouted. 'I've found a fold in his shirt. I can snap it off and he'll be OK, but you've got to take the weight to stop him falling.' Zsa's all right, I remember thinking to myself. She's all right. I'm not exaggerating when I say she may well have saved my life.

I couldn't feel anything, of course, but I watched a group of them gather round beneath me and each take a hold. I heard a definite click as she snapped off the fold of my expensive goalkeeper's jersey and suddenly it was like the TV had been switched on and turned up loud in an empty house. Sensations rushed in through the hole in my jersey and I was buffeted, even though I stayed right where I had been since the cast formed: tucked away in the gloved right hand. Zsa did well. Not only because she chose to break off a piece of the shirt, but because she chose the shirt in preference to snapping off one of my fingers. It's so often fingers that are sacrificed in these situations. In my case that would have had far-reaching implications. It would have been like tearing a hole in the fuselage of an aircraft flying at 30,000 feet. You know what I mean.

They lowered the cast and me inside it to the ground. A guy in a red shirt had collected the ball from behind the goal and taken it to the corner flag. He was determined to restart the game. It hurt but in a funny sort of way I wanted the game to continue and for us not to lose, so that it would be worth it. The group who had lowered the cast to the ground were discussing with Zsa what was the best thing to do. Eventually it was decided that they would carry me to her car and Docs would go with Zsa back to my flat. Stud meanwhile was to collect my stuff from the changing room. But there was pressure from some of the others on Docs to stay and finish the game. So they carried me down to the car, laid me on the back seat and Zsa sat and waited in the driver's seat while Docs and Stud ran back up the hill and the game was resumed.

I sat there wondering what was going on in Zsa's mind and hoping we wouldn't concede a goal in the dying minutes of the game. Zsa didn't talk to me but I saw her looking at me in the rear-view mirror. Did she know I was able to hear? I don't know. She put a tape on. I didn't know who it was but she'd played it in the car before.

Docs reappeared, flying down the hill, his arms raised in victory. I heard him whoop. 'We did it.' He grinned at Zsa as she opened the passenger door and he jumped in. He turned and looked at me. 'We did it, Bob,' he said with a big smile. 'We bloody won. We've never won before and we won today. That means we won't go down. And it's thanks to you.' It was nice to be addressed directly and obviously I was delighted about the result but I could see that Docs was a bit uneasy about the cast. He seemed to want to touch me to communicate his pleasure and share the victory but didn't know whether to or not. Zsa settled it by starting the engine and swinging out into the road.

It was weird being driven home like that. Not only the whole cast thing, but lying in the back gazing at the backs of their heads, looking for all the world like those of a bloody married couple.

Zsa parked outside the flat, bumping the front tyre against the kerb in a way that would have made me wince. Together they carried me upstairs and laid me down on the grubby landing carpet to unlock the door to my flat. It was the first time I'd entered my own place in such a way. It all looked so different. Like a stage set all got up to represent my flat. The details were all there but they weren't quite put together right.

'What do we do now?' Docs asked.

Zsa had known all the answers up to now. 'We put him somewhere he'll be comfortable and leave him.'

'Comfortable?' Docs queried, possibly wondering where comfort came into it for a statue.

'Yes. Let's put him on the sofa. That's where he sits when he's at home.' She was right again. Nice one, Zsa.

So they left me there and walked out. It upset me a bit that neither of them said anything to me like 'See you in a few days' or anything. Something encouraging like that would have been nice. Still. I watched them go and Zsa stuffed the keys back through the letter box after she'd closed the door. She was that sure.

In fact, she had a spare set of keys to my flat but still I had the strong impression she knew I'd be out of there in a few days' time and back playing in goal.

As it happened it took only a day and a half. It's hard to describe those thirty-six hours. If you've been through this yourself you'll know anyway. So this is for anyone who thinks they might be losing it. What normally happens to you after you get drunk? And I don't mean a-few-beers-and-a-couple-of-glasses-of-wine drunk; I mean a-whole-bottle-of-spirits-and-maybe-half-a-dozen-tequila-slammers drunk. Like, paralytic. OK, you get the same thing after a heavy evening down the pub but just not as intense. What happens is you fall asleep. You come home, you forget all about drinking loads of water to pre-empt the hangover and you collapse into bed. You're out cold before your head hits the pillow.

But imagine if you came home and you didn't fall asleep. You have to deal with this drunkenness while remaining awake. Maybe it's never happened to you but you can imagine it. You're just not tired or you've simply got to stay up for some reason. Whatever. The process of moving from drunk to sober, which usually takes place while you're asleep, happens in full view of your conscious mind. It's not particularly pleasant.

Well, getting out of the cast is something like that. You maintain a high level of self-awareness, constantly asking, is this it, am I OK yet? Some people flip. They can't handle it. But like I said, for me it was relatively quick. One state recedes and the other fades in. You don't do anything; it just happens. But your mind won't shut up, going on and on at you, wanting to be able to get a grip.

There must be a moment when you cross over. When you come out of the cast and find yourself suddenly looking at it, thinking, what the hell happened? But it's like when you fall asleep after hours of trying to stay awake to watch the late election results or just because you thought it would be a crazy thing to do. You fall asleep just for a second, you think, and then bang, you're awake and it's four hours later and you've missed it, whatever it was. You feel cheated and stupid.

With me it was like one minute I was curled up inside the right hand, thinking, what's going to happen next, how will I get out? And the next I'm walking out of the kitchen into the living room and there I am lying on the sofa. Only it's not me. I'm me and that's the cast, now completely hollow and lifeless.

I kept it, of course. You don't throw something like that away. What more perfect souvenir could you want of when you were happiest? For half an hour or so I sat there looking at it, all sorts of questions buzzing round my head. But none of them really needed asking. The important thing was I had made that save, I had been that fulfilled, we had won the game. Now I was whole again.

But not quite.

I looked down at the goalkeeper's jersey I was still wearing. There was a small uneven hole in the material just below the badge with the three lions. In the same place on the cast was a rough edge where Zsa had snapped off a fold in the shirt.

I carried the cast up the stepladders and found a safe place for it in the loft. Whenever I wanted I could come up here and look at it.

I changed out of my football kit and had a shower. It was late afternoon. By the time I got round to Zsa's she would be back from work. I wanted to thank her for what she'd done for me. I drove round but there was no answer. I kept ringing for a while until someone poked a head out of a neighbouring flat to see who was making all the noise. OK, OK, I'm going. I had spare keys to Zsa's flat as well but I didn't know how long I'd have to wait. She could be out for the evening, I thought, and I wanted to see someone, a friend, anyone. I'd had quite enough of my own company.

Docs lived a few miles further out but his flat was nicer than mine or Zsa's. Being further out he could enjoy the luxury of having enough space to spread himself around. As I drove I thought about the game. It didn't matter that I had to call him Docs. He was my friend whatever we called each other. I parked across the street, noticing the light on in his window, and pushed open the street door, which was always left open. I'd warned him about the risks but he'd said it wasn't for the lack of trying to get his neighbours to cooperate. They were just lazy. It was too much trouble to give the door that final push.

I climbed the stairs to Docs' flat and knocked on the door. I knocked again but no one came. The light had been on so I felt sure he was in. Docs didn't leave lights on. I knocked again then bent down and pushed open the letter box. The hallway glimmered. The main room was at the end on the left. I could hear music as well. It was familiar but I couldn't place it. I realised I hadn't been round to Docs' for at least a couple of months. He'd been round to my place and we'd seen each other for the games, but I hadn't made the effort to visit him at home.

Anyway, the fact that he had music playing convinced me he was in but hadn't heard the door. Perhaps he'd had a particularly hard day at work and was having a nap. It crossed my mind that he could have got lucky, but this seemed like an unlikely time to be doing it. I knew what Docs was like after a day at the office. Mr Bad Tempered or what? So I reached in through the letter box and caught hold of the string with his spare key on it. I'd told him about that as well, but he'd said, 'When you lose things as easily as I do, that spare key is essential. I've lost count of the number of nights I've come home pissed as a fart and used it because it's easier than searching through me pockets.'

I unlocked the door and stepped inside. 'Docs,' I called gently, but there was no answer. The music was infuriatingly familiar but still unplaceable.

Do you remember I said how you sometimes know someone's there before you see them? Well, it's not always the case, because I felt nothing like that as I turned out of the hallway and into the main room. The first thing I saw was the CD player with the red repeat light on. As I took in the sight of Docs and Zsa cast in a lasting moment of mutual rapture in the middle of the floor I recognised the music. It was what had been playing in the car stereo when they'd driven me back to my flat, a statue on the back seat oblivious to what was going on.

I said that Docs had plenty of space to spread himself around. He had done just that with himself and Zsa. Their casts littered the floor at the far end of the room under the bay window. There were too many of them to count, like a sea of bodies. Clearly he gave Zsa something I couldn't. Perhaps if she'd said something, given me a chance to understand? But I'm kidding myself. I stared with morbid fascination at all the different casts, at the ecstasy on her face, the evidence of her complete abandonment to sensation. The awful traces of vulnerability on Docs' face, which I half pitied and half envied. Yes, I knew how he'd felt and I'd seen that look on Zsa's face before, but I guess it was all in the timing. Or something like that.

Don't ask me how they got out of their casts. I really don't want to think about it too hard. But they found a way. Lovers always do, after all.

But this latest cast was one souvenir they wouldn't get to keep. Feeling numb and empty inside, I went looking for the baseball bat.

CHRISTMAS BONUS

In the cold, brittle weeks towards the end of December, two strange discoveries were made within a few days of each other. Two closed spaces on opposite sides of London were broken into by demolition teams who worked with the eagerness of children tearing the wrapping off Christmas presents.

In Rivington Street, EC1, workers entered a boarded-up photographic studio that had hundreds of photographs pinned to the walls – photographs of the same girl – and, in the middle of the floor, a pile of ashes containing fragments of negative film.

While over in Royal Oak, another team sledgehammered their way into part of a former BR building to find a reasonably expensive camera attached to a tripod – in a room that had been sealed from the inside.

Since neither was a crime scene, no one dusted for fingerprints – the only conclusive evidence that would have linked the two finds.

Andrew Kerner blamed his eviction from Rivington Street on the Young British Artists, who, with the help of gullible collectors, crafty gallery owners and lazy-arse magazine editors, converted ideas into money faster than they could sign their names on Hoxton Square rental agreements. The swift transformation of what had for many years been an unremarkable, largely ignored, working-class district, in which artists, photographers and others had lived and worked alongside ordinary Londoners, had now started to affect the neighbouring districts. Kerner had read in a magazine that the Hoxton/Shoreditch nexus had already acquired its own name. More than one, in fact. Take your pick. Shoxton or ShoHo. NoSho, more like.

Rents hit the roof, and lesser mortals like Kerner hit the streets, priced out of the (art) market. He'd been in Rivington Street several years, using his first-floor studio as both living and working quarters. Being on the Northern line meant he could, if he wished, pop up to Archway and revisit old haunts. But the flat where he'd lived in the early 1980s, where he'd let a room to the projectionist Iain Burns and introduced him to the four film-makers who would change his life for ever (i.e. not very long), had been bulldozed.

The day he left Rivington Street, he removed or destroyed all his stuff apart from the prints of Jenny Slade, hundreds of them, which he pinned to the walls. He'd acquired the use of Jenny Slade, just then breaking into movies from modelling, through his association with the four film-makers who had done for Iain Burns. One of them, Frank Warner, had got him Jenny Slade, in return for his promise to look out some of his old stills from the film they'd made of Burns's 'suicide'.

'Why Jenny Slade?' Frank had asked him.

'She reminds me of someone.'

'I didn't know you knew anyone.'

Jenny Slade blanked him until he lifted the camera and shot off a few frames. Then she went down on the lens, date-raped the camera. She strutted, pouted, snarled. She spent half a day in the studio and would do whatever he asked, except that she didn't need leading. She prowled around the studio like a panther, her hair jet black, her skin as smooth, in the diffuse light from a series of high narrow windows, as a pelt. Kerner felt himself become invisible, redundant, edged out of the frame. He was a voyeur. He knew, as the camera moved slickly as oiled machinery in his hands, as he ejected a spent film and loaded a new one in seconds, that this was the best work he had ever done and would ever do. But it was kind of beside the point. He shot her until he could no longer dry the sweat running down his face, until he ran out of film. At the end of the session she put her clothes back on and he gave her the old stills Frank wanted. She left the studio and stepped into a waiting cab. It was only once she'd gone that

Kerner realised she hadn't spoken a word the whole time she'd been there.

In a sense she'd remained unseen as well as unheard, because although he'd been looking at her, he'd seen someone else. Someone she resembled. The colour of her hair, the shape of her eyes, were the same, but it was more in the way she carried herself, the jut of her chin, the look she gave you. She reminded him of someone he had once known, someone long gone, someone with whose abrupt loss he had never come to terms. Anya. Poor, lost little Anya, who would never let him photograph her, and now it was too late. Doing the shoot with Jenny Slade, he hoped, might help him to bury the dead.

He spent a week developing and printing the results, blowing them up to ten by eight and poring over them morning, evening and night. He didn't hang a single one until the day he left.

Once he had cleared the space of any last trace of himself and thumb-tacked the images of Jenny Slade to the wall, Kerner burned the negatives, leaving the ashes in a little pile on the floor, and sealed the studio from the outside. He nailed boards across the doorway, determined to protect the space from intruders, his hope being that the planned redevelopment of the block would not follow on immediately, allowing some kind of energy to build up in the enclosed space.

It was after he left that the flickering began.

Without money, he couldn't rent. Rivington Street had eaten up the last of his cash. He wandered west, since half of that side of London seemed to be up for major refurb. From White City to Paddington, along the Westway, traffic cones, tarpaulins and scaffolding gave the game away. Cranes punctuated the skyline, skeletal outlines softened by fairy lights. He probed the interstices until he found an open window into a condemned railway property at Royal Oak.

He chose a space on the first floor that seemed to offer a balance between the considerations of seclusion and escape, and held a house-warming party to which he, the only guest, brought three bottles of Laphroaig lifted from Praed Street.

When he woke up, he didn't know what day it was. Trains rattled past the dirt-streaked windows every few seconds, bright morning light caught in the train windows and thrown back at his own. A reflection of the passing carriages flickered across the opposite wall, but there was a further flickering in Kerner's eye. It felt like a nervous tic, but when he stared into a fragment of mirror in one of the building's shattered bathrooms he couldn't detect any movement. He gazed at his gaunt image: the ponytail and whiskers of earlier, less solitary years had given way to a severe look of shaved head, permanent stubble, grime gathering in his crow's feet and purple shadows under his eyes.

The flickering came and went. Whether its return coincided with the passing of a train, he couldn't be certain, so frequent were the trains, so regular the interferences. His head pulsed with pain, his mouth was dry, his stomach invaded by a nauseating sense of an expanding velvety darkness. He lay down again, but instead of sleep came a series of hypnagogic hallucinations: a pile of smoking ashes on the floor, a curled edge of film, sprocket holes, a passing train, Iain Burns's body wrapped in coils of celluloid – a twentieth-century mummy – Jenny Slade's flat stomach, identical to Anya's but for the absence of a birthmark in the shape of a comma.

He slept and dreamt that he was back on the set of *Auteur*, the suicide film, reprising his role as still man. In Iain Burns's place on the battered old sofa sat Anya, naked but wrapped from head to toe in videotape.

He woke in darkness, convinced someone was in the building with him. He tried to move but couldn't. The flickering scattered an iridescent sparkle over the cobwebs in the corners.

He felt the darkness in his stomach creeping up to cast a shadow over his lungs. As sleep stole over him once more, he noticed that his breathing had become slow and shallow.

The noise of the trains woke him in the morning. As he watched the sun-bright image of the passing carriages on his wall, the breaks between one frame and the next shuttling back and forth to give the illusion of motion pictures, he remembered the moments that had never been captured on film because she would not allow it. Anya leaning over him in bed, her white man's cotton shirt open to the waist. Anya standing by the window watching the rain, unaware of his gaze. Her eyes in candlelight. The curve of her spine as she bent to pick up a book from the floor.

With the help of the light playing on the wall, they processed in an unbroken series, a short film playing inside his head.

Kerner had slept in an awkward position and one of his legs had gone dead. His left eye was gummed shut.

Somewhere, at some stage, his camera had gone missing.

He made his one-legged way, painfully, to what was left of the bathroom. There was no water to wash his eye and his throat was too dry to produce saliva. Leaning heavily on the cracked and dusty washbasin, he stared into the shard of mirror. His skin was tented across his cheekbones, new planes emerging, sharper angles. It wasn't just the effects of dehydration and starvation: he couldn't ignore the fact, even if it made no sense, that his physiognomy was changing. He stared intently through the flickering of the good eye at the gummed-up eye: the lashes were encrusted with thick deposits of yellow sediment. He doubted he'd be able to open the eye without tearing the delicately veined skin of the eyelid.

With the last of his strength he tore the last piece of mirrored glass off the wall and slipped it in his pocket.

He returned to his spot and sat watching the shifting light on the wall. His dead leg had not recovered. He had read, in the same magazines that filled pages and pages with fashion 'stories' shot in Hoxton, about the Death of Affect, but he had never understood it. He thought now that he was beginning to, but all too late. Emotion drained from him like moisture from a corpse in sand. He sensed his memories fading like reverse Polaroids, and, despite a general low-level ache, he no longer felt any real pain. He placed the mirror fragment on his tongue and swallowed it.

The weight of his body settled on its two arms and one good leg, while the aperture that was his single functioning pupil remained open, so that light could still get in.

One of the lads on the demolition team, left alone with the camera for a moment while the foreman went outside to get a signal on his mobile and the other lad took a piss, flipped open the back

and palmed the film. He took the Tube back to Shepherd's Bush,
where he rented a room in a house draped with Australian flags.
Not that that narrowed it down in Shepherd's Bush, the new
Earl's Court. The constant reminders caused him a little distress,
but being among compatriots was a comfort. Christmas was a
bummer of a time to be dumped, but then Vicky had always been
good at bad timing.

He got the film developed, not expecting much, so the glossy
prints of the beautiful girl with the raven hair were a welcome
surprise. They caught her climbing in through the window,
nervously approaching, then visibly at ease with the camera,
smiling, losing the clothes. Flat stomach, comma-shaped
birthmark. He laid them out on his bed. Not a bad Christmas
bonus.

THE INLAND WATERWAYS ASSOCIATION

If Birmingham was the Venice of the Midlands, in Sir Reginald Hill's appropriated phrase, what did that make Venice? The Birmingham of the Veneto? From where I was sitting, sipping a glass of *prosecco* at a café terrace overlooking the Grand Canal, I couldn't see it catching on. The bright sunlight and fresh breeze turned the broad expanse of water into an inverted version of the Artex ceiling in my Yardley flat, white and choppy. I tried to picture the Grand Union Canal at the end of my road midway between Acocks Green station and the Swan at South Yardley and found that I could do so all too easily. Tench-green, oxygen-starved and barely two rod-lengths across, it would have a job making it on to the World Heritage list. To be fair, though, I'd seen canals in Venice that were not dissimilar. Only the setting was markedly different.

This was my last night in La Serenissima, the so-called most serene republic, my last night of a week-long visit that I had nearly cancelled. Only two things had stopped me: first, the fact that the travel company offered no refund in case of cancellation, and second, Martin Weiss.

I left the café terrace and headed back towards the hotel to shower and change before dinner.

Martin Weiss was a friend from school days. In fact, although he and I had been at school together in Acocks Green, we hadn't been particularly close. But then we found ourselves attending the same college at London University. Anything to get out of Birmingham had been pretty much my approach to further education, whereas Martin, if our conversations in the union bar were anything to go by, missed the Midlands and looked forward to going back as soon as he'd completed his degree, if not sooner. It seemed to me the particular area of London in which we'd chosen to study, the East End, was not much different from Birmingham anyway. Urban deprivation, a divided community, the subtle, yet constant, threat of violence: Martin should have felt at home.

For the first few months, Martin and I saw little of the neighbourhood, in any case, since we spent most of our free time in the union building. I would be reading, either set texts or potboilers, but I made little progress owing to Martin's constant interruptions as he showed off his talent for solving the *Daily Telegraph* crossword. Martin didn't read the *Telegraph* (I don't think he read a paper at all; he got it for the crossword), but that didn't stop the Labour Club types who controlled the union glaring at him disapprovingly. He made no effort to justify his choice to them.

'The *Guardian* crossword's too fucking hard,' he confided. 'Now, what about three down? "Bubblegum, chewed, loses fellow but gains one in country." Seven letters.'

'I struggle with the *quick* crossword,' I said.

'It's easy. Look.' He pointed with his pen. 'Bubblegum, chewed, i.e. anagram of bubblegum, but minus a word meaning "fellow". That's "bub". Then you add "i" – that's "one" – and the answer is the name of a country. Belgium. See? Piece of piss.'

'You're not just a pretty face, are you?' I said, smiling at him.

There was no warmth in his hazel eyes as he replied sharply, 'Fuck off back to GaySoc.'

The college had a good reputation for science-based courses, but I was doing English, while Martin was doing – or, to edge closer to the truth, *not* doing – history of art. He didn't last long. A term and a half into the second year, Martin vanished for two weeks, then reappeared, not as a remorseful student begging the vice-dean to let him stay, but as the featured artist of a one-man show at a scabrous basement gallery in Bethnal Green. His blurry photographs of East End murder sites, under the title *Echoes of the Past*, showed that he had, after all, found something to hold his interest in Whitechapel: the district's lasting association with the crimes of Jack the Ripper.

The show was both an inauspicious debut in the art world and his 'Goodbye, I'm off' note to the corridors of academia. He wasn't seen on the Mile End Road again, although the college paper was the only journal to include a review of *Echoes of the Past*. A rather overlong, not entirely uncritical but largely positive write-up, it marked my own first appearance in the world that would later claim me for one of its own, newspaper journalism. In particular I praised the cryptic captions Martin had given his photographs: each, like a crossword clue, had to be worked out, making you think about the pictures.

When I eventually left college with my predictably average degree, it was back to Birmingham that I went, working for a spell as a sub-editor on the *Post*, then as a reporter on the *Evening Mail*. Gradually, telescoping a series of various staff positions, freelance gigs and 'rest periods', we return to the present day, which sees me employed as a crime reporter on a launch project for a rival publisher to the bunch that owns the *Post* and the *Mail*. A new daily paper for the West Midlands, it's likely to ditch into Edgbaston Reservoir within a year of launching, if we even get that far, but it seemed like a golden opportunity in the final dismaying weeks of 2001, when I was staring out of the window cursing the name of Patricia Cornwell.

If it hadn't been for Cornwell, I would have been getting on with my book. For about eighteen months, I had been writing this book, on spec, entitled *The Art of Murder*, and had just reached the chapter about the Victorian painter Walter Sickert, in which I would explore the conspiracy theories that placed him at the centre of the Jack the Ripper case. Whether you buy the Sickert-as-Ripper theory or not (and I didn't), the work of the founder of the Camden Town Group is full of interest for those drawn to the representation of murder in visual art, with paintings such as *The Camden Town Murder* and *L'Affaire de Camden Town* indicating his own close interest in the subject. The chapter on Sickert was always going to be the beating heart of the book, but then Patricia Cornwell tore it out with her widely reported act of monumental stupidity. By buying up thirty-two of Sickert's paintings and having one ripped asunder in the hope of finding evidence to back up her '100 per cent certain' view that Sickert

and the Ripper were the same man, she had rather taken the wind
out of my sails.

I remember e-mailing Martin Weiss on the day the story
broke. I asked him whether he'd seen it. He e-mailed me back and
said he had, but added, 'So what?'

'Well, it's obviously a publicity stunt,' I sent back. 'Guess what
her next book's going to be all about?'

The phone rang. It was Martin.

'Listen,' he said, without preamble. 'She won't be the first
person to argue in print that Sickert was the Ripper. Nor will she
be the last.'

'Well, I might as well cancel my trip to Venice,' I grumbled.

Sickert had lived in the Italian city, producing numerous
pictures of its people and places.

'Bollocks,' snapped Martin. 'Fuck Patricia Cornwell. She
doesn't own Sickert or Jack the Ripper or the right to conjecture
over any links between them. Of course you should still go.'

As I showered in the hotel I thought of Martin back in
Birmingham. We hadn't seen that much of each other since
college, despite my occasional promptings that we should get
together. I missed his company, but he had his own circle of artist
friends, or so I presumed. It was Martin, though, who put me on
to Sickert, sending me a series of postcards of his work: *Ennui,
Sunday Afternoon, Mornington Crescent Nude*. He had e-mailed
me a web address, which turned out to be a Masonic site with an
endless screed devoted to the Sickert/Ripper theory, and the seed
for my book idea was sown.

I tried to maintain contact with Martin, sending him a long,
chatty e-mail when I started researching the book and asking
him what he was working on, but he didn't reply. Months later, I
received another Sickert card in the post, *La Hollandaise*, another
downbeat nude, a prostitute perhaps, on the back of which Martin
had scrawled a note to say he was working on a big project that
required all his energy. It would be the making of him, he wrote.
I took the hint and got on with my research into Sickert, and the
material for the other chapters, on my own.

For all its licentious reputation over the years, even earning the soubriquet Sea-Sodom from Lord Byron himself, Venice these days is rather tame and a man may have to travel away from the centre of things to satisfy his carnal desires, especially if those desires are of a homosexual nature. I selected a restaurant in between San Marco and the Rialto bridge, so that I could cruise Il Muro in search of a potential livener. The guidebook said there might not be that much action out of season, but it was even quieter than I'd feared, and I ended up eating on an empty stomach.

From the restaurant it was a short walk back to the Rialto, and thence to the hotel, but there was always a chance I might get lucky.

I didn't. I got unlucky.

As I approached the Rio di San Salvador by the Calle dell'Ovo, I noticed a large crowd gathering on the bridge. With my reporter's instinct, I eased through the crowd to the front. As long as you're polite and don't push too hard, no one really minds, especially in a country like Italy, where queuing is hardly a way of life. When I reached the parapet, I saw the humped shape in the water, the dark hair floating like seaweed. A police launch was just arriving and so I witnessed the body being pulled out of the water. She looked about twenty-five, still clothed, and couldn't have been in the water more than a day, although her face was a waxy grey under the harsh spotlight. Her eyes, thankfully, were closed. Mine were not, and even when I did close them later that night in the hope of finding some relief in sleep, I couldn't banish the image of her grey face, water trickling off the end of her nose back into the canal, drop by sickening drop.

There were even more upsetting images of the dead girl in the papers when I got home. They showed a pretty, lively twenty-three-year-old management trainee called Hannah Power, from Balham in south London, who had gone to Venice with a group of girlfriends and never come back. Initial reports indicated a high level of alcohol in the bloodstream, so it was assumed she had simply strayed, slightly drunk, too close to the edge of a canal. According to her friends, she had left the bar they'd been in just to get some fresh air. When she did not reappear and then later failed to show up at their hotel, the girls raised the alarm, but by then it was too late.

Fortunately, I didn't have much chance to dwell on my memory of that last night in Venice. At work on the Monday morning, we were summoned to a meeting in McCave's office – James McCave was the editor – and told to prepare a dummy issue of the paper to an unpopularly tight deadline. The launch date had been brought forward by three weeks. We weren't told why.

With three days to go to the deadline, a new story broke. I was the crime reporter and this story wasn't a crime story, at least not yet, but the news guys couldn't keep up with the stories they were already chasing, so I volunteered, as my desk was pretty clear. I don't really know why I volunteered. Well, I do, but I don't, if you see what I mean. I'll tell you what I mean. The story was that of a Birmingham girl who had fallen into a canal in Amsterdam and drowned.

I should have realised, when volunteering for the story, that it would mean interviewing the grieving parents, but for some reason that didn't occur to me, not until the news editor gave me that specific instruction as he handed me a Post-it bearing the dead girl's name, Sally Mylrea, her parents' names, Bob and Christine, and their address on the Old Birmingham Road beyond the Lickey Hills. I was to get a cab, the news editor said, adding that I should make sure I got a fucking receipt.

'You want me to go now?'

The news editor, a hard-bitten, hot-metal throwback called Paul Connelly, happened to be not very tall and suffered from Small Man Syndrome. Actually, it was the rest of us who suffered as he strutted about the office cursing and scolding whoever was daft enough to get in his way.

'No, I want you to go next fucking week,' he retorted. 'Of course I want you to go fucking now.'

As I walked out of the office into Frederick Street, the last thing I felt like doing was finding a cab to take me to see Bob and Christine Mylrea. I wasn't a parent, so I could only imagine what they might be feeling. It was a bright January morning, almost lunchtime. Our office was located between Brindleyplace and the Vyse Street cemetery, which meant that most lunchtimes I would end up sitting in one or the other eating my sandwich in silent contemplation. That day in particular I could really have done

with some time to sit and think. I find it impossible to relax stuck
in the back of a taxi.

On any other day, on any other mission, it would have been
good to get out of the city. The long straight run down the Bristol
Road past Longbridge, the hills ahead full of the vague promise
of wind in the hair, a spring in the step. But today I was rooted to
the back seat of a Cavalier, dreading the moment when it would
pull up by the side of the road and the driver would turn round
to demand his fare.

The dreaded moment arrived. The Mylreas lived within yards
of the Gracelands garage; its zoot-suited mannequin loiterers out
front and lifesize Elvis on the roof seemed, for once, like a bad
joke in poor taste. I paid the man and stepped out of the car, only
remembering as he U-turned in the garage forecourt and headed
back up the hill that I had forgotten to ask for a fucking receipt.

As I arrived, a photographer was leaving. Bob and Christine
were standing at the front door holding a framed graduation
picture of their daughter. Dazed, they invited me in and the three
of us sat in an isoceles triangle formation in the front room, Bob
and Christine, red eyed, taking up their expected positions next
to each other on the low-backed, high-cushioned sofa, while I
perched on the edge of an armchair opposite them, notepad on
my knee. As soon as I offered my condolences, the tears began
welling up in Christine Mylrea's eyes. She lowered her face and
her husband did the talking in a cracked voice, but I couldn't look
away from the grieving mother, her tears dripping off the end of
her nose, reminding me of the water that trickled off Hannah
Power's nose as she was hoisted out of the Rio di San Salvador.

Sally Mylrea's death didn't strike me as anything more sinister
than a macabre coincidence – there had been no evidence that she
was pushed or that she might have jumped, and trace elements of
cannabis and alcohol in her blood were hardly surprising, given
where she'd gone on holiday – until a month later.

Our dummy issue had been well received and we were starting
to gear up for the actual launch. My piece on the Mylreas, on to
the end of which I had tacked a brief, factual mention of Hannah
Power's death in Venice, earned me a nod of acknowledgement

from James McCave (and a disguised snort of derision from Paul Connelly). In a brief lull before the intense pressure of the next few weeks, I took a couple of days off, intending to decorate the grottiest parts of my flat. I lived in a modern conversion above a tools reclamation workshop (and if you know what one of those is, you're one step ahead of me) at the bottom end of one of the short ladder of streets that run between the Yardley Road and the canal. The view from the back of the flat (my living room/study) was of Yardley Cemetery, while from the front (my bedroom, where decoration was most urgently needed) the vista was dominated by the green ribbon of the canal.

I wandered down the road to get a paper. As I was walking back, my eye fell on a story on page four: 'Canal death treated as suspicious', ran the headline. 'The body of Marijke Sels, 25, was recovered from the Regent's Canal in London's Camden Town yesterday. Ms Sels, a student from Amsterdam enrolled at London University, is believed to have drowned, but police are treating as suspicious certain marks found on her body, which could possibly have resulted from a struggle, and are appealing for witnesses.'

Decorating forgotten, leave cancelled, I was at my desk inside half an hour.

Paul Connelly spotted me.

'What the fuck are you doing here?' he enquired.

I showed him the story.

'Don't waste your time,' he muttered.

'They must be related,' I persisted. 'The three deaths: Hannah Power, Sally Mylrea, Marijke Sels. It's too much of a coincidence. There must be a common thread.'

'Of course there's a fucking common thread. They're all dead. Now stop wasting your time. Since you're here, you might as well do something useful. Sub that.'

He dropped a galley on my desk and stalked off. I wasn't a sub, but nor did I fancy a four-hour wait in Dudley Road A&E with a broken nose, so I had a look at what he'd left me. It was copy for a canal walk, the first of a weekly column 'by our environmental correspondent Julie Meech'. This had run in the dummy, so shouldn't have needed subbing; but again it didn't seem my place to point this out, so I read it, marked up a few little things and scrawled Connelly's initials in the top right-hand corner before sticking it in the internal mail.

I spent the rest of the day digging up everything I could find on the three dead girls. Apart from the fact that they were all around the same age, nothing seemed to link them. I lay in bed that night unable to sleep as I turned the girls' names over and over in my head and watched their grainy newspaper faces swim past me into the murky depths. A phrase from Julie Meech's canal walk kept coming back to me: the Inland Waterways Association. Writer and still-water enthusiast Robert Aickman had co-founded (with L. T. C. Rolt) the Inland Waterways Association in 1946, Meech had written, to promote the restoration of his beloved canals and encourage more people to use them.

I got out of bed and walked to the window. I'd taken the curtains down in preparation for the now abandoned decorating. The link between the three girls was staring me in the face. The canal. There was no other common thread. Whether they fell or were pushed, the three had died in canals. Different canals. One in Venice, one in Amsterdam and one in London. Gazing out into the darkness, I was struck by another thought, which hit me like a hammer in the back of the head.

There was no reason to assume that the killing of the Dutch girl was the end of it.

In fact, I realised as I hurried to work the following morning, there was one very good reason why it wasn't the end of it.

If the news editor had been anyone other than Paul Connelly, I would have gone straight to him – or her – with my theory. You could argue I should have gone straight to the police. But I waited, and while I waited I did some research. Using the phone book, the *A–Z* and the Internet, I scoured Birmingham for Italian communities or associations. I discovered that part of Digbeth had become a thriving Italian quarter following an influx of migrant workers from southern Italy more than a century ago. Whether their legacy amounted to more than a couple of Italian restaurants in the area was unclear, but even if it did, what good would that do me? What did I think I was going to do? Distribute flyers? Stand outside with a sandwich board? No. What was the point of working for the press if you didn't use it as it was meant to be used?

Assuming the intervals between the other deaths had set a pattern, I had at least a week before the final piece of the puzzle was slotted into place.

I wrote my article, describing the pattern I believed had been set and issuing the warning I thought necessary. I e-mailed it directly to McCave. Half an hour later the phone rang. I was to see the editor in his office.

'What's this?' he asked, waving a print-out of my story.

'I'm completely serious about it,' I said.

'So I see. Why didn't you follow procedure and send it to the news editor?'

I looked at McCave as if seeing him for the first time. Broad shouldered, straight backed, he looked at home in his tailored suit. There was a tiny shaving cut just below his left ear.

'He seems to have a bit of a downer on me,' I said.

'He's got a downer on everybody, but he's good at his job. Pull a stunt like this again and *you* will be looking for a *new* one. Is that clear?'

'Yes.'

'Close the door on your way out.'

Close the door on your way out. So people actually said that.

My piece appeared in the launch issue. I had no illusions about why McCave had ordered Connelly to run it: it was bound to generate publicity and McCave was gambling that it would work for us rather than against us. Connelly had barely looked at me over the last four days, which I found more alarming than his usual confrontational methods of intimidation.

The reception was mixed. Briefly, I'd stated the facts. Hannah Power, from London, had been found dead in the Rio di San Salvador in Venice. Sally Mylrea, from Birmingham, had drowned in the Keizergracht in Amsterdam. Marijke Sels, from Amsterdam, had been pulled out of the Regent's Canal in London. While the possibility remained that one or two or even all three of the deaths were accidental, if you considered the details, the coincidence seemed too unlikely, and once you factored in the evidence of assault in the Marijke Sels case, it became almost impossible not to conclude that all three girls had been murdered, presumably by the same person, who we should be expecting to strike once again. The missing piece in the jigsaw puzzle he (again, a presumption) was assembling would be the drowning of a Venetian girl in a canal in Birmingham.

The police didn't waste any time in calling to say they were dispatching two detectives to interview me at the office. The Heart of England Tourist Board were not best pleased, faxing the ad sales director to complain that this had set them back years. And readers – in their dozens – e-mailed, telephoned and even turned up in person at the Frederick Street offices to report suspicious sightings of strange men by canals throughout the Birmingham area.

I'd half expected to hear from Martin Weiss, so when I didn't, I e-mailed him and, later, called; but if he was there, he didn't pick up.

I did, however, get a card the following morning. It was another of Martin's trademark Sickert postcards, *Nude on a Bed*, which showed a woman sitting on the edge of an iron bed with her hands clasped behind her head. On the back, Martin had written: 'Nice tits. I hope your bosses appreciated your "news story" as much as I did.' Unable to work out whether he was taunting me – the pointed reference to the model's breasts seemed uncharacteristically vulgar – I slipped the postcard into my inside pocket and it went home with me at the end of a long day of police interviews and difficult phone calls, as many from cranks as from anxious Italian parents. What could I tell any of them that I hadn't put in my piece? Everything I knew for sure was there, and most of what I suspected. Should I have told them of my vague suspicions regarding an old friend? Such thoughts would have seemed monstrously fanciful with no real evidence to back them up.

The evidence arrived the next day in the shape of another postcard. Again it was a girl on a bed, lying back, one leg on the floor, the other hanging in the air. As with one or two of the Camden Town paintings, it was impossible to say whether the woman was asleep or dead. The title was the one I should have been expecting if I'd done my research thoroughly: *Fille Vénitienne Allongée.*

On the back, in Martin's handwriting: '4 down. Birmingham noir (10)'.

I took it straight to the photocopier, then to Connelly.

'Fuck's that?' he asked.

'Look,' I said, turning it over. '*Fille Vénitienne Allongée.* Venetian girl lying down. It's a direct reference to my piece.'

'I can see that,' he said icily. 'What about the fucking crossword clue?'

'Bournville?' I suggested hesitantly.

When I got to the stretch of the Worcester and Birmingham Canal that passes through Bournville, alongside the railway line that runs right past the Cadbury factory, it was like a film set. Police cars, ambulances, reporters, TV crews, lights, lines and lines of police tape strung up like bunting between the trees, and crowds of onlookers.

I bitterly regretted that I was too late, but I was glad of one small thing: that I was too late to see the girl's limp body emerging from the dark water in the arms of a police diver. I saw the pictures later, but they didn't have the same power that seeing her in the flesh would have had.

I often go back there. Some kids have built a rickety stepladder up the side of a tree, leading to a couple of strategically placed sheets of hardboard where you can sit quite comfortably. It doesn't look new and has probably been there for years. It's as good a place as any to sit and brood. I tried to work out how far in advance Martin had planned everything. Did he get the idea only once I became interested in Sickert and decided to go to Venice, or had he been planning it from the moment when he first introduced me to the painter's work?

I don't know, but I remember his telling me he was working on a big project. So this was it. Right from the beginning, since his photographs in the Bethnal Green gallery, he'd been drawn to the overlap between violent crime and visual art. His series of murders, perfectly constructed, deftly executed, had been signed just like a painting. The police investigation proved that he'd flown to Venice while I was there and that he'd returned to Birmingham via Amsterdam. Apart from that, they were no nearer catching him than I had ever been, in any sense of the word.

The canal at Bournville is quite beautiful, especially at dusk. Sometimes I sit there for hours, until the sky turns purple over the chocolate factory, and I wonder about Martin, still out there somewhere. Is that it? Has he finished? Or will there be more? I realise that asking 'Why me?' implies a solipsistic attitude when the tragedies have affected so many lives, but I can't help wondering whether the responsibility for the murders should really be all Martin's. Clearly, he used me because he knew I would be interested. He engineered things in such a way that I was *bound* to be interested. He wanted the world to hear about his work, just as it gets to hear about the work of any great artist, and I could be relied on to make sure of that. But was I not also being punished, or at the very least put in my place?

THE SPACE—TIME DISCONTINUUM

*'First we shape our buildings, and then our buildings
shape us'* — Winston Churchill

As I climb the spiral steps, I have a sense not so much of my
entering the building, as of the building entering me. I feel its
presence, its soul if you like, begin to seep into my pores. Its dust
sinks into my lungs. Colours are imprinted on my retinas. The
curve of the tiled wall stimulates the pads of my fingertips. The
signatures of the graffiti writers who have been here before me
are gently tattooed on to my back. Known. Demo. Tox. It might
not be expected that these streetwise kids and I would have much
in common, but suddenly they feel like my brothers. Dex. Fume.
Shade.

Somewhere below me, in the bowels of the building, a guy
in a suit waits, pacing up and down. I can no longer hear him.
He's forgotten. Of the Aristotelian unities, only place holds good.
Action is doubtful. Time is finished.

What was this place? A railway building, but so close to the
motorway! Someone's idea of a joke. The Westway, immediately
adjacent, runs on three decks; the lowest has been blocked off
for as long as this building has lain empty. It – the lower deck
of the motorway – has offered one way into the building for the
kids who have decorated the walls. They could access it from the
deserted cobbled remains of Paddington Goods Yard, skirting the
puddles of diesel and rainwater, and the rough patches of nettles
and dock leaves where black-eyed rats would wait patiently for a
bared ankle. The only other way into this building – let's give it
a name, the former Paddington Maintenance Depot – would be

from the two motorway decks that remain operational, dancing across from the hard shoulder, sashaying in through an open window. One foot wrong and you'd sleep the big sleep. I can feel them now all around me, these graffiti desperadoes, running on bravado and adrenalin, the law at their heels.

My own means of entry is above board. It's business, ostensibly. Hence the guy in the suit. But once I'm in, my heart is with the outlaws. I'm as excited as they are by the emptiness, the sense of potential. I assess the volume, grasp the space.

On the second level, I leave the stairs and step into the main triangular body of the building. There are windows on the two longer sides. I gravitate towards those that give on to the Westway. A breeze cools the sweat on my face as I watch the cars flash by. They come from Oxford, White City, Shepherd's Bush. But where are they going? Oxford Street? The City of London? Shepherd Market? I stick my head out of the window and look across the Westway towards Paddington, expecting to see the familiar low ragged skyline, but instead it's once again farewell, my lovely London, as I see escaping clouds of subway steam, water towers like B-movie rocket ships, the glass buttes and concrete mesas of Manhattan. Behind me, instead of the Grand Union Canal slipping gloopily into Little Venice, the grey expanse of the East River. In front of me the cars chugging along the FDR Drive are guzzling gas. The horns sound different. The cabs are yellow, not black.

I've gone away again.

My name is David Rosen. I am a bespoke property consultant. You can call me a commercial estate agent, if you prefer. What I am is a kind of private detective, sitting by the phone waiting for a client to ring with the next job. 'I want you to find me a building.' Except building doesn't really get it. Not unless you buy all that touchy-feely stuff about buildings having a soul, and the windows are the eyes of the soul, and something of the past lives on in the fabric of the bricks and mortar. I do. I buy it. I get it wholesale. My latest case? Missing kid. Kind of. This one's different. No one called the case in. It's sort of a personal project.

It wouldn't be true to say I became aware of Shade on my

first job. But, with the luxury of hindsight, I would say there was something slightly weird right from the very start. Like a patch of a photograph that's inexplicably out of focus. I don't mean in terms of the job, which went off perfectly. The Design House was a conversion from a 1950s car showroom at the top of one of the quirkiest streets in what was then London's trendiest neighbourhood, Camden Town. As the job progressed, and the beautiful blue glass butterfly emerged from the chrysalis of contracts and scaffolding, I found that I would occasionally experience the sensation of watching proceedings from outside myself. I knew this to be a common phenomenon in times of stress. But I wasn't stressed. Quite the reverse. This was my first big job and I was still in my late twenties. I was bursting with confidence. This was going to set me up. I knew what I wanted and it looked pretty much like I was going to get it. It looked as if I was getting it already. Maybe it was my own sense of significance of the moment that got to me.

The job done, I walked back to Camden one day to check out the new building like any other passer-by. I stood on the pavement and caught my reflection in the smoky blue mirrored glass and for a second I thought there was someone standing behind me. I turned round, but there was no one there. Then there were two guys walking past and they gave me a look and I thought, what the hell, I'm seeing things.

From the high window of my office on Savile Row, I can gaze down Old Burlington Street and appreciate the front elevation of the former Museum of Mankind. Only the 1960s Economist Building behind it has altered the view from this point since my maternal grandfather fled the pogroms that heralded the Russian revolution and settled in the East End of London. My grandfather's brother kept going all the way to America, past the lady in the lake, the Statue of Liberty, docking at Ellis Island, where he and hundreds of thousands of other immigrants were processed. He settled in the Lower East Side.

During the Second World War, rubble from bombed British cities was carried as ballast in ships sailing from England to America. Much of this was used as supporting landfill for the FDR Drive where it passed Bellevue Hospital between East 23rd Street and East 30th Street, a stretch that became known as Bristol Basin. The road there curves to the left, to the right and then to the left again as you're heading downtown. The effect in a fast-moving car is similar to that felt on the Westway, when you appear to be driving directly at the former Paddington Maintenance Depot, only to veer off to the right at the last moment, before dropping to the level of Paddington Green.

After my inspection of the former maintenance depot, we cut across to the Rotunda, the low oval-shaped glass-roofed building in the middle of the roundabout between the Westway and Warwick Avenue. At first sight the little sister of the maintenance depot, the Rotunda reveals her seductive appeal only once you get inside. In the late 1970s and early 1980s, the building was squatted by anarcho-hippy artists Mutoid Waste. I know, because I encountered them when I used to enter the building myself as part of my own urban explorations. I remember turning a corner and finding myself face to face with the owner of a green Mohican that prefigured Winston Churchill's on May Day 2000. The wall paintings left in the Rotunda by Mutoid Waste were no less vivid. The trick would be to find the right client for the space so that the graffiti would not have to be removed.

Graffiti, like the fabric of the city itself, is a palimpsest, and these had been interwoven and elaborated since the departure of Mutoid Waste. Lots of familiar tags were here: Fume, Fiza, Chop, Touch, Teach, Rote, Hear. And, as ever, Shade.

Shade – relative darkness; a position of relative obscurity; a shield; a slight amount; *literary* a ghost; *archaic* shadow.

After the car showroom became Design House, the phone started to ring. Clients came looking. I encouraged them to be adventurous. Tell me what you're looking for and I'll go out and find it. This is what I did, and wherever I went, it seemed, Shade came – or had been – too. As the signs of habitation quickly fade, other elements enter the abandoned building as surely as seawater seeps into the hull of a ship that cracks on a rock. Rot, vermin, graffiti. Subversive life forms. In the old Anello & Davide shoe factory in Covent Garden, Shade's tag was among those that had to be stripped from the walls before the building could be turned into the Saunders design studio. When I walked out into Drury Lane, I thought I was in Alphabet City. I saw the same bars, print shops and bargain record stores. It didn't last long, but it was the first time I daydreamed NYC on the streets of London. After that, it happened time and again and it became more realistic, more convincing. Not on every job, but on enough. I skipped out of the Edwardian school that would metamorphose into the Imagination Building and immediately hallucinated the Empire State Building rearing up in front of me, as if Store Street had become 34th Street. In a few seconds it resolved into the more manageable outline of Senate House.

But it was as if a switch had been thrown and thereafter London and New York seemed to coexist in my mind. I remember an early Compaq computer with a button that enabled you to toggle between two screens. Fabulous for fooling the boss. But I *was* the boss. And I had a toggle switch in my head. The only difference was I didn't control it. It controlled me. I wondered whether it had anything to do with my meddling with space. Here I was taking a space devised for one function and handing it over to someone else to use for an entirely different purpose. Was I breaking the rules? Was the city resisting me? Was Shade – my imaginary friend, my elusive cousin – trying to give me a warning?

On later projects, there weren't always graffiti. Maybe we started to use spaces that had better security. Or places that were off the writers' routes. I didn't see his tag at the Wallis Gilbert-designed Daimler garage in Herbrand Street and the walls were bare inside the old tax office on Rockley Road, Shepherd's Bush. But I sensed him nevertheless. I felt him as surely as I felt the vibrations of the old railway line that I knew had run under the building – in a cutting where the long narrow building now stood – eighty years ago. I thought I saw him dodging behind one of the thick pillars thirty yards ahead of me, so I quickened my step, but so did he: when I reached the west end of the building, there was no sign of him, just an open window. I followed him out on to Rockley Road and down to Shepherd's Bush Green. The streets were busy and I couldn't be sure I wasn't following a phantom, but it seemed to me he turned left off Goldhawk Road on to Richford Street. At the bottom of Grove Mews, I lost him. Across Trussley Road were the remains of the viaduct that had carried the same old railway line down to Hammersmith. I wondered whether he'd climbed up there and scampered off along the disused High Line that runs from West 34th Street to Gansevoort Street on the edge of Greenwich Village.

On the second Tuesday in September, I occupied my usual seat in Highbury's East Stand. Premiership champions Arsenal were entertaining Manchester City, recently promoted from the First Division. All eyes were on City's star striker Nicolas Anelka, who had left Highbury under a cloud and ghosted through three other clubs before joining the Blues. This was his chance to edge it over fellow Frenchman Thierry Henry. All eyes, that is, except mine.

I was looking out of the ground to the right, watching the railway line from King's Cross as it swept around to the north. InterCity 125s and local services used the line and each time I watched one slide past, a regular series of yellow rectangles, I was transported to an equivalent seat in Yankee Stadium with a clear view of the elevated No.4 subway carriages rattling by.

Anelka did score, but so did two other Frenchmen, Arsenal's Sylvain Wiltord and, later, decisively, Henry. City captain Ali Benarbia faced the long goodbye as he was sent off for a second bookable offence with only six minutes to go.

I looked at the railway line. Just out of sight, around the edge of the stadium, was Finsbury Park overground station. Among the many tags that covered the walls there was one that was especially familiar to me. Underground, too. I remembered standing in a Tube train waiting for the doors to close, reading his name vertically off two yellow poles.

The day soon came when Nissan firmed up their interest in the Rotunda. It would be their design studio and they would undertake to preserve the graffiti, employing a series of removable panels. The same day I got a call from an American client. I was out at lunch at the time. When I returned, I hit playback on the machine and listened to this guy telling me he wanted me to find him a space in London just like one he'd photographed in New York. He'd e-mailed the pictures, he said.

I logged on to the server and picked them up. There were three shots, two exteriors and one taken inside. The interior walls were covered in graffiti.

I leaned closer to the screen, looking for something.

> *'But down these mean streets a man must go who himself is not mean, who is neither tarnished nor afraid...'* — Raymond Chandler

FLYING INTO NAPLES

Flying into Naples the 737 hits some turbulence. It's dark outside but I can't even see any lights on the ground. I'm a nervous flyer anyway and this doesn't make me feel any better. It's taking off and landing that bother me.

But when we're down and I'm crossing the tarmac to the airport buildings there's a warm humid stillness in the air that makes me wonder about the turbulence. I wander through passport control and customs like someone in a dream. The officials seem covered in a fine layer of dust as if they've been standing there for years, just waiting.

No one speaks to me and I get on the bus marked 'Centro Napoli'. I'm on holiday. All I've got in Naples is a name, a photograph and a wrong number. The name is a woman's – Flavia – and the photograph is of the view from her apartment. The phone number I tried last week to say I was coming turned out to belong to someone else entirely.

I've worked out from the photograph and my map that the apartment is on a hill on the west side of the city. There's not much more to go on. It's too late to go and look for it tonight. Flavia won't be expecting me – beyond occasional vague invitations nothing has been arranged – and she could take a long time to locate.

I knew her years ago when she visited London and stayed in the hotel where I was working the bar. We knew each other briefly – a holiday romance, if you like – but something ensured I would not forget her. Whether it was the sunrise we saw together or the shock of her body in the quiet shadow of my room over the kitchens, or a combination of these and other factors – her smile, my particular vulnerability, her tumbling curls – I don't know, but something fixed her in my mind. So when I found myself with a week's holiday at the end of three difficult months in a new, stressful job, I dug out her letters – two or three only over eight years, including this recent photograph of the view from her apartment – and booked a last-minute flight to Naples.

I'd never been there, though I'd heard so much about it – how violent and dangerous it could be for foreigners, yet how beautiful – and I would enjoy the effort required to get along in Italian.

I'm alone on the bus apart from one other man – a local who spends the twenty-minute ride talking on a mobile phone to his mistress in Rome – and the taciturn driver. I've come before the start of the season, but it's already warm enough not to need my linen jacket.

I'm divorced. I don't know about Flavia. She never mentioned anybody, just as she never revealed her address when she wrote to me. I've been divorced for two years and a period of contented bachelorhood has only recently come to a natural end, and with the arrival of spring in London I have found myself watching women once again: following a hemline through the human traffic of Kensington, turning to see the face of a woman in Green Park whose hair looked so striking from behind. It may be spring in Berkeley Square but it feels like midsummer in Naples. The air is still and hot and humid when I leave the bus at the main railway station and begin walking into the centre of the city in search of a cheap hotel. I imagine I'm probably quite conspicuous in what must be one of the most dangerous areas but the hotels in the immediate vicinity – the pavement outside the Europa is clogged with upturned rubbish bins; the tall, dark, narrow Esedra looks as if it's about to topple sideways – look unwelcoming so I press on. It's late, after 10.30p.m., and even the bars and restaurants are closed. Youths buzz past on Vespas and Piaggios unhelmeted, despite the apparent dedication of the motorists here to the legend 'Live fast, die young'. I hold my bag close and try to look confident, but after fifteen minutes or so the hotels have disappeared. I reach a large empty square and head deeper into the city. I ask a gun-holstered security guard if there is a *pension* in the neighbourhood but he shrugs and walks away. I climb a street that has lights burning but they turn out to be those of a late-night bar and a fruit stand. Two boys call to me from a doorway and as I don't understand I just carry on, but at the top is a barrier and beyond that a private apartment complex, so I have to turn back and the two boys are laughing as I walk past them.

I try in another direction but there are only banks and food stores, all locked up. Soon I realise I'm going to have to go back down to the area around the railway station. I cross the road to avoid the prostitutes on the corner of Via Seggio del Popolo, not because of any spurious moral judgement but just because it seems I should go out of my way to avoid trouble, so easy is it innocently to court disaster in a foreign country. But in crossing the road I walk into a problem. There's a young woman standing in a doorway whom in the darkness I had failed to see. She moves swiftly out of the doorway into my path and I gasp in surprise. The street lamp throws the dark bruises around her eyes into even deeper perspective. Her eyes are sunken, almost lost in her skull, and under her chin are the dark, tough bristles of a juvenile beard. She speaks quickly, demanding something, and before I've collected my wits she's produced a glittering blade from her jacket pocket that she thrusts towards me like a torch at an animal. I react too slowly and feel a sudden hot scratch on my bare arm.

My jacket's over my other arm so I'm lucky that I don't drop it and give the woman the chance to strike again. She lunges but I'm away down the street, running for my life. When it's clear she's not chasing me I stop for breath. One or two passers-by look at me with mild curiosity. I head back in the direction of the railway station. Down a side street on my right I recognise one of the hotels I saw earlier – the Esedra. Then I hadn't liked the look of it, but now it's my haven from the streets. I approach the glass doors and hesitate when I realise there are several men in the lobby. But the thought of the drugged-up woman makes me go on. So I push open the door and the men look up from their card game. I'm about to ask for a room when one of the men, who's had a good long look at me, says something to the man behind the little counter and this man reaches for a key from room 17's pigeon-hole. I realise what's happening – they've mistaken me for someone who's already a guest – and there was a time when I would have been tempted to accept the key in the desire to save money, but these days I'm not short of cash. So I hesitate only for a moment before saying that I'm looking for a room. The man is momentarily confused but gets me another key – room 19 – from a hook and quotes a price. It's cheap; the hotel is probably a haunt of prostitutes but right now I don't care. I just need a bed for the night. 'It's on the third floor,' the man says. I pay him and walk up. There are light bulbs but they're so heavily shaded the stairs are darker than the street outside. On each landing there are four doors: three bedrooms and one toilet-cum-shower. I unlock the door to room 19 and close it behind me.

I have a routine with hotel rooms: I lock myself in and switch on all the lights and open all the cupboards and drawers until I feel I know the room as well as I can. And I always check the window.

There are two single beds, some sticks of furniture, a bidet and a washbasin – I open the cold tap and clean up the scratch on my arm. The window is shuttered. I pull on the cord to raise the shutter. I'm overlooking the Corso Uberto I, which runs up to the railway station. I step on to the tiny balcony and my hands get covered in dust from the wrought-iron railing. The cars in the street below are filmed with dust also. The winds blow sand here from the deserts of North Africa and it falls with the rain. I pull a chair on to the balcony and sit for a while thinking about Flavia. Somewhere in this city she's sitting watching television or eating in a restaurant and she doesn't know I'm here. Tomorrow I will try to find her.

I watch the road and I'm glad I'm no longer out there looking for shelter. Small knots of young men unravel on street corners and cross streets that don't need crossing. After a while I start to feel an uncomfortable solidity creeping into my limbs, so I take the chair back inside and drop the shutter. I'd prefer to leave it but the open window might look like an invitation.

I'm lying in bed hoping that sleep will come but there's a scuttling, rustling noise keeping me awake. It's coming from the far side of the room near the washbasin and the framed print of the ancient city of Pompeii. It sounds like an insect, probably a cockroach. I'm not alarmed. I've shared hotel rooms with pests before, but I want to go to sleep. There's no use left in this day and I'm eager for the next one to begin.

Something else is bothering me: I want to go and try the door to room 17 and see why the proprietor was about to give me that key. The scratching noise is getting louder and although I can't fall asleep I'm getting more and more tired so that I start to imagine the insect. It's behind the picture where it's scratched out its own little hole and it's lying in wait for me to go and lift the picture aside and it will come at me, slow and deadly, like a Lancaster bomber. The noise works deeper into my head. The thing must have huge wings and antennae. Scratch…scratch…scratch. I can't stand it any more. I get up, pull on my trousers and leave the room.

The stairs are completely dark. I feel my way to the next landing and switch on the light in the WC to allow me to see the numbers on the doors. I push on the door to room 17, feeling a layer of dust beneath my fingertips, and it swings open. The chinks in the shutter admit enough light to paint a faint picture of a man lying on the bed who looks not unlike me. I step into the room and feel grit on the floor under my feet. As I step closer the man on the bed turns to look at me. His lips move slowly.

'I came straight here,' he says, 'instead of walking into the city to find something better.'

I don't know what to say. Pulling up a chair, I sit next to him.

'I found her,' he continues. 'She lives above the city on the west side. You can see Vesuvius from her window.'

I grip his cold hand and try to read the expression on his face. But it's blank. The words rustle in his mouth like dry leaves caught between stones.

'She's not interested. Watch out for Vesuvius,' he whispers, then falls silent. I sit there for a while watching his grey face for any sign of life but there's nothing. Feeling an unbearable sadness for which I can't reasonably account, I return to my room and lie flat on my back on the little bed.

The unknown insect is still busy scratching behind the ruins of Pompeii.

*

I wake up to heavy traffic under my window, my head still thick with dreams. On my way downstairs I pause on the landing opposite room 17 and feel a tug. But I know the easiest thing is not to think too much about it and just carry on downstairs, hand in the key and leave the hotel for good. Even if I don't manage to locate Flavia I won't come back here. I'll find something better.

I walk across the city, stopping at a little bar for a cappuccino and a croissant. The air smells of coffee, cigarettes and laundry. Strings of clothes are hung out in the narrow passages like bunting. Moped riders duck their heads to avoid vests and socks as they bounce over the cobbles. Cars negotiate alleys barely wide enough to walk down, drivers jabbing at the horn to clear the way. Pedestrians step aside unhurriedly and there are no arguments or remonstrations.

The sun is beating down but there's a haze like sheer nylon stretched above the rooftops – dust in the air. I'm just heading west and climbing through distinct areas. The class differences show up clearly in the homes – the *bassi*, tiny rooms that open directly on to the street, and higher up the huge apartment blocks with their own gates and security – and in the shops and the goods sold in them. Only the dust is spread evenly.

As soon as I'm high enough to see Vesuvius behind me I take out the photograph and use it to direct my search, heading always west.

It takes a couple of hours to cross the city and locate the street. I make sure it's the right view before starting to read the names on the bell-pushes. The building has to be on the left-hand side of the road because those on the right aren't high enough to have a view over those on the left. I still don't know whether I'm going to find the name or not. Through the gaps between the buildings I can see Vesuvius on the other side of the bay. By looking ahead I'm even able to estimate the exact building, and it turns out I'm right. There's the name – F. Sannia – among a dozen others. I press the bell without thinking about it.

When Flavia comes to open the door I'm surprised. Perhaps it's more her place to be surprised than mine but she stands there with a vacant expression on her face. What a face, though, what extraordinary beauty. She was good looking when we first met, of course, but in the intervening years she has grown into a stunning woman. I fear to lean forward and kiss her cheeks lest she crumbles beneath my touch. But the look is blank. I don't know whether she recognises me. I say her name then my own and I must assume her acquiescence – as she turns back into the hall and hesitates momentarily – to be an invitation. So I follow her. She walks slowly but with the same lightness of step that I remember from before.

As I follow her into the apartment I'm drawn immediately to the far side of the main room where there's a balcony with a spectacular view over the Bay of Naples and, right in the centre at the back, Mount Vesuvius. Unaware of where Flavia has disappeared to I stand there watching the view for some minutes. Naples is built on hills and one of them rises from the sea to dominate the left middle ground, stepped with huge crumbling apartment buildings and sliced up by tapering streets and alleys that dig deeper the narrower they become. The whole city hums like a hive and cars and scooters buzz about like drones. But the main attraction is Vesuvius. What a place to build a city: in the shadow of a volcano.

It's a while before I realise Flavia has returned and is standing behind me as I admire the view.

'What do you want to do while you are in Naples?' she asks with a level voice. 'You'll stay here, of course.'

'You're very kind. I meant to give you some notice but I don't think I had the right phone number.' I show her the number in my book.

'I changed it,' she says as she sits in one of the wicker chairs and indicates for me to do the same. 'I've been widowed six times,' she says and then falls silent. 'It's easier.'

I don't know what to say. I think she must have intended to say something else – made a mistake with her English – although she seems so grey and lifeless herself that the statement may well have been true.

We sit on her balcony for half an hour looking out over the city and the volcano on the far side of the bay, during which time I formulate several lines with which to start a fresh conversation, but each one remains unspoken. Something in her passivity frightens me. It seems at odds with the élan of the city in which she lives.

But Flavia speaks first. 'With this view,' she says slowly, 'it is impossible not to watch the volcano, to become obsessed by it.'

I nod.

'My father was alive when it last erupted,' she continues, 'in 1944. Now Vesuvio is dormant. Do you want to see Naples?' she asks, turning towards me.

'Yes, very much.'

We leave the apartment and Flavia leads the way to a beaten-up old Fiat Uno. Her driving is a revelation: once in the car and negotiating the hairpin, double-parked roads leading downtown Flavia is a completely different woman. Here is the lively, passionate girl I knew in London. She takes on other drivers with the determination and verve she showed in my room overlooking the hotel car park when we took it in turns to sit astride each other. She rode me then as she now drives the Fiat, throwing it into 180-degree corners and touching her foot to the floor on the straights. She's not wearing her seat belt; I unclip mine, wind down my window and put my foot up on the plastic moulding in front of me. At one point – when I draw my elbow into the car quickly to avoid a bus coming up on the other side of the road – Flavia turns her head and smiles at me just as she did eight years earlier before falling asleep.

We skid into a parking place and Flavia attacks the handbrake. Once out of the car she's quiet again, gliding along beside me. 'Where are we going?' I ask her. Beyond the city the summit of Vesuvius is draped in thick grey cloud. Out over the sea on our right a heavy wedge of darkest-grey thunderheads is making its way landwards, trailing skirts of rain. In the space of two minutes the island of Capri is rubbed out as the storm passes over it and into the bay.

'She must want to be alone,' Flavia says, and when I look puzzled, she continues: 'They say that you can see a woman reclining in the outline of the island.'

But Capri is lost behind layers of grey veils now and just as Flavia finishes speaking the first drops of rain explode on my bare arms. Within seconds we are soaked by a downpour of big fat sweet-smelling summer rain. My thin shirt is plastered to my back. The rain runs off Flavia's still body in trickles. She seems impervious to the cleansing, refreshing effect that I'm enjoying. Dripping wet with rain bouncing off my forehead I give her a smile but her expression doesn't change. 'Shall we walk?' I suggest, eyeing some trees in the distance that would give us some shelter. She just turns and starts walking without a word so I follow. The trees – which I realise I have seen previously from Flavia's balcony – conceal the city aquarium, housed in the lower ground floor of a heavy stone building. I pay for two tickets and we pass in front of a succession of gloomy windows on to another world. It's so damp down there I feel almost as if we've entered the element of the fishes. My shirt clings to my back, getting no drier under the dim lights. Flavia's white blouse is stuck to her shoulders but there's no tremor of life as far as I can see. She stares unseeing at the fish, the sinister skate and lugubrious octopus, which regard us with an expression I recognise but can't put a name to. Because I'm beginning to feel quite anxious I hurry past the shrimps and seahorses – which I see only as a blur of commas and question marks – and I'm relieved to get back into the open air.

Flavia takes me to a restaurant she knows and I eat cousins of the creatures we've just seen in the aquarium. Flavia orders mineral water and oysters but then hardly touches them. My teeth grind on tiny particles of grit or shell in my sauce but I don't say anything because it seems to be a city-wide problem. The waiter's black patent-leather shoes are matt with a fine layer of dust.

I watch Flavia as I eat and she stares out of the window at the teeming rain. When she moves it's with an incredible slowness that sets up a tension within me. Her stillness makes me want to protect her. She must have suffered so much, like a tree that's been buffeted by so many storms it's been stripped of leaves and twigs, but still stands, proud and defiant. I want to reach across and touch her cheek in the hope she might soften and smile, but such a deliberate act seems reckless. The worst thing would be if she remained indifferent to my advance.

As I continue eating, however, I'm filled with desire for her. I want to take her to bed and hold her and stroke away the years with her thin layers of clothing.

The feeling grows throughout what remains of the day. We go to a couple of basement piano bars and a club where crowds of strikingly beautiful people spill out on to the street. The atmosphere of intoxication and sexual excitement does nothing to spark Flavia into life. She simply trails her fingers through the dust that seems to coat the tables in every bar we enter.

Only in the car does she come alive as we race from one venue to another, bouncing down noisy cobbled escape routes and diving into alleys thin as crevices. The car's headlamps startle cats and in one hidden piazza a huddle of unshaven men emerging from a fly-posted door. 'This is a dangerous quarter,' she says, pointing at streets I remember from my first night. 'Camorro. Our Mafia. They kill you here as soon as look at you.'

Way past midnight we end up in a park above the city on the same side as Flavia's apartment but further round the bay. 'This newspaper,' she indicates piles of discarded newsprint lining the side of the road. 'People come here in their cars and put the newspaper up to cover the windows. Then they make love.'

I look at the vast drifts of newspaper as we drive slowly around the perimeter of the park. 'Why?' I ask. 'Because they live at home? It's their only chance?'

She shrugs. 'They do it in the cars then throw the newspaper out of the window.'

'And what a view they have,' I say, looking across the bay at the brooding shadow of Vesuvius.

Back home again she retreats inside her shell. The sudden change throws me. I want to touch her, sleep with her, but suddenly it's as if we're complete strangers. She sits on the balcony staring at Vesuvius and I bring her a drink. As I put it down I place my other hand on her arm and give it a brief squeeze. She doesn't react so I pull one of the wicker chairs round to face hers and sit in the darkness, just watching her watch the volcano. The moon paints her face with a pale wash. I can see the shape of her breasts under the white blouse and as I concentrate I can see the merest lift as she breathes. Otherwise I might have doubted she was still alive. 'Do you want to go to bed?' I ask.

She just looks at me. Inside me the tension is reaching bursting point. When Flavia gets up and walks to her bedroom I follow.

She undresses in front of me. The moonlight makes her flesh look grey and very still. I undress and lie beside her. She doesn't push me away but neither does she encourage me in any way.

When I wake in the morning she's gone. The pillow on her side is still indented and warm to the touch. I wish I'd done something the night before but her terrible passivity had killed my desire. A night's sleep, however, has returned it to me. If she were here now I'd force her to decide, whether to accept or reject me, either being preferable to indifference.

I get dressed and step out on to the balcony. The top of Vesuvius is covered with cloud. The air over the city is hazy. On the little table there's a note for me from Flavia. She's had to go out for the day and hopes I'll be OK. I'm to help myself to whatever I want. She suggests I visit Pompeii.

The Circumvesuviana railway trundles out of the east side of Naples and skirts the volcano, calling at St Giorgio and Ercolano, the sun beating down on the crumbling white apartment buildings. I avoid the modern town at Pompeii and head straight for the excavations. German tourists haggle over the entrance fee. I pay and go through, detaching myself from the crowd as soon as I can. They saunter off down the prescribed route armed with guidebooks from which their self-elected leader will read out loud, peculiarly choosing the English-language section, as they pass by the monuments of particular note. The same man – he's wearing a red shirt that bulges over the waistband of his creamy linen trousers – carries the camcorder and will listen impassively to anyone who suggests they operate it instead. They're a distraction from my surroundings: a city preserved to a far greater degree than anything I had been expecting. I wander off into an area of recent excavations where I'm alone with the buzzing insects and basking lizards that dart away at my approach. The heat is overpowering, and after a quarter of an hour threading my way through dug-out paved streets bordered with shoulder-high walls and great swaths of overflowing undergrowth I have to sit down for a rest. I look up at Vesuvius, a huge black shape jiggling from side to side behind the thickening haze.

A bee the size of a fat cockroach lumbers towards me, buzzing like a whole canful of blowflies, and I have to duck to avoid it. Even when it's gone I can still hear it, as if I hadn't managed to get out of the way quickly enough and somehow it got inside my head. The sun, even through the dust in the air, amplifies the noise and cooks my skull so that everything inside it rattles like loose beans. Off down a long straight street to my right I recognise the party of German tourists standing to attention as they listen to the man in the red shirt with the stomach, the camcorder and the guidebook. His words are just a low hum to me amid the constant buzz in my ears. My limbs tingle as if electricity is being passed through them, then they go completely numb and the buzzing gets slower and even louder. At the far end of the long straight street the Germans have frozen in position. The man in the red shirt is in the act of raising the camcorder to his eye, a woman in a wraparound top and shorts is caught in the act of leaning backwards – not ungracefully – to correct the fit of her smart training shoe. The air between them and me is thick with shiny dust, glittering in the golden sunshine. The tiny particles are dancing but the figures remain petrified.

Suddenly they're moving but in a group rather than individually. They are shifted silently to one side like a collection of statues on an invisible moving platform. It's as if they're being shunted into another world while I'm left dodging the insects in this one and I want to go with them. Maybe wherever they're going there won't be this terrible grinding noise that is giving the inside of my skull such a relentless battering.

By the time some feeling returns to my arms and legs the German tourists have completely disappeared. I stumble over the huge baking slabs, trying to escape the punishment. Pursuing the merest hint of a decrease in the noise level, I turn in through an old stone doorway and begin a desperate chase after silence: over boulders, through tangles of nettles and vines where enormous butterflies make sluggish progress through the haze. As the pain levels out and then begins to abate I know I'm heading in the right direction. A couple more sharp turns past huge grass-covered mounds and collapsed walls where lizards the size of rats gulp at the gritty air; the noise fades right down, the pain ebbs and warm, molten, peaceful, brassy sun flows into my bruised head. I fall to my knees with my hands covering my face and when I take them away I'm looking directly into the empty grey eye sockets of a petrified man. His face is contorted by the pain he felt as the lava flowed over him. I'm screaming because the man looks so much like me it's like looking in a mirror, and a lizard suddenly flits out of one of the eyes and slips into the gaping mouth. The pain is back and this time it doesn't go away until I black out.

I'm out for hours because when I come to, rubbing my forehead, the sun casts quite different shadows on the stony face. Dismayingly I have to admit he still looks like me. For several minutes I sit and watch the insects that use his cavities and passages as they would any similar rock formation.

Later I tell Flavia how closely his volcanic features resembled mine.

'It's quite common to hallucinate after an eruption,' she says, applying a piece of sticky tape to the newspaper covering the driver's window.

That's all very well, I think, but I'm two thousand years too late. Or did she mean him? But I don't want to dwell on it because the faster the newspaper goes up the sooner I can have her.

It clicked with me that I could make the most of Flavia's car-bound vivacity so that her passivity at home would not matter as much.

Through a narrow gap at the top of the windscreen I can see Vesuvius rising and falling as Flavia and I punish the old Fiat's suspension.

In a few hours' time I'll be climbing Vesuvius herself.

Flavia's away somewhere – working, she said – so I'm to tackle the volcano alone and although I could have taken a cab to the tourist car park halfway up the mountain I decided to walk all the way from Ercolano, which, as Herculaneum, was itself covered by the same lava flows that buried Pompeii. The road folds over on itself as I climb. The routine is soon automatic as I maintain a regular ascent and efficient breathing. My mind is rerunning

the night before in Flavia's car. Six times her emotions reached
bursting point and boiled over. In the early hours the air in the
car was so thick and cloying we had to wind down the window,
which meant losing part of our newsprint screen, but the park
had emptied hours before.

In her apartment, where I swallowed glass after glass of fresh
orange juice, Flavia was once more still and grey. I was thinking
about getting her out in the car again but I knew I had to climb
the volcano before I left: it had been calling me and this was my
last day in the city.

If the air were not so thick with dust, the view from halfway
up the mountain would be spectacular. I can just make out a
darker shadow, which is the centre of Naples, and a thin line
separating the land from the sea. Only the island of Capri is clear
in the distance but its profile is still no more like a woman than
the trembling slope beneath my feet. Down here there are trees
either side of the road, but I can see that higher up the ground
is bare. The sun still manages to break through the thickening
air and once caught between the ground and the dust the heat
cannot escape. I've taken off my shirt and tied it around my
neck to soak up some of the sweat. The mountain seems to get
no smaller even though I know I'm climbing. The road hugs
the side and disappears some way around the other side before
twisting back on itself to reach the car park and refreshment
stand. I have the sense, the higher I get, of the volcano as an
egg, its exterior thin and brittle and cracked open at the top. I
stop for breath, lean back and stretch. The summit and crater
are covered by cloud.

Beyond the empty car park the narrow path zigzags into the
clouds. I climb with the same sense of purpose that took hold
of Flavia and me in the car, and I sense that the prize is not
so far removed from that sweet and fiery memory, which even
now stirs me. The earth and trees have been left behind and the
slate-grey cloud thickens about me like hospital blankets. The
mountain is loose cinders and disintegrated volcanic material,
a uniform grey-brown, like a dying horse in a burnt field. I'm
suddenly engulfed by a wave of sympathy for Flavia and her
years of suffering. They have turned her into a brittle shell, but

life lingers within her, a dormant energy that last night we fired up. She deserves longer-lasting happiness and yet I know she wouldn't even flicker in some other city; Naples is her only home. Some things are rooted too deeply in the earth to shift.

Never in my life have I felt so alone as I feel now, wrapped in cloud, buffeted by sea winds, following a path to a crater. I can't see more than ten barren yards in any direction.

When I hear the music I think I've died or am still asleep in Flavia's bed and dreaming. Soft notes that gather a little power then fade quickly as the wind blows new ones slightly up or down the scale. I've already called Flavia's name three times before I realise I'm doing it. The name is taken from my lips and wrapped in this soiled cotton wool that surrounds me. Her name rolls on with the cloud over the top of the mountain where the crater must be. It mustn't fall in.

The source of the music comes into view – an abandoned shack supported by an exoskeleton of tubular steel shafts. The wind plays them like panpipes. A sign still attached to the side of the shack advertises the sale of tickets to the crater. I begin to laugh at the absurdity of such an idea and wade on past the chiming tubes and up towards the edge. I know it's up there somewhere although I can't see it and I stumble blindly onwards, scuffing my shoes in coarse, loose material. Then suddenly the ground disappears beneath my feet and I'm clawing at space for a handhold. Somehow I manage to fall back rather than forward and I crouch in the harsh volcanic rubble peering over the edge of the crater. Below me the cloud twists in draughts of warm air. I'm muttering Flavia's name to myself and thinking I should never have gone to look for her. Then I'm thinking maybe I never did go, but stayed in the insect-ridden hotel instead.

As I watch the updraughts of ash and dust I see a recognisable group of shapes take vague form in the clouds. The German tourists – he with the red shirt, the camcorder, the stomach, she of the shorts and smart training shoes, still frozen as an exhibit of statuary – descend through the rising dust as if on a platform. The thicker swirls beneath me envelop them.

They pass into the throat of the giant and are followed by a facsimile of Flavia, falling like a slow bomb. A cast of myself

– whether from Pompeii or the hotel, I don't know – is next, slipping in and out of focus behind curtains of clogging ash.

The last thing I remember is the buffeting and turbulence the 737 went through as it passed over Vesuvius on its descent into Naples, and suddenly the whole crazy city with its strange visions and coating of fine dust – from a waiter's shoes to the air rattling in lungs – makes perfect sense.

THE CHURRING

Corpse fowl. Goatsucker. The nightjar is inside my head. Its ghostly, premonitory clicking. The ironic applause of its wing-beat handclap. A summer visitor, Sylvia Plath's 'Devil-bird' casts its deadly shadow from May onwards. I have just one bird-spotting book (I'm not a twitcher. I don't need the ticks) and it's one my father gave me when I was ten. 'To Alexander,' he wrote inside it, 'on becoming amphibious.' Underneath, in my own childish hand, I have added a key: a pencil tick indicates that I have seen a particular bird, a tick in green ballpoint means my sister has beaten me to it (I needed the ticks then, but not now). The nightjar is ticked by neither of us. The cuckoo, on the page before, has a green tick, which strikes me as unlikely. The swift, which follows the nightjar, has two entirely plausible ticks.

The book is inaccurate. The nightjar, it says, 'is more often seen than heard'. In fact, the reverse is widely known to be true. I wonder whether the text, which appears to have been translated from the Czech (of Jaroslav Spirhanzl Duris) *by* a Czech (Hedda Veselá-Stránská), has been adequately checked. I do, however, like how the writer describes the nightjar's song, as 'a cry like that of a sewing machine in action'. I'm so used to seeing the goatsucker's song described in print as a 'churring', for some reason always with inverted commas, that the sewing-machine analogy always makes me hear it afresh. At first I thought it missed the mark: the sewing machine is too noisy, the whirr of the turning wheel, the rustle of the fabric. But I've ended up thinking it's actually quite a good comparison, especially when I remember that my mother's sewing machine, constantly audible on the soundtrack of my childhood, was a Singer. It's difficult to describe birdsong, but here is someone who's had a go, and maybe a Soviet-era Czech sewing machine (the book was published four years before the Prague Spring) sounds a little different to today's cutting-edge equivalent.

I close the book and notice that the head of the goldfinch on the spine has faded, its red face a pale ochre. I return the book to the shelf and go downstairs, picking up stray books and magazines as I go.

I'm in the middle of getting the house ready for the annual meeting of the Fallowfield Film Society, which falls, as it has done for the last ten years or so, on the second weekend in May. For the benefit of those group members who are parents, it has to be scheduled for after Easter and the May Day bank holiday, but before Whit Week, so that it doesn't interfere with school holidays. Childless myself, I don't object. 'Child free', I recently read in the newspaper, is preferred by some to 'childless', as it accentuates the positive side of not having children, the having taken a decision not to have any, rather than suggesting the terrible lack of something, the unbearable regret. That was in a column by a young woman who never misses an opportunity to express her displeasure at children and her impatience with over-indulgent parents. She comes across as chippy and vituperative. In any case, I don't have a problem with children. I like children.

The kitchen is a mess, newspapers and CDs everywhere. I collect the jewel cases together and stow them on the shelf in the alcove. I eject Bartok's nerve-jangling string quartets from the CD player and replace them with Beethoven's more restful piano sonatas. As an afterthought, I check the cassette deck. It contains a very old green BASF C90. I take it out and sit down on one of the stools at the island in the middle of the kitchen. I turn the cassette over in my hands, studying it, as if it were unfamiliar to me, as if I hadn't spent long nights listening to it over and over again. Play, rewind, play, rewind, play. On the label, in my father's handwriting, I read: 'Wed 28th June 1978. Cannock Chase'. I move my fingertips lightly over the line of text as if reading Braille.

Unsure where the cassette case is, I slip the tape into my top pocket and start stacking the newspapers that have accumulated on the island during the week. A headline catches my eye, as it had the day I'd bought the paper it was in: 'CAN YOU CATCH CANCER?'

Pretty effective. It made you stop and think. It certainly made me stop and think, although it didn't make me read the article. Not because I'm squeamish or anything, but because the question more or less contained its own answer. Can you catch cancer? What was the piece likely to go on to say? It wouldn't be a flat 'no', obviously, or the headline would be a bit cheap. Hardly a resounding 'yes' either, or the feature would surely be headed 'YOU CAN CATCH CANCER' and everyone would read the article and it wouldn't be the lead story in the second section, either. It would be front-page news.

So, probably, the piece would weigh up some recently uncovered facts and statistics and end up saying, 'Well, perhaps. Sort of. Maybe.'

Responsibility for hosting the meetings rotates around the group. This year it's my turn. People start arriving on the Friday afternoon and by mid-morning on Saturday everyone is present. I make it sound like a bigger event than it is, perhaps. It's not a real film society with a projector and an audience. The invite list is basically three couples, plus children. And me. Luckily I have a big house.

If you went to university in Manchester in the early 1980s and had the sense to get on the housing ladder at that time, twenty years later you could, like me, be living in a house worth half a million. That's assuming you didn't fritter away your student grant and then hit the overland trail the moment you graduated. If you lived sensibly and walked straight into a local-government job on graduation, a flat or even a small house in Fallowfield wasn't beyond your means. Sell that for a tidy profit five years later and buy a Victorian terraced in Chorlton and you were halfway there. By that stage it's hard to go wrong. Before you know it you've landed in Didsbury, owning the sort of house the estate agents in the village would be describing as a 'prestige property' by the end of the next decade.

Everyone gathers in the kitchen and I make coffee and open a packet of biscuits for the kids. The newspapers on the island have become unstacked again, plus there are more of them now. I make an effort to gather them up. On top, by chance, is that piece about catching cancer. Still unread. I move the papers to the alcove, where they will be out of the way and the headline won't upset anybody.

I hand a cup of strong black coffee to Iain, who is here with his partner, Steph.

'I can't remember how you take it, Steph.'

'White without, please, Alex.'

Steph is pretty, with a short dark bob, a severe pair of glasses and an odd line in 1950s dresses worn over leggings and suchlike. All a bit 1980s, in fact. She works in advertising. She's a few years younger than Iain, who's my age, early forties. For years Iain struggled with hair loss. He didn't seem to know what to do with what he'd got, whether to grow it or crop it, whether to use gel and make a feature of it or hide it under a baseball cap. One day he shaved it all off, what was left of it, and this became his regular look. He has the overhanging brow of a Ralph Fiennes and the amused, somewhat untrustworthy glint of a Clive Owen or a Ciaran Hinds in his smile. Iain and I were on the same landing in halls of residence at Owens Park in Fallowfield and I became his friend primarily because I liked his then girlfriend, Jenny, whom I'd met through the Student Labour Club. The three of us hung out together a lot, and in our visits to the Aaben in Hulme, making full use of its four screens showing a mixture of schlock, art-house and new releases, lay the origins of the Fallowfield Film Society.

Iain and Jenny surprised everbody, including themselves, when Jenny became pregnant in 1986. The following year three momentous things happened: their son, Jacob, was born; Iain and Jenny got married shortly after; and within four months Jenny was diagnosed with breast cancer. She died two years later, while the Berlin Wall was being torn down. Whenever those scenes are replayed on television, which happens more often than you might think, Iain finds himself instantly catapulted back into the grieving process. It can throw him out for up to a week, which may be a little disconcerting for Steph, but it's not as if she didn't know what she was getting herself into. Jacob is grown up and away doing his own thing, but Iain and Steph have a child of their own, six-year-old Thomas. I want to like him, but to be honest he's a bit precocious, which I attribute to Steph. Thomas is in the front room with the other children, where I've put on a video for them.

Nina is a beautiful, delicate-featured Indian woman. Her wavy hair is going elegantly grey, in streaks, a bit like Susan Sontag. She's wearing a blue sari. When she was going out with my best friend Richard Salthouse in the early 1980s, I would join them for pub crawls around Withington and film screenings at CineCity. In those days Nina wore the same as me and Richard – jeans, T-shirts, secondhand jackets. When I became friendly with Iain and Jenny, I introduced the two couples to each other and everyone got on, the five of us spending time together as a group.

The following year, investigating the social potential of the Federation of Conservative Students, I met James, who would become the sixth member of our group, which had by now been given its name.

Later, Richard started fitting and having blackouts. They took him in for tests and found an aggressive malignant brain tumour the size of a tangerine. His condition was terminal and his decline mercifully swift; nevertheless, the shock of his disappearance from our lives was like a punch in the gut. Nina dropped out of college and withdrew from everyone who'd known her and Richard as a couple. She went to India and came back in a sari. An arranged marriage, which she'd previously resisted, followed, but it didn't last. Nine years ago she met Sunil, a lecturer in statistics at Manchester Poly. He's not very exciting, but he seems to make Nina happy, so that's fair enough. They have a boy and a girl, Vishnu and Raji, aged eight and six respectively. Right now they're in the front room with Thomas.

'What film have you chosen for us, Alex?' asks Steph.

I smile.

'Nice try, Steph,' says James with a laugh, raising his dark eyebrows above the gold glint of his round-eye frames.

James is reminding Steph that the choice of film, which is the prerogative of the host, is kept secret until the screening is ready to begin.

'Are you not bringing anyone, James?' Steph asks him. 'Or has he yet to arrive?'

'You never know who's going to turn up,' James says, with a little look in my direction. 'Actually, I did meet a very nice young man in Taurus last night, but I'm not sure this would be his scene.'

'Not enough rubber?' Steph asks. She delights in bringing out the queen in James.

'Oh, I don't think he's into rubber, although I haven't yet got to know him *that* well.'

At this point there's a clatter of wings and a loud ratcheting cry from the back garden.

'What's that?' Nina asks, and I notice that Sunil looks relieved at the change of subject.

'Magpie,' I say as I watch the delicate, springy branches of the cherry tree take its weight.

'What a racket!' Nina exclaims. 'Alex knows all the different birds,' she adds for Sunil's benefit, although he's known me long enough perhaps to know of my avian enthusiasms. 'You know, when we started, we didn't meet in people's houses. After all, we didn't have houses, did we?' She looks at me and at Iain. 'Remember when we went to Dorset?'

'*Five Go Mad in Dorset*,' says Iain.

'Except there were seven of us,' I remind him. 'You and Jenny, Nina and Richard, James and whoever he was with that weekend – and me.'

'I'm trying to remember,' Iain says, looking at James. 'Didn't you pick someone up there?'

'No, I wasn't that bad. Well, not then,' James says with a laugh. 'Wasn't I with Tim then?' he adds, looking straight at me.

I kick myself for having given him the prompt. Tim was an obsessive Smiths fan who James went out with for a few weeks. He did come on the trip to Dorset. How could I forget? Quite easily, if it wasn't for what actually happened in Wareham, because in any gathering he blended into the background. I can quite imagine having him in the back of my car, so to speak, and not being aware of him, as his lips move in silent autistic repetition of Morrissey's hallowed lyrics.

'He was the Smiths fan, wasn't he?' Iain asks.

'Who wasn't in those days?' says Nina. 'Richard certainly was.'

I remember that Richard was. He used to try to convince me that I should listen to their albums. I told him I liked Joy Division and the Passage, that they were my Manchester bands. A Certain Ratio. The Fall. There was no room for whiny self-obsessed losers in my record collection, I told him.

Having mentioned Richard's name, Nina gazes out of the window. I've noticed that whenever he is the subject of conversation, everything about her seems somehow to slow down. Sunil always tries to take her hand and she lets him, but there's a moment when you can see how she still misses Richard badly. How it still hurts.

'I think Tim did go to Dorset,' James says. 'Surely you remember, Alex?' he presses me.

I return his look.

'Why should Alex remember?' Nina asks, snapping out of her moment of sadness and withdrawing her hand from Sunil's.

'It was Alex's weekend, wasn't it?' James says, turning to face me again. 'You organised it. You were in charge. Alex is a born organiser, aren't you, Alex?'

I did organise it, although it didn't take much organising. Two cars, mine and Richard's. Iain and Jenny went in Richard's car with him and Nina, leaving James and Tim to go in my car. I remember James sitting alongside me, so Tim must have been in the back. He really was one of those forgettable people. I've certainly forgotten him. If only James could.

We drove down in convoy on a Saturday in April. The Rex in Wareham was the country's only gas-lit picture house. The cinema itself would have been worth the trip on its own, but it was playing host to a mini-festival, a horror all-nighter. According to what had already become a tradition, I didn't tell anyone where we were going, merely that it was a very long drive and we would be coming back the following day. That we didn't need accommodation was what especially intrigued everyone.

The festival opened early on Saturday evening with an

irresistible splash of gore: Lucio Fulci's *Zombie Flesh Eaters*. The second film, the rather silly *Blood Beach*, was one I had already seen and I persuaded Richard and Nina to give it a miss. 'You're missing nothing,' I assured them. We drove the short distance to Canford Heath, north of Poole, and parked on the edge of a housing estate, then took a path on to the heath. In the twilight, away from the street lamps and lit windows of the estate, the sky became a liquid electric blue. The trees and shrubs around us formed vaguely suggestive shapes in the gathering gloom.

'What are we looking for?' Richard asked.

'Dartford warblers, nightjars,' I said. 'Nightjars really. Bit late in the day, perhaps, for Dartford warblers, but it's just the right time of day and the perfect environment for nightjars. Slightly early in the season, but we might get lucky, especially this far south.'

'What does a nightjar look like?' asked Nina.

'A bit like a kestrel or a cuckoo. In fact we're very unlikely to see one. More likely to hear one. It sounds like…It's almost more like a knocking sound than a song. Like a woodpecker, only not on wood, more, I don't know, metallic somehow. They call it a churring. Rhymes with whirring.'

'We're not looking for Dartford warblers at all, are we?' said Richard.

'No, we're not. As you very well know.'

Nina gave us a look.

'We're looking for nightjars,' I said. 'Have you not told Nina, then, Richard?'

'Told me what?'

'I would have thought couples told each other stuff like this.'

'You told me it was personal,' Richard said.

'It was. I just imagined…'

'A lot of couples share everything, but if you tell me something and tell me it's personal, it goes no further.'

'Well, that's…nice, I suppose.'

'Is someone going to tell me what's going on?' Nina asked.

'It's nothing really,' I said. 'Just that I'm interested in nightjars. My father had a special interest in them, so in a way they're my link to him. My only link, really.'

'Your father died, didn't he?'

'Yes, he died in 1979, when I was sixteen. Lung cancer.'

'That must have been very hard.'

We came to a fork in the path. We split up. It was Nina's idea. She suggested she go one way and Richard the other.

'I'll go with Nina,' I said.

'I can manage,' she said. 'You go with Richard.'

In the end, it was decided that since we would have to return to the car by the same path, Nina and I would each explore one of the two forks, while Richard would wait at the point where the path divided for us to come back. The left fork, mine, led quite quickly into full forest, which I knew was the wrong terrain for nightjars, so I went back and rejoined Richard. While we were waiting for Nina, we suddenly heard a sound. It came from the open ground to the left: a steady uninterrupted clicking. We looked at each other, eyes wide, and I nodded. 'That's it,' I whispered. 'That's a nightjar. No question.'

'Are you sure?'

'A hundred per cent.'

'The tape recording your father made?'

'Identical.'

We strained our eyes in the dark, but there was nothing to see. No bird sat in a tree silhouetted against the sky. No hawklike shape flew past us questing for prey. The nightjar was on the ground somewhere, churring, and given that they were practically invisible by day, thanks to the superb camouflage provided by their grey-brown feathers and mottled, barred markings, what chance did we have of seeing it in the darkness?

None. But it didn't matter. We had heard it, and with the nightjar, that counted.

The churring continued for up to a minute, rising and falling in pitch. Richard and I breathed slowly and quietly, leg muscles taut from standing on tiptoe, focusing all our efforts on listening. Eventually it stopped. We waited, tense and expectant, for it to start again, but it didn't. We relaxed, let the tension flow out of our bodies. Richard bent over, pressing his hands against his knees. I rested mine on Richard's shoulder. My legs felt wobbly. It was the first time I had heard the churring in the flesh, my first actual encounter with a nightjar. Even if we hadn't seen it, I had had a clear image in my mind of its enormous black eyes and cavernous mouth, its beak edged with bristles. I pictured it on the wing, hoovering up moths and beetles like a whale shark gorging on plankton.

'It's like a Geiger counter,' Richard said.

'What?' I said, keeping my eyes averted.

'It sounds like a Geiger counter.'

I thought of the blasts of radiation my father had had to endure at the Christie Hospital. All for nothing.

Shortly after that, we heard Nina returning along her fork of the path. We told her about the churring and she wanted to wait around and see whether we would hear it again. We gave it ten minutes or so, but the night was as quiet as the grave, and eventually we headed back to where we'd left the car.

We got back to Wareham in time to watch child actor Mark Lester touching up Britt Ekland in the third instalment in that night's programme, *Night Hair Child* – and rather wished we hadn't.

Richard fell ill later that year. After he died, Nina told me how happy he had been in the days after the weekend in Wareham. Specifically it seemed to have been hearing the nightjar that had moved him so deeply. Hearing it, moreover, in my presence, because he had a pretty good idea what it meant to me.

'If you could have seen his face,' she told me, 'you'd have known it was worth all the effort of getting us down there.'

We go for a walk in the afternoon. Fletcher Moss Gardens, with its south-facing hillside rockeries and botanical riches, attracts a lot of birds. In the low flat meadows between the park and the River Mersey I once saw a fieldfare (slightly dubious pencil tick in the book) and more recently a small bird I thought might be a bullfinch, but which I doubt since I discovered how rare they've become.

The children run on ahead. Iain and Sunil walk together and I'm flanked by Steph and Nina. James is hanging back, making a phone call. I wonder who he's calling. I even let Steph and Nina dictate our slow pace in the hope that he might approach within earshot. James lives in an apartment in one of the big conversions in town. India House. Very much the bachelor lifestyle. The single gay man's lifestyle, to be precise. The anonymity of the corridors. Could almost be a hotel. I wonder whether he ever sees Tim these days. Maybe he's calling the lad he met in Taurus, trying to persuade him to join us for tonight's screening.

'So what have we got to look forward to tonight?' Nina asks, as if reading my mind.

'You'll find out soon enough.'

'More horror, I suppose,' she adds, with a sigh of mock impatience.

'I don't always pick horror films,' I protest. 'Didn't I pick a film about birds last time?'

'Yes,' says Steph. 'Hitchcock's *The Birds*.'

'Ah, yes. Look, next time, I promise. I'll find something different. Although don't assume you're going to hate tonight's film. It has local appeal, I'll say that much.'

Nina and Sunil moved out to Cumbria, close to the M6, to facilitate Sunil's commute to the poly, now MMU, while Steph and Iain live in north London. Steph is a big cheese at one of the ad agencies in Fitzrovia; Iain works part time for a housing charity and does the school run.

I notice that Iain and Sunil have stopped and Sunil is pointing at a small bird in a tree.

'What is it?' he asks me when we catch up.

'A chaffinch,' I say.

Sunil looks hopeful. 'Are they rare?' he asks.

'No, they're very common,' I say, and I wonder whether it was a chaffinch I saw when I thought I'd seen a bullfinch, except there's a marked difference in size. A hawfinch, then, perhaps.

Sunil, Steph, Nina and I are still watching the chaffinch, the UK's second-commonest breeding bird, hardly deserving of our attention, when I realise Iain has left us and is walking off towards the children.

The 1987 meeting was always going to be tricky. Jacob was less than three months old, yet Iain and Jenny, to their credit, said they were not going to let the side down and would attend. There may have been one or two members slightly less excited at the prospect of a small baby joining the group, but those people kept their opinions to themselves.

It was to be Nina's first meeting since Richard's death. She was back from India but the arranged marriage was not yet in the bag, so she came on her own. James was definitely a solo act that year. (The previous year had been James's turn as host and he had taken us all to the Aaben, where we each drew lots to decide which film we saw. Somehow he and his then partner, Andrew, ended up together in screen number four, but didn't see much of the picture. I sat through Wim Wenders' *The Goalkeeper's Fear of the Penalty Kick*, having had my request to swap with Iain, who'd landed a double bill of *Halloween* and *Assault on Precinct 13*, turned down.)

I had hired a small farmhouse on the edge of the North York Moors. There was neither a VCR nor a television. On the first night Iain, James and I went to the pub, leaving Nina and Jenny with the baby in the farmhouse. Iain and Jenny tended to give each other breaks from childcare, and Nina said she would prefer to stay behind with Jenny. I waited until we were on our second pint apiece to ask Iain and James whether they felt like a walk in the forest.

'Cropton Forest,' I said. 'It's just up the road.'

'Go on, then.'

The road allowed us to drive into the forest, then turn on to a bridleway. I pulled over when it narrowed to a track and we got out and walked.

'What are we looking for?' Iain asked.

'Any cleared section,' I said. 'This is nightjar country. They like it where the trees have been cut down.'

I told them what to listen for if we did come across any man-made clearings. Eventually we did, but if there were any goatsuckers present, they were keeping quiet about it.

On the way back to the car James asked why I was so interested in nightjars.

'No special reason, except they're extremely rare,' I said, 'and there's a whole mythology grown up around them. They're supposed to steal milk from goats, which of course they don't.'

People say they presage misfortune and even death, hence "corpse fowl" – another nickname. If one lands on the roof of your house, you're fucked, basically. Fortunately they don't tend to come into residential areas.'

The following day we drove to Whitby and toured the Dracula sites, visiting the abbey and St Mary's churchyard. In the afternoon there was a special screening of Terence Fisher's 1958 adaptation of Stoker's novel at Whitby Museum. This wasn't a great success, with baby Jacob screaming the place down when he woke up and tried to get out of his pushchair halfway through. As we left, Nina told me she wanted to go home to Manchester and asked me whether I would drive her to York so she could catch a train. We tried to persuade her to stay another night, but she was adamant. In the end, James took her. He said he needed to get back to Manchester as well to take care of a work matter and so the two of them left that year's meeting before it was really over. A sense of anti-climax hung over the farmhouse and I asked Jenny whether she wanted to go out hunting for nightjars, assuming it was Iain's turn to look after the baby.

As Jenny and I walked through the forest on a different path to the one I had taken with Iain and James the night before, we talked in low voices. I had always been close to Jenny. I think it was because I sensed in her an acceptance of me, a lack of judgement. She was constant, happy with herself and secure in her opinions. Even having had a child didn't seem to have changed her a great deal.

'It's a bit weird, James and Nina leaving early,' I said.

'I think it's been hard for Nina,' Jenny said, casting sidelong glances into the darkness between the trees. 'You know, it was her first meeting since losing Richard. She's been in India, getting her head straight. Probably the last thing she needed – and I'm not criticising your choice – but maybe a Dracula weekend wasn't the ideal one to come back on.'

'Oh,' I said, disconsolately, 'yeah.'

'I think whatever it had been, even if it had been someone else's turn to choose, she would have struggled.'

Jenny was being kind to me. We walked in silence for a while.

'Alex,' she said after a bit, 'can I ask you a question?'

'Um, of course.'

'Why do you never have anyone with you on these weekends? I mean, why have you been on your own for so long? I hope you don't mind me asking, but are you gay or do you just not like girls or what?' It had come out in a rush and for a moment all either of us could hear was the sound of our feet landing on the path and the occasional crack of a broken twig.

Eventually, I opened my mouth to answer and Jenny started speaking at the same time.

'You know what?' she said. 'Ignore all of that. It was a mistake. I shouldn't have said it.'

'No…No…It's fine. It's…I…' I was having trouble formulating a response. 'Am I gay? I don't know. I watch James, I see what he gets up to and who he gets up to it with, and I think to myself I could do that. I see guys I like the look of. But could I really, *really* go through with it? I don't know.' I thought for a moment as I looked into the forest ahead of us. There was a clearing coming up. 'Why am I always alone? It's not that I want to be, but I can't seem to get my head round the alternative. I'm not sure I'm very comfortable with people. With a few exceptions. Like you. But you're taken and you have been as long as I've known you, and I'm not the kind of person who can do anything about something like that. Ssh!'

I stopped and put my hand out and Jenny held her breath alongside me. The clearing on the right was just a few yards away. We listened, but there was nothing to hear. Slowly we advanced, taking care to step lightly on the path. Then, what I'd thought I'd heard I heard again. The unmistakable churring of a nightjar. It was very close to us. No more than twenty feet away. We stood transfixed. I felt Jenny's hand take hold of mine and squeeze it. I held tight as we listened. I felt enormously privileged. I felt the very edge of something I suspected was happiness, or the possibility of happiness, but also I felt like a pauper touching the hem of the king's robes. Then I remembered the last time I had heard the churring, with Richard, and I felt a strange sensation in my stomach. It wasn't sadness or regret. It didn't make me feel wholesome. It was not unlike a caffeine high. I felt apprehensive and a little excited, and I didn't know whether I liked it or not.

As we walked back, Jenny took my arm and leaned her upper body against mine. At the time I interpreted it as a caring, protective gesture. With hindsight and the knowledge that only a matter of weeks lay between that night and the diagnosis of Jenny's breast cancer, I wonder whether it was the other way around and whether it was that she was seeking support from me.

The night contained one further surprise. As we reached the car and separated and I walked around to the driver's side, Jenny said, 'What about Tim?'

'What *about* Tim? What do you mean?' I looked over the roof of the car at Jenny. It was too dark to read her expression.

Eventually she shook her head and said, 'Never mind.'

On the drive back to the farmhouse a barn owl flashed across the road in front of the car, its moon-like face briefly caught in the headlamps. Jenny gasped, but neither of us spoke.

I've made chilli. On our return from Fletcher Moss, I heat it up and open a couple of beers and a bottle of wine. Everyone's in the back room apart from me. I'm in the kitchen chopping up coriander to sprinkle on the chilli. Nina comes through and asks whether she can help. I tell her there's nothing to do and she leans back against the cooker, raising her wineglass to her lips. She asks me how my job with the council is going, am I enjoying it, am I being sufficiently stretched? Nina can be quite direct. I tell her it's fine. Then I tell her it's a bit dull, actually, and not terribly rewarding. Out of the blue I tell her I'm thinking of standing for Parliament.

'To be an MP?' she asks incredulously.

'Why not?'

'No reason. I'm just surprised.' She looks at me quizzically, then adds: 'For which party?'

'Wherever I'll do best.'

'You mean do the best work for people or have the best chance of getting in?'

'I wouldn't be going into politics in order to lose.'

'Yes, but left or right? Red or blue?'

'Whichever's going to get in. It might even be yellow. It's yellow round here nowadays. Dirty tricks over Christie's. According to Labour.' Nina is staring at me in apparent bafflement. 'Just a thought,' I said. 'Will you give me a hand with these plates?'

'What if the party that stood the greatest chance of winning was the BNP? What would you do then?'

I paused, appearing to give the question serious consideration.

'Alex!'

'No, of course I wouldn't join the BNP,' I said, smiling. 'They're still not respectable. I need to be respectable. I *am* respectable.'

'But what if they managed to make themselves respectable while still pursuing the same policies? Would you go against what you believe in merely to gain power?'

'Go against what I believe in?' I stopped serving chilli for a moment and looked at her. 'That's my great strength, Nina. I don't believe in anything.' I looked away as her face creased in disapproval. 'That's why I quite like the idea of the Liberal Democrats.'

'Skeletons in the cupboard?' Nina asks, changing tack.

'If I've got any I'll take care of them. Trust me. I'm serious.'

We take the plates through.

We're ready to start the screening. I put the DVD on and no one recognises the title that comes up on screen, *Let Sleeping Corpses Lie.*

'What's this, Alex?' Iain asks.

'That's the American title. The British title was *The Living Dead at the Manchester Morgue.*'

Nina groans and Iain laughs.

'Watch these opening shots,' I advise. 'It's Manchester in the early seventies. Orange buses. Miserable-looking shoppers. That antique shop is right near the cathedral, just this side of Victoria station.'

'Great,' says James. 'The Manchester everybody was glad to see consigned to the dustbin of history.'

'By the IRA,' adds Iain.

'I'm not sure they should take full credit,' says Steph.

'The end justifies the means?' says Nina, without looking away from the screen, but I know for whose benefit she said it.

'Are we watching the film or what?' I say.

'Sorry.'

'Soz.'

The choice of film is a qualified success. Its unusual blend of American lead (Arthur Kennedy), Euro zombies (director Jorge Grau) and English pastoral (most of it is shot in the Lake District) was never going to make it a mainstream hit, but it works for me.

'It's a bit derivative of *Night of the Living Dead*, don't you think?' says Iain.

'Well, it's a zombie movie.'

'We saw that in Wareham, didn't we?' Iain says.

'Did we?' I say.

'Some of us did,' says Nina. 'It was on in the early hours. I remember you and James and James's friend Tim squeezing past me to leave the cinema when it had only just started.' She's watching me as she says this, as if to gauge my reaction.

'I'd seen it before,' I say. 'I must have needed some air.'

I could do with some air right now.

'The three of you were gone for some time,' Nina says.

I notice Sunil take Nina's hand.

'Well,' I say. 'I'm going to put some coffee on.'

Iain follows me into the kitchen.

I'm filling the kettle, aware of Iain sitting down at the table next to the alcove. I hear him pick up a newspaper.

'Did you read this?' he asks.

'What's that?' I say, turning round. 'Oh, that. No, I intended to, but haven't got round to it yet. So what does it say?'

'I read it the other day. It's about how cervical cancer develops from one virus and stomach cancer from another. That sort of thing. Kaposi's sarcoma from HIV. It's good news, though. That they're making these discoveries, I mean. If they know that a particular virus might cause cancer, and if they can flick a switch to stop us getting the virus, then we're less likely to get cancer. Well, that cancer, anyway.'

'That's good,' I say, pouring the water into the cafetière.

'Jacob's boyfriend had a scare recently.'

'What?' I look up.

'Jacob's boyfriend. He had these red marks on his back, got

them checked out. Harmless, thank goodness, but we were worried sick for about a week.'

'Jacob's gay?' I say, putting the cafetière down.

'Yes. Didn't you know?'

'How would I know?'

'I don't know. I thought everyone knew.'

'How do you feel about it?'

'How do I feel about it? Great! I mean, why wouldn't I?'

'Jenny...'

'Jacob was two when Jenny died. A bit young to be hanging out down Canal Street.'

'It's just a shock, that's all. I mean, I had no idea,' I say, sitting down at the table across from Iain.

'There are a lot of things about Jacob that Jenny never got to know. His sexuality is only one of them. It's not a problem for you, is it?'

I shake my head. 'Of course not. I'm just trying to take it in.'

Iain smiles and folds the newspaper.

'It's just a pity,' I say, 'that more fathers can't be as forgiving as you've been.'

'What's to forgive?' A trace of scorn has crept into his voice. I suppose if I don't explain, he can't understand.

'Accepting, then. Not forgiving. Accepting.'

'It's just the way things are. Times change.'

We sit in silence for a while.

Eventually I speak. 'I wish I could be more like you. More accepting. More forgiving, in my case. But I can't. I've tried and I can't.'

'Forgiveness breeds forgiveness. The inability to forgive creates rancour, and that can spread like a cancer,' he says equably, replacing the newspaper on the pile. 'That coffee should be ready by now.'

When everyone has retired for the night, I unplug the stereo from the kitchen and take it up to my bedroom. I crawl into bed and drop the green cassette into the machine, close the little door and press play. It plays for thirty seconds and then has to be rewound and played again, over and over. The churring of a nightjar recorded at Cannock Chase, Staffordshire, on 28 June 1978.

It was the year I took my O-levels and for some reason the German and French oral exams took place about six weeks before the written papers, which we sat in June and July. The German oral was first, towards the end of April. That spring I'd been hanging out with a kid from another class. I never knew his real name, but everyone called him Faz. He had floppy blond hair that fell down low over his eyes and he was forever sweeping it out of his face like my sister. When you could see his eyes, they sparkled. We never really questioned why we'd been spending time together. We didn't have a lot in common. I collected bus numbers; he played cricket for the school. But if I look back at my diary I see that throughout March and April I spent a lot of time at his house and he at mine. The German orals took place on the Tuesday and Wednesday in the last week in April. Faz came to ours on the Saturday. Whether you blame the pressure we'd been under to get through the oral, or we just took 'oral' too literally, we ended up in my bedroom on the Saturday afternoon, believing ourselves alone in the house. Maybe we were at the start, but we became too involved in what we were doing and didn't hear my father climbing the stairs. He pushed open the door – maybe he'd knocked, I don't know – and saw us, Faz sitting on the edge of the bed and me kneeling on the floor. I turned and looked at him and he looked at me and I braced myself for an assault of some kind, whether verbal or physical, but none came. He just stepped back out of the room and closed the door.

Faz is not mentioned in my diary again after that. My father never spoke to me about what he had witnessed, nor did he tell my mother, as far as I could tell. He'd always been interested in ornithology and had a special fondness for nocturnal birds, the nightjar in particular, although he had never seen or heard one. He started going on longer bird-watching trips, staying out overnight, sometimes longer. If my mother asked him for an explanation, I don't know what he said to her. One afternoon I arrived home and my father's car was standing in the drive. The Philips cassette recorder that was his normal means of listening to tapes in the kitchen was sitting on the passenger seat. Through the little perspex window I could see a green BASF cassette. I was peering at this equipment when my father came out of the house and approached the car. When he saw me, he stopped and looked down. He seemed almost frightened of me. I waited for a moment, but he didn't look up, and I walked past him into the house.

I dealt with the situation by focusing solely on my exams, which finished in early July. We were supposed to be going on a family holiday to Cornwall, but it was cancelled. My father had to go to Christie's for tests.

He died the following May, just as the nightjars would have been arriving from Africa.

In the morning, Iain, Steph and Thomas set off for London straight after breakfast. Nina and Sunil are in less of a hurry, allowing Vishnu his regular Sunday morning lie-in. Raji watches DVDs while waiting for her brother to get up. James sits in the kitchen doing the cryptic crosswords in the Sunday papers, one after another. After a late lunch Nina and Sunil start packing their car. I go out to say goodbye. Nina winds down her window to thank me for the weekend.

'It was my pleasure,' I say.

She smiles and looks through the windscreen, then back at me. 'Were you serious about running for office?' she asks.

'Absolutely. Skeleton removal work begins today.'

This makes her laugh. I laugh, too. Sunil waves and they drive off, the children's noses buried in their Gameboys.

I go back into the house. James is working on the final corner of the *Observer* crossword.

'Do you want to go for a walk later, if you're not in a hurry to get back?' I ask him.

'Sounds good,' he says without looking up.

'Bit of a drive first, but it's something to do, if you're sure you don't have to be home by a particular time.'

'I've got nothing on till tomorrow morning.'

'Perfect.'

He completes the crossword. 'There!' he says, dropping the paper on the table. 'Where are we going, then?'

'Cannock Chase,' I say, 'but there's no hurry. We can drive down on the A34, take it slowly. Find a nice little pub and have a couple of drinks, then have a walk in the forest and drive back up the M6. I'll drop you back in town.'

'Whatever,' he says as he sifts through the papers on the table looking for another crossword.

I sit and watch the light outside the window, waiting for the first signs of it beginning to fade.

NEGATIVES

If night-time motorway driving didn't have such a numbing effect on the mind and the senses, he wouldn't have needed to wake himself up by accelerating down the inside lane and into trouble in the way that he did.

The queues out of London had begun thinning out near Luton and disappeared after Milton Keynes. There were still plenty of cars on the road but now they were moving at a proper speed.

He kept to a steady seventy in the inside lane, aware that it was a little too fast for the car over a long distance, and he would probably have to top up water and oil at Rothersthorpe or Watford Gap.

The road was straight; the distance to the next car in front remained constant. He'd tried listening to music but couldn't hear it over the noise of the engine. Now and again he looked over at the passenger seat and smiled at Melanie. Despite the noise and her conviction that she wouldn't, she'd managed to fall asleep.

For a brief moment he had a detached view of himself: sitting in a small chair hurtling through the darkness encased in this strange little shell called a car. It was like sitting in a chair at home and being taken somewhere. He felt as if he should be able to get up and go and make a coffee. The steering wheel and pedals seemed incidental. Then with a jolt he was back there driving the car again.

The road disappeared under the car, perfectly uniform from one bridge to the next. He opened his eyelids and wondered how long they'd been closed: a split second, or two or three seconds? He needed only to nod off for two seconds and unconsciously depress the accelerator and they'd be up the back end of the car in front. He knew he should stop but also knew he wasn't supposed to. Where would he stop if he decided to? On the hard shoulder, obviously, but where? After a mile, half a mile, a hundred yards? Its invariable aspect offered no invitation to pull in.

Instead, he shifted in the seat and straightened his back. Gently he accelerated. The car ahead was drawn into sharper focus. It was a Fiesta, a new model. He eased the pedal down further. He glanced in the mirror and saw just red lights; it must be reflecting the other carriageway; the vibration had caused it to slant; he straightened it.

He was suddenly right on top of the Fiesta.

With a tug on the steering wheel he missed the car in front and sheered into the middle lane. A horn blared, tyres screeched. There *were* cars behind him. He stood on the accelerator and leapt into the empty space ahead. A large BMW passed him on the outside, faces peering his way. Ignoring them, he concentrated on eating up the middle lane. Drowsiness snatched away, like a veil from a bold, thrusting sculpture, he bent over the steering wheel. Out of the corner of his eye he saw the speedometer needle leaning round the clock face to point at numbers it had not seen before.

The needle was just tipping at ninety-eight when the back end suddenly collapsed at one side and the car began to veer.

His immediate reaction was one of enormous relief that Melanie was not with him. She'd been working out west and was going up in her own car to meet him there.

Although he detested actually going to work, he was glad when they'd had to move from the old office to new premises. It had taken two months to find suitable new office space and they'd ended up having to move right out of Soho (much to Egerton's regret) as far north as the Angel.

Linden had been pleased because it meant he could now drive to work and find somewhere to park. In Soho it had been impossible.

Of course, it meant sitting in traffic jams at the bottom of Holloway Road and where Essex Road joined Upper Street, but wasn't it nicer to be stuck in your own car rather than suffocating in a Tube tunnel surrounded by the barely alive, still smelling of their beds?

He crunched into first and edged forward, but the Citroën in front had only been moving into space between it and the next car: the queue itself was not moving.

He realised he'd still got the choke out a fraction. He pressed it home and the revs dropped to normal. It was still running a little low; it could easily cut out waiting in a queue like this. Still, the man at the garage who'd tuned it only last week said it was better that it should be running too low rather than too high. It would keep his fuel consumption down and that had been quite a problem before. For a twelve-year-old Mini, the man had said, it wasn't in bad nick.

In front of him in the rear-view mirror he saw someone cross behind the car. He knew he was rolling back so he brought the clutch up and stepped on the gas. Then the queue started to move.

He parked in the private car park in the courtyard of the new complex. The start of another week. He cursed at the thought of five more days in the company of Egerton. Five more days staring at that damned computer screen. He didn't know which he disliked more – Egerton or the computer. That was a lie. The computer was not sentient; it had no excuse. (Come to think of it, Egerton was barely sentient either.)

Egerton was slowly climbing the stairs when Linden pushed open the ground-floor door. Not that the other man had, like Linden, just arrived – Egerton always got in at nine, an hour early – no, he'd come down to get the post so he could look at it before anyone else. That was why he was climbing the stairs so slowly, because he was devouring every bit of information the morning's delivery had to offer. Linden didn't care about the post – he wasn't in the slightest bit interested in the industry that employed him – it was Egerton's rapacious enthusiasm for everything connected with the job that irritated him.

'Good morning, Brian. How are you today? Did you have a nice weekend?'

Please somebody tell me why he has to be so bloody cheerful every Monday morning, Linden thought. The weekend, ah yes, the weekend – that precious island of time when he could escape.

He knew Egerton often came in on Saturdays. He didn't ask why any more.

Egerton was grinning at him, waiting for an answer. He couldn't bring himself to speak to the man.

The computer was waiting for him. He sat down, switched it on and nothing happened.

'Good morning, Brian.' Whitehead had come into the room. 'It's down. You'll have to use the other one. You *were* working on floppies, weren't you? Just stick them in the other machine.'

Linden nodded. Whitehead was the boss. He pretended to be everybody's equal. Until it came to writing out the salary cheques.

He worked without a break all morning. The computer had a green screen, which he wasn't used to. His eyes were tired by the time he'd saved all he'd done and was ready to go to lunch. One good thing about Egerton's keenness was that Linden never had to worry about the man inviting himself along to lunch: Egerton generally worked right through, occasionally getting in a McDonald's or a beanburger or something else equally Egerton-like.

When Linden tried to read his paper, waiting for his food to arrive, he found he couldn't concentrate properly. There were red dots all over the page. Wherever white was enclosed by black, as in a 'b', an 'o', a 'p' or an 'A', the little white space was now red. Consequently, the effect on a page of small newsprint was to turn the whole page red.

He worked all afternoon on the computer. Egerton annoyed him with his exaggerated mannerisms – grasping his chin, swinging his arms, clicking his fingers. When he wasn't striding around the office he was making telephone calls, mainly to the company's debtors. It was a matter of *personal* betrayal if someone had lapsed with an invoice payment. When Egerton uttered the company name he did so with chest-swelling pride.

Linden looked from the screen and grimaced at the tight little curls of blond hair on Egerton's head.

Driving home, Linden was tense. Occasionally he wavered over the red line in the middle of the road. A Triumph Vitesse barked its horn at him.

The red effect didn't wear off and allow Linden to read a book without straining his eyes until he was too tired to read anyway.

'It's the green, you see,' Whitehead explained. 'After looking at the green screen for long enough, you look away at something white and you see it as red. Green and red are the reverse of each other, or negatives or something. It's to do with that. Take a photo of a man in a red jumper and on the negative the jumper will be green.'

Because the maintenance contract on the old computer had expired and Whitehead was too tight to get an engineer in, Linden had to work with the green screen all week. It only affects some people, Whitehead had said, but it's not dangerous and is only short term.

He knew he shouldn't sit in front of the machine for too long at any one time but try telling that to Whitehead. They had a big job on – correction: Linden had a big job on. He was editing a four-hundred-page handbook and it had to be done by the end of the week. Each page resembled the next; three entries on a page, all with their identical lists of superfluous information. Every decimal point had to be checked. The spelling, as usual, was abysmal.

He ran off a hard copy of all he'd done, but the pages were bright red: it dazzled him. The material should be checked by someone else before it went off, but Egerton and Whitehead could barely spell their own names.

Negotiating Highbury Corner, Linden almost killed a pedestrian.

He'd thought the old man was in his rear-view mirror, but the wrinkle-smoothing shock on the aged face when the Mini snarled forward brought Linden's foot crashing down on the brake pedal. The car juddered and stalled. Linden sank his head on to the wheel and waited for the old man and several bystanders to stop screaming at him.

As soon as he got in he went to the fridge for a long drink of cold milk. He opened the fridge door and recoiled. There were two bottles of blood on the shelf.

He washed and shaved to see whether that would remove

some of the tension. He looked awful in the mirror. His eyes were bloodshot.

He switched on the television, but the newsreaders' eyes were all bloodshot as well, and their red teeth made them look like they'd just been eating raw hamburgers with Egerton.

He got hungry but couldn't bring himself to touch the eggs that were all that he had in the way of food. He went out to a restaurant and ordered a salad. He shouted at the waitress: how dare she put tomato ketchup on his salad? Drawing angry red stares he stalked out of the restaurant and crossed the road to a fish-and-chip shop, but the woman started sprinkling little dried flecks of bloody dandruff on to his chips, so he left in disgust.

By morning there was milk in his fridge again and he could enjoy a normal breakfast before driving to work.

'Are you all right, Brian?' Whitehead wanted to know.

'Yes. Why?' he snapped.

'You look a bit harassed, that's all.' Defensive. 'You will get that editing done, won't you?'

There seemed to be more red cars on the roads than ever. The days were already getting shorter: as he drove up Holloway Road the premature sunset was turning low clouds vermilion.

He finished at the computer on Friday morning and spent the rest of the day checking the hard copy in spite of the eye strain. There would be no use anyone else in the office proofing it. Although he considered himself underpaid for the work he was doing, he wanted to make sure it was right, in the unlikely event of someone, somewhere appreciating the hard work that had gone into the handbook.

He drove away from the Angel, down towards the roundabout. An enormous sense of release jostled with him for space in the Mini; the end of another week in the office, no more Egerton for two days, liberation from that infernal green computer screen. Since he'd finished on-screen editing before lunch, the effect had already begun to wear off.

He just had to call in at the flat to collect his bag and any messages, then head off up the A1 to the M1 and freedom. Melanie had been working out in W14 and so was going up in her own car. She would probably have been able to get away early, so would be first at the cottage. By the time he got there she'd have it all cosy for him.

The northbound lanes on Holloway Road were chock-a-block, as Linden knew the motorway would also be when he finally reached it. Through the windscreen he admired the beginnings of the sunset; the skies above Highgate were aglow with strange lilacs. Hadn't he seen yesterday's sunset in his rear-view mirror rather than through the windscreen? A small detail.

He reached the turn-off for Sussex Way and his flat. The traffic being as bad as it was, he was glad he'd put his bag in the car that morning and didn't have to make the detour to go and get it now.

He watched a Beetle worm its way out of a side street between two Escorts into the traffic flow. If this was a stream of traffic then it was a stream of mud. He looked for the Beetle again: was it an old one with a tiny back window and semaphore indicators or a more recent model with big rear-light clusters and fat bumpers? But he couldn't see it, and when he thought about it he couldn't remember whether he'd caught sight of it in his rear-view mirror or through the windscreen.

On the other side of the road a red Escort nosed out from beside the snooker centre and was allowed to pass between two VW Beetles. The driver of the Escort waved her thanks. Behind Linden impatient drivers pipped their horns, making him jump: the queue in front of him had moved forward.

The traffic didn't get any better; when the M1 intersected the M25 and then merged with the M10, it got worse.

He asked Melanie to put on a tape. She chose the Organ Symphony; at least while they proceeded at ten miles per hour he was able to hear it.

'Why don't you go to sleep?' he asked her.

'Your car's too noisy,' she said. 'I wouldn't be able to.'

Every few hundred yards the congestion would just dissolve and Linden would get up to thirty or forty. It was always a brief respite, however, and inexplicably the queue tightened up again. Eventually, though, thanks to the domestic attraction for the majority offered by places like Luton, Leighton Buzzard, Milton Keynes, Newport Pagnell and Bedford, there were fewer cars sharing the same lanes and all of them were doing at least sixty-five miles per hour. The novelty soon wore off and the tedium of motorway driving set in, exacerbated by the fact that it was by now quite dark.

The tape clicked off, but since he hadn't been able to hear it for the last half-hour he didn't bother putting another one on. He wished Melanie were with him to keep him awake. Would she be at the cottage yet? he wondered. He tried to guess who might be driving the Fiesta in front. What kind of person? He accelerated to get closer. A woman, he decided, but not like Melanie, more of a career woman, someone who saw great intrinsic worth in *belonging* to a company, a Company Girl. A female Egerton. He toed the accelerator again. Her hair would be fixed in a go-ahead style like some kind of fossilised bird's nest, the brain-eggs long since hatched and flown the nest, leaving only the corporate gloss of cranial vacancy in her eyes.

He was suddenly right on top of the Fiesta.

When the back end collapsed at his side and the car began to swerve, he had no idea what had happened.

He glanced at the passenger seat and seized the steering wheel as if it were the reins of a bolting horse. Steer into the skid, they always said. But what did that mean? Go with it or against it? He swung to the left, trying to aim the front of the car at the hard shoulder and braking as gently as he could without sliding into a new skid.

He never knew how close he came to being hit by the cars that flew past him as he shuddered to a halt on the hard shoulder. He didn't need to hold his hands out to see how much he was shaking: he was still holding the steering wheel and it was trembling, and not on account of the engine, which had stalled. Climbing over the empty seat, he got out on the passenger side, and walked unsteadily round the back of the car to see what had happened. A blowout. The back tyre on the driver's side was shredded. He could just make out the word REMOULD.

He got back in the car and told Melanie what had happened. She was calmer now; the shock had been greater for her since she'd been asleep when it had happened.

He took his spanner and a jack from the boot and set about taking the wheel off. The first nut was a bit difficult so he worked at the other three, which all came off after some effort. The first one wouldn't budge; the spanner's grip began to slide on the nut.

'Shit!' He leant against the Mini, watching the cars streaking past.

He tried the nut again but the spanner was now far too big for it; he was just wearing the edges away; if he continued, it would become impossible to remove.

Linden stopped for breath and looked back up the hard shoulder to see whether he could still see the Mini. The car itself was invisible but the hazard lights flashed on and off and on again. They were much brighter than he would have imagined and he was grateful for them. He continued walking.

Cars sped past him, occupants' faces blank white spaces turned towards him, yet he'd never felt more alone. The sky was black, clouded over; the darkness of the land beyond the motorway uninterrupted by lights. Not even farmers lived here. People only drove through. He fastened all three buttons of his jacket and pulled up the collar. Where the hell was the emergency telephone? One just a few yards from his car was out of order. As was its opposite number, which he had reached illegally by crossing all six lanes of the motorway.

Eventually he came upon a telephone that worked and he was able to call for assistance. It seemed so unlikely that there should be a man waiting by a telephone to take his call and send another man out in a van to rescue him. And yet that was the system he paid for. He was of course glad now that he *had* subscribed.

He began to walk back. The cold penetrated his thin jacket. Cars swept by only a few feet away, making him feel vulnerable. He lost count of the bridges he passed under. The horizon failed to yield the flashing orange of his hazards. He began to worry that somehow he'd gone wrong. He'd not crossed back after running over to try the telephone on the other side. 'Don't be stupid,' he said out loud, but the sound of his voice, so feeble and vain, frightened him. He decided that he would turn back at the next bridge, and as the next bridge came into sight, so too did the hazard lights.

They belonged to a P-reg Ford Cortina. A woman with bad teeth sitting in the passenger seat threw him a nervous glance then looked away.

The Mini was another two hundred yards farther up. As he narrowed the gap from behind, a trick of the shadows cast by passing headlamps made it look as if there were two people already sitting in the front seats.

He clambered in and waited for the van to arrive.

Each passing car shook the little Mini. He put some music on but imagined that it prevented him from hearing the footsteps of an interloper approaching the car. He pressed EJECT. Melanie said: 'They won't be long.'

It started to rain. Big fat drops exploded on the windscreen. He pictured Melanie at the cottage: making a drink, running a bath, watching the television. He wished he were with her. How long would it be before she started to worry? The rain rattled on the roof as if it were a tent. Suddenly a brilliant flash created a second's daylight in the night. Then the thunder began to roll, like a solo by a drunken timpanist.

When the serviceman arrived, Linden joined him in the teeming rain, but the man couldn't shift the nut either. 'It's only a mile to the next services,' the man shouted over the noise of the storm. 'I'll tow you there. It'll be easier. I'll be able to get this nut off. More space, more light.'

Linden nodded and climbed into the cab as directed.

'It's not far,' the man said, when he'd hitched up the Mini to his truck. They moved off and stayed on the hard shoulder. After ten or fifteen minutes the lights of the services sparkled through the rain. Linden left the man to change the wheel and walked across the rain-slick tarmac to the complex.

In the self-service restaurant he sat down in a red plastic seat with a cup of stewed tea. He was alone in the place apart from a smartly dressed couple who stared miserably at each other's shoulders across a crumb-strewn table.

He stood looking at the telephones, wishing they'd gone to the trouble and expense of installing one in the cottage.

Crossing over the covered footbridge, he stopped in the middle and watched the traffic sweeping underneath in both directions. He felt like a pivot between the two carriageways, as if with his mind he could just switch them. A flash of lightning printed a colour negative on his retina, sending a shiver down his back and dropping a chilled weight in his stomach. With a vague sense of foreboding he reached the end of the bridge and walked down the steps. In the hall area a number of people were grouped around a video game. He joined the back of the group, which was murmuring its praise of the game-player. Someone moved to give Linden a better view. He stood behind a man with tight curly blond hair, whose hands, he now saw, were manipulating the game's joystick and firing button.

Ships and creatures fell from the top of the screen towards the bottom. The game-player had his own unit, which he had to defend and from which he could attack the ships and creatures that, if they came into contact with his unit, would destroy it. The game was probably an old one, but the curly-haired man was obviously playing it extremely well to have attracted spectators.

The screen was bright green.

Linden was transfixed. He barely registered the man clicking his fingers as he relaxed between one attack and the next.

The screen seemed to get brighter, like a television in a darkening room.

Linden leaned closer. Slowly he began to turn his head to see the face of the man who was playing. But before he finished the turn he shot round the other way and barged his way out of the crowd, running for the doors.

His head pounding, he searched for his car. On the far side of the parking area he saw the serviceman's truck, its orange light still revolving. The man was bending down at the Mini's rear, just tightening the last nut on the changed wheel.

'Quickly,' Linden croaked. 'I've got to go.'

'All right, all right,' the man said, kicking the wheel trim into place. 'You've got to sign my forms.'

The man walked too slowly to the cab of his truck and shuffled some papers around on a clipboard. Linden hovered at his shoulder.

'There,' the man said, pointing with a stubby finger.

Linden leaned over. The paper was red. He looked at the man, who pointed again and rubbed a sore red eye with his free hand. Linden scrawled his signature.

'And there.'

He signed again and dropped the pen on to the floor of the cab in his haste to get away.

He jumped into the Mini, rammed it into first, thrust the key into the ignition and started the engine as he released the handbrake and turned the wheel. He accelerated and stamped on the brake when he thought he was going to run the serviceman over: but he was behind him in the rear-view mirror, waving his arms and shouting something Linden couldn't hear. He screeched away and built up speed, aiming for the slip road to get back on the motorway. He ignored a road sign he didn't recognise – a solid red circle – and sped between two bollards. The man's alarmed face receded to a fleck in his mirror.

The motorway was fairly clear so he accelerated straight into the centre lane, pressing the pedal to the floor. He soon caught up with the red lights ahead. Too quickly, in fact. Suddenly there were swarms of red lights apparently speeding towards him in all three lanes, as if reversing down the motorway at seventy miles per hour.

He turned to Melanie in bewilderment and fear.

But she wasn't there.

And within seconds neither was he.

THE MADWOMAN

It wasn't until the French girl stopped going on about it and finally got her saxophone out that I realised I'd never sleep with her. Up to that point it had been a possibility. It was a rough old night. One of those hurricanes we don't have in this country, which now seem to come round every October, was blowing umbrellas into trees and nonsense out from between the ears. Catherine's light glowed invitingly from her Tottenham first-floor window as I was on my way home from the station. I rang and she invited me in, clearly pleased despite it being so late. I followed her up to her room, nodding and murmuring at her flatmate who was leaning against her own lintel. Catherine shut the door, offered me a seat and there began another round of will we or won't we, conducted, as always, entirely within our heads.

I'd met Catherine three weeks or so previously at some dive in New Cross, a hot, steaming pie of a place stuffed to the crust with travellers and people wearing rainbow jumpers and trailing scraggy dogs on bits of string. There'd been some group of losers playing strange folk music on a makeshift stage behind the pool table and I happened to make eye contact with this not-bad-looking dark-haired girl whose eyes swam this way and that behind a huge pair of blue glasses. I asked her whether she wanted a drink. Not half, she said. God knows where she picked that up from, being French. Anyway, several drinks later we shared a cab back north of the river and I asked whether she wanted to do this again some time. She went all cool and said she was taking life pretty much one day at a time. OK, I said, and got out of the cab thinking I'd probably never see her again and that would be no great tragedy.

She called me at the place where I was working a week or two later. Presumably I'd told her where that was. Did I want to go out? Sure, why not. To a French play in Chelsea? Ah, tonight, you say? I'm sorry, Catherine, I'm busy tonight. What a shame, eh? Good play, is it? Narrow escape, that one. Even *she* told me later it was boring, so take my word for it, it must have been very bad news. We did go out a few days later for a drink and went back to my place for a coffee after. She didn't live far away, but come 2 a.m. she was yawning and saying it was a long walk back to her flat. So, entirely reasonably, I thought, I asked her whether she wanted to stay. Oh no, she said, you've only got one bed. Well, you know, you can share it with me. She didn't like that idea, and who can blame her? But what was she doing round my flat at 2 a.m. saying it was a long walk home if she wasn't after an invite to stay? Will you walk me back? she asked. Better still, I said, I'll call you a cab. And as I was dialling, the roof creaked, the roof or the ceiling, I didn't know what it was. What was that? she wanted to know. Just settlement, I said. It's a new flat. She seemed bothered by it; I was getting bothered by her. For someone who wanted escorting back to her flat at 2 a.m. she was getting pretty invasive with my personal space, leaning over me while I spoke to the cab office. I think your flat's falling down, she said. Do you? Well, it's a good job you're going home, then, isn't it? Her cab arrived soon after that and I didn't see her again until after I'd been out with Alysson the mad clairvoyant.

I met Alysson at a dinner party. I'm not a great dinner party person. Never have been. When I do accept an invitation, which is rarely – because I don't get many – I tend to go along well tanked up already just in case it's too dull or I can't cope with the formality. I suppose I went to this one because I'd been on my own for a while and Catherine was far from being a safe bet. As I was getting ready to go I was drinking those little bottles of Belgian beer with the defective glass you could buy in the supermarket and I was beginning to wish I wasn't going, and then the ceiling creaked like a special effect in a bad film and that made me think of Catherine in her flat only ten minutes' walk away. I could go round there, maybe end up in bed with her, have a good time, or I could go to some poncey dinner party down in Fulham and sit next to some suit on one side and his Sloaney girlfriend on the other. As I said, Catherine wasn't exactly a safe bet, and if she was the prize I wasn't even sure I wanted to win.

I was impressed by Alysson, who was sitting opposite me (amazingly the suit and the Sloane I had pictured were indeed planted either side of me), as soon as she started talking. Had she told me there and then how she spelt her name we could have saved a lot of wasted time and effort. But still. She told me I was on an upswing. I saw it as soon as you walked in, she said. The suit was smirking. He thought it was a chat-up line. I thought he was a twat but I wasn't sitting there smirking about it. In any case, I reckoned Alysson was dead on and I told her so. I've never been wrong, she said. Come over and see me. I'll give you a free reading. She passed me her card. I said I wasn't sure, liked to think I was in control of my own destiny, all that. She said I should go round and see her anyway, there were some nice bars down the end of her street.

Something else happened before I saw Catherine again. I met Anne. I met her in a pub. Amazingly, at thirty, this was the first time I had met someone in a pub. Actually it was a drinking club but let's just call it a pub that stayed open late. Two girls were playing the quiz machine and making quite a bit of noise about it, so it seemed OK for yours truly, accompanied by Decko, an old friend of mine, to wade in there. Such was the nature of that night, I don't recall much of what was said. Anne remembers even less. But Decko didn't hang about, I remember that much. He had his arms round Anne's friend before you could answer Lionel Blair to the hairdressing question. So when he and Lizzie disappeared on to the stairs, or the roof for all I know, Anne and I had to talk about something. And films it was. I asked whether she'd seen such and such, and she hadn't, so I suggested we go and see it together. She made doubly sure by asking straight out whether this was a date and I'd had enough to drink that I could just say yes, and beam at her.

It had been a good evening. For me. Decko, who was staying with me while he was down in London for the weekend, rolled in around 5 a.m. having walked from Finsbury Park to Tottenham because some twisted old cab driver had dropped him there saying it was Seven Sisters. Plus, he'd stayed at the club with Lizzie till the bitter end expecting he wouldn't have to come back and sleep on my floor again and she'd said she'd love to invite him back but she couldn't, as she thought her boyfriend might take a dim view. So he ended up with an aching jaw, which was no doubt fun in the acquiring, but I had a date. I felt absurdly old fashioned next to Decko, but quite proud of it.

Incidentally, while I'd been hanging around waiting to see whether Decko would reappear, I listened to some music before going to bed. I stuck on this old Psychedelic Furs album, *Talk Talk Talk*, which in one song has the line 'Ha ha ha'. And that line came up just at the exact point when I happened to scan a magazine cover on my desk and noticed the cover line 'Ho ho ho'. Coincidences. Apparently they come in clusters. Yeah, well, I can confirm that. And they carry some significance, though the jury is still out on that one. A couple of weeks earlier I was sitting in my kitchen spooning the contents of a tin of cherry pie filling into my mouth. I knew I'd never make the pie and the can was taking up valuable shelf space. I was hungry, couldn't be bothered to cook. Need any more reasons? And on the radio I had some football commentary on Radio 5. So I'm noshing on this gloopy cherry stuff and the commentator talks about the substitute who's about to come on. I bite into a cherry just as he says this guy's about to get his first bite at the cherry of the season.

I'm not making this up. I mean I wouldn't, would I?

I was walking down Oxford Road in Manchester on my way to Maine Road one Saturday afternoon before all of this started, reading the paper, a piece about Highgate Cemetery, and the writer mentioned vampires just at the moment when I turned a corner and saw the Contact Theatre's huge banner advertising their next show: *Dracula*.

So, I went over to see Alysson the clairvoyant. It was a bit of a trek but I was curious. Mainly, I suppose, because of these coincidences. She already had a bottle of each colour open so I couldn't really say no to the wine she offered me. I leant over to smell her Christmas tree, then, So what about these coincidences, I asked. I told her about them. You're very intuitive, she said. How do you know, I wanted to ask her, but that was the point. Any minute now she'd say I was sensitive, wasn't like other men. I asked how is it you can wait for months and nothing happens, then two or three opportunities come along at exactly the same time. She explained that she'd had the Beijing flu that was going round and had called in this Tibetan healer who had pummelled her spine a tad excessively. Couldn't you just take a Lemsip, I asked her. Like the rest of us. No, she had to get this weird guy in. She said he was one of a small group of healers – I forget the name – who operated by plunging their hands into your flesh, actually entering the body to play around with the vertebrae, but leaving no surface wound. Fuck knows how that was relevant. In case she *was* on the scent and to put her off it, I told her I'd met someone. She said she knew. She knew when I'd sniffed at the Christmas tree. Bollocks, I thought, and left not long after. It was freezing cold, teeming with rain and herds of black cabs were consistently failing to come rumbling over the horizon. It wasn't a good night, to say the least, but it had served the purpose of focusing my mind. From now on I could concentrate on Anne. And Catherine. Because it was on that night, having returned to Tottenham by Tube, that I passed beneath her window and, seeing the light on, rang the bell.

We circled round each other, parry and counter-thrust, a little teasing, a touch of satire. All of it verbal. There's a piano in the other room, she said, squeezing past me in the doorway to get to the boxroom, which did indeed contain a piano. She played, badly, a couple of things from sheet music, then stood up. Because of the size of the room we were right up close. I could show you my saxophone, she said. Sure, why not? Make-or-break time. Back into the other room, more choreographed squeezing past each other to get there, and suddenly there was the saxophone.

She announced something by Charlie Parker – which is a pretty hard act to follow – and blew into her horn. What can I say? It was terrible. It lacked finesse. It lacked class. It lacked being in tune. She had the rhythmical sense of a stag beetle. I could go on but it would be unkind. Suffice to add that she had an essentially basic playing style, so you could just about recognise the songs being mutilated, which I can't remember being either a good or a bad thing. I couldn't wait to get away. I was just thinking about

Anne, who for all I knew could be a suicidal anorexic with a history of child sexual abuse and a collection of toenail clippings, but there are times when you have to make a judgement based on the flimsiest of evidence, and in these matters I tend to trust my intuition. What else have you got to go on? As far as I could tell, Anne was the only one who wasn't mad. Alysson was clearly a basket case and Catherine played the saxophone badly, insisting she played it well – grounds for desertion on suspicion of potential madness. And that's an area in which I have some experience, having known the Madwoman. Someone who dragged me through the hedge of mental anguish backwards so that I came out with my personality awry. Couldn't do a thing with it. Took months of psychic combing to straighten it out.

On my way out of Catherine's flat that night she got me, draped her arms about my neck like a damp scarf and pouted for a kiss. I'm weak in these situations. I didn't want to hurt her so I kissed her. She kissed well but despite that, and the promise of so much more, I knew what I wanted. It was regrettable from her point of view that it took that kiss further to focus my mind, but that's the way it goes sometimes.

I walked back through the windswept, leaf-scattered streets of N15, and when I got home the ceiling was creaking like one of the old Central line trains.

In the morning the steam from my bath outlined a message written on the bathroom mirror. Help me, it said. It could have been there days, since Decko's visit.

Anne and I were due to meet in a pub in Soho. I was so nervous I rang Bob and asked him whether he'd have a drink with me first. We drank in one of those dark, little-used pubs behind Piccadilly Circus and I jokingly asked him whether he'd take my place and tell her I'd been unable to make it. He agreed and I could see he half meant it, so I grinned foolishly and said I couldn't bottle out now. She might be really nice, he said. Yes, I said, but I've been wrong before. He bought me another drink and we sat there silently for a while.

When I met Anne outside the pub we'd arranged to meet in she kissed me in welcome. A nice, quick, friendly kiss on the lips, completely natural, totally without self-consciousness. I knew I'd made the right decision. Even if it didn't work out in the long run, even if she turned out to be mad in the medium term, she was clearly the only woman I'd met in a long time who it made any sense at all to see more than once. Inside the pub with a couple of drinks, the conversation, which I'd feared would dry up in the first ten minutes, flowed as easily as if we'd known each other for years. But we really only met that night – she remembered almost nothing of the night in the club – and it was simply that we wanted to get to know each other better, so there was no end to the questions, no sense of duty in the replies.

For the next couple of weeks we met regularly in town, at first choosing different venues, then we started to return to favourites. We never ran out of things to talk about, I never tired of looking at her, she of telling me not to stare. We took things slowly because I think we both sensed this could be good, but not if we rushed it. Too many times I'd been told not to be so intense, to give a girl some time to herself, to back off, for fuck's sake. I didn't want to make that mistake again. The only person who'd ever really lapped up the attention and demanded more, more than I could manage, was the Madwoman. I wanted to tell Anne about her but she didn't want to know. I could understand that. If she'd started telling me about Geoff or Bill or Todd, and about what really great guys they'd been, I wouldn't exactly have been a full house at the Festival Hall sitting down to hear Ashkenazy play Brahms's second piano concerto. But the Madwoman had made a lasting impression, which I was hoping might by now have faded like any physical scar.

But Anne was right. We didn't need to dig up any of those bodies from the past. They were best left alone.

She pinned her hair up with a slide, which I liked because when we did get to the touching stage I could remove it and watch her hair fall to her shoulders. Then she'd sweep it out of her face. One day she'd get it all cut off perhaps and I'd be a bit sad. But she'd let it grow again.

Then she did it. The Madwoman dropped in.

We were at my flat one night. The video we'd been watching had finished and was rewinding, the takeaway containers were stinking out the kitchen, and we were lying on the sofa just feeling pretty good about things. There was a bit of a draught getting through the cracks in the window frames but nothing the curtains couldn't handle. There wasn't much noise. The video ran right back to the beginning and clicked off. I was combing my fingers through Anne's hair and she was laughing every time I got stuck.

The ceiling creaked. Once. Twice. We both looked up.

At the far end of the room the ceiling opened up with an ear-splitting crack. Anne leapt to her feet and pressed her body against the wall. I was aware of something tumbling on to the floor amid the fractured plaster and clouds of dust. I got to my feet slowly and walked across the room. Powder was still streaming down from the edges of the hole in the ceiling. I looked at the bulky black shape on the floor. It was like something wrapped in a jacket. I turned it to see. It was her. It was the Madwoman.

She was wearing the black jacket she always wore, the dark grey slacks and stocking feet. Her skin was desiccated as if mummified. How she had achieved that I didn't know. Slowly Anne approached and looked over my shoulder. I felt as if I should protect her from the sight, but then thought my instinct an absurd one and made no real effort to shield her. A jumble of questions, like a knot of wires in a Channel 4 animation, tugged my thoughts this way and that before shrivelling up into nothing and leaving my mind completely blank. I wanted to sit down, put my head in my hands and look up again to find the whole mess cleared up, the body never having even been there.

She was crouched up in a fetal position as if she'd fallen asleep.

Not knowing what to do, I suggested to Anne that we try to get some sleep and I'd deal with it in the morning. She nodded dumbly. I remember thinking that no girlfriend should have to put up with her partner even talking about his ex. But this was something else. Quite why she didn't order a cab and leave me there and then I don't know. I guess she was nicer than that, or just tired.

The following day after breakfast – all either of us could manage was a strong black coffee – I said I was going to have to clean up. Anne did leave then. She walked right out and

didn't look back. To my considerable surprise she returned that
evening, to find me drinking beer on my own with the lights
out and listening to an REM CD that was on repeat. How many
times has that played, she asked, spying the little red repeat
light. I shrugged. Why had she come back? She was clearly no
ordinary woman, though that was not necessarily a good thing.
The Madwoman herself had been quite extraordinary. Instead
of, say, telling me I'd had enough to drink, Anne got two beers
from the fridge and sat next to me on the floor. So I told her
about the Madwoman. About the sacrifices she'd made and the
way she'd missed her husband so badly she cried herself to sleep
as she lay next to me. About the times she insisted on sleeping
in the bathroom, curled up on the drip mat, resisting my efforts
to return her to the bedroom by beating on my chest with her
fists as if she wanted to get inside. About the day she decided she
was going to go back to him and even phoned him to arrange
that he should come down in his car to pick her up. We'd talked
and it seemed her mind was made up, so I just kind of accepted
it. I went out for the evening and wandered round in a kind
of daze, looking into people's houses and envying them their
ordered lives, standing stock still in the middle of the 7–11 for
two minutes until an assistant took hold of my elbow.

When I came back he was still there, he was just leaving, on
his own. She'd been unable to do it when it came to it. He looked
right through me and drove off. She collapsed on the floor,
screaming, sobbing, tumbling down the stairs of hysteria. Then
she tried to get him on his car phone to tell him to come back and
get her. She'd go this time. But his phone was switched off and
she had to stay. That was the evening that did it for me. That was
the evening it finished. The top of the slide. From then on it was
downhill and it was a fuck of a long way. Only then did I realise
how far up we'd climbed.

She had nowhere to go. After that night she couldn't go
back to him. She would have left me but she had nowhere to
go, no money to afford a place on her own, not while she was
still paying half their mortgage. Of course, I felt like a shit. I'd
promised her the world and given her nothing, as far as she was
concerned. When things had been good we had enjoyed a lively

and balanced sex life. Now it descended into nightmare. I had no desire to touch her, except to comfort her; she needed me still to show I needed her if only in that way. But I didn't and I couldn't pretend. My greatest failing is that I've never seen any alternative to telling the truth. There's no respect for either party in unwanted sex. She thought sex was a bandage that could be used to wrap around our problems. It just covered up wounds that grew steadily deeper and began to weep, the longer we stayed in the same space. The dimensions of my flat shrank about my shoulders as her recriminations rained down on me. And they were all justified. I was the world's biggest bastard.

Over the next few months, even after she'd scaled down her mortgage payments and moved into a bedsit, she nurtured my guilt. It grew till it was the size of a wasps' nest. She only had to stir it with a repeated question – what *did* go wrong? – or a few tears and my head buzzed with sudden heat. I never knew guilt carried such a sting. Slowly she got better, she got over it as she pushed me steadily further under. I didn't see the slightest thing wrong with that. I deserved whatever came to me. I don't know how I got up in the mornings, how I went to work. You carry on. You're a shit and everybody knows it, but you carry on.

Anne listened to all of this and like any balanced person said I shouldn't blame myself. I know, I said. But it took me months and months to realise it. And by that time the Madwoman had gone away, taken a job in the States.

When you're in my position, I said to Anne, cranking up that old Napoleon Wilson line in *Assault on Precinct 13*, days are like women. They all end up leaving you.

But you wanted her to go, she reminded me. Of course, I said. I wanted *her* to go. But I didn't want Anne to go anywhere. We'd only just met and already the past was squaring its shoulders as it rushed up behind me. Why didn't you phone me, I once asked the Madwoman. Because I was waiting for you to phone me, she said. But we agreed, I said, that you would phone me because you wanted to leave it for a few days. Yes, well, she said, pulling the draw-string of her lips together, I knew you were waiting for me to ring you so I waited for you to ring me. Wow. Say goodnight to the folks, Gracie.

And in any case, Anne said, changing the REM CD for Kissing the Pink's new album, she didn't leave you. You left her. True, I said, and will she ever let me forget it? She's gone now, honey, Anne said, and you should forget her.

Then the phone rang.

It was the Madwoman.

I'm in Seattle, she said. Just wanted to wish you a merry Christmas.

Anne must have seen the look on my face. What's wrong, she asked. Who is it? I couldn't answer her. I couldn't speak.

Thought I'd surprise you, the Madwoman said.

I tried to hang up but the receiver missed the cradle and I could hear her still talking. I screamed at the phone. I remember thinking that Anne looked terrified. She replaced the receiver for me while I gathered my knees up under my chin and rocked backwards and forwards. The phone rang again and I snatched at it, breaking the connection with my other hand and leaving it off the hook. I got up, my body quite unfamiliar, and walked unsteadily into the bathroom to look at myself in the mirror. My face was haggard. What's going on, I heard Anne call, her voice breaking. I went back into the other room and sat down next to her. She held me. It was her, I said. It was the Madwoman. I cremated her this morning and that was her on the phone.

It can't have been her, she said reasonably. I quietly and calmly told her that it was and that I thought I was going mad. What did you do with the body, she asked. I burnt it this morning. Carried it down to the waste land by the railway and burnt it. What else could I do?

How did she get into your loft, she asked. I don't know, I replied angrily. I told Anne I needed to think. I didn't know what was going on and I needed time to get things sorted out in my head. After a little more encouragement she left and I went and stood in the middle of the flat looking up at the jagged hole in the ceiling.

You can come out now, I called into the darkness. She's gone.

The ceiling creaked and a thin trickle of plaster whispered down through the air in front of me.

KINGYO NO FUN

Everybody knows one. You've either met one or you know one by reputation. Not everybody suffers, however, to the extent that James has suffered. And while that's partly circumstance, it's also partly James's own fault, through his innocence – which has a lot to do with why I love him myself.

This one's name was Simon but it could have been anything. It could have been William or Terry, or Carolyn or Suzi. They're all the same. They're all *kingyo no fun*. I've known them, you've known them. And James has known them. Only James doesn't know how to shake them off like most people do.

We were in Amsterdam for the weekend. A long weekend. It was late spring some time in the mid-1990s. I think it was late May. That summer would break all records for mean temperatures and hours of sunshine and already by the end of April it was beginning to get seriously hot. James was doing publicity for his new book and I was hanging around with him. He likes me being around when he's doing this stuff. It's not that we make a big show of it, but I'm always there, if anybody wants to know. If anybody's wondering. About James, you know. There's a light. OK? And it's a red kind of a light.

He's not a gay writer, he's fond of saying. He's just a writer who happens to be gay. You come on as a gay writer and you get asked to do all the representative stuff. Act-up and Outrage and fund-raising for Aids charities. James says he's got nothing against doing some of that stuff – and he works hard for a good cause – but he doesn't want to get labelled. And I think that's cool. He doesn't want to cut his sales by half in order to please a minority. So I hang around and meet people but I don't, you know, stick my tongue down his throat and my hand down his pants while he's schmoozing some new agent or flirting with pretty-boy publishers. I do have a sense of restraint. I can be diplomatic. It's not half as much fun but I can do it.

The gig was some weird conjunction of writing and visual art in a small gallery off the Herengracht – *gracht* being the Dutch word for canal. The place was crawling with conceptual artists being studiedly unkempt and unshaven – boys *and* girls, this being the year Della Grace famously 'stopped plucking' – and, frankly, a little bit dirty. I longed to take one of them aside and ask why they thought it necessary to go around looking like extras out of some Eastern Bloc movie of the 1970s. In whose eyes could it possibly make them look better artists?

But I didn't, because I had to think of James.

The artists were all meant to be exhibiting new stuff and the writers reading from recently published work. One video artist showed his new 'piece', which consisted of him wearing a gorilla suit and jumping up and down – quite strenuously for a self-proclaimed slacker. Over the course of twelve minutes – the over-generous running time of this video – the gorilla suit gradually falls apart, leaving the artist naked and generally looking a bit of an asshole. Wouldn't have been half as bad if he'd had a decent body, I said later to James. Another artist showed a glass case full of miniature houses pinned down like dead butterflies. The work was entitled *Househunting 1995*.

There was worse, believe me, but hey, you know, life's too short.

James was doing his thing. There was a microphone but James never uses them because he's blessed with a mellifluous, sonorous voice – he can project to the end of next week. And if he's reading from a book or script he prefers to keep one hand free. He ranges to and fro in order to include the entire audience, trying to give good value. He's a real pro. There was a photographer guy climbing all over the seats and crates that were stacked up at the side of the gallery, taking shot after shot after shot, and sometimes getting right in close, but James just carried on, totally unfazed. When he cracked jokes people laughed. His timing was good and I noticed he'd give them a look as he delivered a new gag. He knew that even given the language barrier he could make them laugh if (a) they liked him and (b) they realised *when* they were supposed to laugh.

When he'd done I noticed this guy go up to talk to him. Nothing unusual in that. People are always going up to get books signed or just to say hi, so they can say to their friends they met a famous author. This guy looked about thirty-six or thirty-seven, unruly hair and a thrift-store jacket, but perfectly normal compared to some of the freaks James occasionally attracts. I watched James politely listen to the guy and respond with some larger-than-life gesture – not to impress, that's just the way he is – and then, because someone else was waiting to say something, the guy stepped back and kind of melted into the crowd.

'Because that was the extent of it,' James was to tell me much later, 'I thought he was OK. But when he came up to me again at the end of the evening, when we'd all hung around with whoever we were hanging around with for just about long enough, and were all about ready to go and move on, he came up to me again and I don't know what he said but he started talking and straight away I knew – I knew this guy was bad news. I don't know how I missed it earlier. I guess because he wasn't talking to me for long enough and didn't have a chance to show what a complete asshole he was. But as soon as he started, when he came up to me again later, as soon as he started I knew I was in big trouble.'

'That look?'

'That look.'

Kingyo no fun always have the look. Always. But you can't always tell on the look alone because other people can have the same look and be OK. It's a kind of crazed look in the eyes. You know this. You've seen the look. You do sometimes get normal people who have the look, or who appear to have it – the lights are on and there *is* somebody at home. With *kingyo no fun*, the lights are burning for sure, every goddam fucking window, but there ain't *nobody* sitting in that house. And that's the whole problem in, like, a real small pecan shell. Never occurred to me before. You got the whole problem right there.

So when I ambled over to join James because it looked like people might be about to make a move, this guy – Simon – was hanging around like a bad smell. He appeared quite impervious to hints. No amount of subtle body language seemed able to shift him.

'So we going, James, or what?' I said with a trace of impatience.

James was turned the other way. 'I think a couple of the guys are joining us for a drink.' He turned to face me. Simon was side on to the two of us; he didn't turn away, just watched, this little smile like a worm making its way slowly across the lower half of his face. 'You wanna go for a drink?' James said, sort of to the both of us. Jeez, that stung. 'Coupla English guys. Writers. They seem pretty cool. Tall guy suggested we go get a beer.'

'A drink's a good idea,' said Simon, the *kingyo no fun*.

Why don't you go fuck yourself? You're not invited, pal, I wanted to say, but I heard James falling over himself to be nice to the guy.

'Wanna go get a beer, Simon? Whaddya say, huh?'

Jesus, James. Didn't God give you eyes? Don't you ever fucking use them? You wanna fucking use them, man.

'Yeah, that'd be cool,' said the *kingyo no fun*.

Cool. Yeah, it'd be *fucking* cool. Mr Kingyo No Fucking Asshole.

Calm, calm, some shrink was going inside my head. Yeah, calm, you don't know what it's like, guy.

So we headed out of the art gallery, James shaking hands with the gallerist on the way, in pursuit of the two English writers, and with Simon, naturally, bringing up the rear.

'Where would you like to go?' I heard the shorter of the two English guys ask James.

'Wherever,' James replied, looking round to include me.

The *kingyo no fun* said: 'There's a nice place just up here. Shouldn't be too busy.'

The tall English guy, whose name turned out to be Ben, acquiesced quite happily, his shorter companion, Matthew, falling uncomplainingly into line, and James, easygoing as ever, nodded brightly. I looked across the canal at a crowd spilling out of a bar, wondered what was wrong with that place, but Ben and Matthew had already struck off in the direction indicated by Simon, who had fallen in next to James and was animatedly talking *art* with him. Because of some major construction work that ran alongside the canal, I couldn't squeeze alongside them and had to follow on behind. This, you will appreciate, pissed me off.

Kingyo no fun operate differently in different countries when it comes to bar etiquette. The goal is always the same: to avoid paying. OK, OK, I know some of you will have come across people you *think* are *kingyo no fun* who *do* buy drinks in order to ingratiate themselves with the people they're leeching off. But hey, get this, they're not real *kingyo no fun* because the *kingyo no fun* conforms to a rigid set of regs.

James and I, although we were both born and raised in New York City, live in London, England, and have done for about ten years. James likes the scene, by which I mean the literary scene, not the gay scene. He likes that too. A little too well. But that's another story. We met in Heaven about three years ago. We had both been in London seven years already, having come from pretty much the same neighbourhood in New York originally, and not having met previously in London. 'Kinda weird, huh?' James would say to me later.

'What's weird?' I asked him.

'Well, you know. It's kind of a coincidence you turning up like that and, you know, we're both from New York, both in Heaven that night, both been on the scene some time and never met up before.'

'Coincidence? There's no such thing,' I said.

When we met, James was with a group of leathermen. I'd been following them with my eyes for about ten minutes when one of them approached me and asked whether I wanted a drink. Sure, I said. Why not? And rather than let this guy take me off to some dark corner, which was what he appeared to have on his mind, I used him to help me enter the group. It was the tallest guy I had my eye on. The one with long sculpted sideburns and a Nick Cave T-shirt. The one with big eyes. The one called James.

So that was the night we met and from then on we stuck together – James slightly less convincingly than me from time to time, but he always came back, always apologised and I always forgave him. Living in England you have to get used to pubs. A pub is like a bar without the sense of being in a bar. You can get a beer and all, but it's like getting a beer in a mall – it's kind of like Bar-Lite, you know, or Diet-Bar. I'm talking about the pubs in London. I can't tell you about the quaint little old country pubs because we didn't go out to the country yet. We did go to High Wycombe once to score some powder, but I don't think that counts. Jesus, I sure hope it don't count. And one of the things about pubs is that groups go there together, or they meet up there, and they kind of take it in turns to go get the drinks. Only there's no bar tab, so by the end of the evening everybody has bought everybody else a drink. Or that's how it's supposed to work. The *kingyo no fun* in any group sits right back in his or her seat whenever the glasses start to look empty. He is not going to buy anybody else a drink if he can help it. Because he's a freeloader. That's his entire philosophy. He's gonna sit right back and let everybody else get on with it. He'll still accept his beer every time some other poor sucker goes up to the bar to get it. And somehow, don't ask me how, he gets away with it.

If you're in a group – Jeez, even if that group is only two people and one of them is *kingyo no fun* – and you're walking towards the pub, the *kingyo no fun* starts to hang back, real subtle like so nobody knows what's going on, but he hangs back and puts an arm around the last person to enter the pub ahead of him, just to make sure. This way he'll be the last person to reach the bar and there's no way he'll have to buy a drink if they're only staying for one or two.

In Amsterdam, Simon, *kingyo no fun*, led us into the crowded bar. *Jesus, what's this guy doing?* I thought. Could I have been mistaken? But once I, and the others, had fought our way through the throng and caught up with Simon, I realised he knew exactly what he was doing. He'd found the only free table in the place. And he'd sat down already. He was guarding our seats. We could hardly expect him to get up and go to the bar now because he was keeping our table for us. That was his job and boy didn't he do it well. So, Ben and Matthew went off to the bar and James and I sat down with Simon. I had this sneaking suspicion that the two English guys would take the opportunity to slip away, unable to take any more of Simon's company, but when I craned my neck I could just make out Ben standing at the bar talking to one of the bartenders – nice-looking guy, about twenty, twenty-one, very tall, blond, healthy tan. Yeah, right – look but don't touch.

James had gone and sat right next to Simon. There was no need for that, I thought. We could both have sat right over the other side of the table – it was quite a wide table – in order to make sure we kept all the seats necessary. But James is like that. He doesn't think. Sometimes I have to think for him. Ben and Matthew reappeared, Ben carrying a tray with five opened bottles of Beck's on it. Matthew helped by distributing the beers and then we were all clinking bottles and saying stuff. Simon was grinning all over his face. Yeah, of course he was. He was doing OK.

No one was saying anything so I thought I'd start the ball rolling. 'So what about all that art shit?'

'Oh, I know some of those guys,' Simon said.

Yeah, he would.

'I think some of their stuff's fascinating, don't you?' He directed his question at James, who raised his bottle to his lips and nodded.

Simon was English and, unlike his two compatriots, talked like he had a ten-pound salmon up his ass. Like someone out of a 1960s movie. Someone who lives in a little mews flat off the King's Road in Chelsea. I looked at him looking at James. His skin was a little too white, like thin dough, and his eyes were punched into it like raisins. The left eye bore a slight imperfection on the iris. A little yellow fleck, like a tendril of broken egg yolk.

'Do you live in Amsterdam?' Ben asked him.

'Yes. I have a rather sweet little place not far from here,' he said, looking around for a glass. 'On Laurierstraat.'

'What do you do?' Matthew this time.

'Oh, you know, I write. Not like you guys.' The word 'guys' sounded forced in his mouth. 'I write about shows and films and art. I suppose I'm a critic.'

'Who do you write for?'

'Oh, there's an English-language magazine, *Time Out Amsterdam*. I do some stuff for them. I speak Dutch so I can write for the local press as well. It's really rather a good set-up.'

Although it was Matthew who'd asked the question, Simon looked at James most of the time while he was answering. And then he went too far. The guy crossed the line. James wore a ring on the second finger of his left hand. It was an impressive ring, a beautiful ring with a serpent design and a polished piece of jet set into it. I'd bought it for him. I'd chosen it and I'd bought it and James wore it always. It occasionally won admiring glances, but people didn't normally go so far as to do what Simon did.

He reached across and touched the ring with his own second finger and his other fingers touched James's. I saw them alight on James's hand, as carefully and gently as Apollo 11 touching down on the moon, while he made pathetic little noises, practically cooing over the ring.

I exploded. I stood up abruptly, jarring the table across the floor and upsetting two bottles of Beck's, and I roared at him: 'Get your fucking hands off him! Right now!' I sprawled across the table in an attempt to grab him. I saw my fingers curl like talons, my nails itching to sink into him. His face went completely pale as he staggered back, murmuring something unintelligible. James looked shocked. Ben was hunched over his Beck's snuffling and spluttering, lost somewhere between hysteria and bafflement. And Matthew had thrust out an arm across my chest to restrain me. Still I struggled to reach him. People all over the bar had turned to watch. Wide eyes and open mouths were everywhere like a bar-load of Munch screamers.

I backed off and glowered at Simon for the last time before turning and stalking out of the bar, knocking the elbow of some guy near the door as I left. He sent me out into the night with a volley of abuse, in Dutch fortunately so I didn't have a clue what he was saying. I was churning up inside, had to get out. It was either that or start a fight. With Simon; with the guy near the door; Jesus, even with James. Or with Ben for finding the whole humiliating episode so goddam funny. Or Matthew for egging Simon on, asking his questions, instead of icing him out right from the start.

I didn't barely slow down for a coupla blocks, then I became aware how my heart was racing and I stopped. I leaned against a handrail on a bridge over one of the city's eighteen million canals. I felt some of the anger pass out of me and float away on the oily wake of a pleasure boat. Only some of it, though. I was still

cursing Simon when I noticed a tall figure loping down the street
from the direction of the bar. At first I thought it was Ben, come
to snuffle at me, but then I recognised James's slight stoop, the
rounded shoulders, the victim look. His long legs covered acres
of cobbled street with each stride. He came alongside me and
leaned on the parapet, looking out at the lights on the water.

'Don't,' I said, expecting a lecture. 'Just…don't.'

I could hear his breathing, slightly faster than normal.

'Let's go back,' he said softly. 'To the apartment.'

Back on Utrechtsedwarsstraat, where we were staying in a cute
little apartment loaned by a former girlfriend of James's, we
chilled out. ('Girlfriend,' I'd said, my eyes popping out on stalks.
Jesus, you just never knew. 'Oh Christ, just a friend. I couldn't
fuck a girl,' he said, grabbing my hand. 'I love them too much. I've
got too much respect for them to do that.' He pronouned 'that'
with genuine distaste.) We drank a couple of beers in the back
yard, where we sat out naked, because it was warm enough. And
because we wanted to. There was a party going on two or three
houses further down and the frantic, hectic techno beats started
to open me up a little. I apologised to James for the outburst in the
bar and James asked me whether I wanted to take an E. I didn't
know whether I did, so I said no, and I knew James wouldn't take
one without me. We do everything together.

'Fuck it, why not?' I said after all.

So James broke out his little wooden pillbox I bought for him
in Paris and produced a couple of white doves. I checked we had
plenty of water in the refrigerator and we took one each and
sat around in the yard listening to the whooping and screaming
taking place a couple of doors down. A Marc Almond single
that I liked at the time came on and I started singing along. 'I
wanna be adored,' I fluted. 'And explored.' I was dancing around
the yard. James was watching me, still drinking steadily. Then I
came on, with a real big whoosh. I just took off like a goddam
rocket. I'd come on so quickly because I'd had nothing to eat
and because, in any case, they were real good doves. James was a
little slower to get it, but pretty soon we were lying on the floor
of the yard, the sounds of the party washing over us, staring

up at the sky. James liked to watch the stars fade in and out. I looked for faces and stuff in the clouds. I ran my hands over his chest. James has a chest covered with thick, dark hair and on E it felt completely different – very, very soft. It seemed as if I could feel every single strand of hair as it passed beneath my hand and each one was indescribably soft. His skin became sort of rubbery. I leaned over him. His pupils were enormous. I told him. 'Your pupils are totally immense,' I said, and he put his hand around the back of my neck, pulling me down on to him, his tongue sinking into my mouth and his lips closing around mine. His free hand sought out my dick and played with it. It was pretty soft but James is an expert. There's never been anybody better. As we kissed he worked at my dick until it had become curiously big and long but still not very hard. This was pretty typical in our experience of E. I broke off the kiss and looked at his dick. It was like mine, lying flopped over his thigh, so I took it in my right hand and moved his foreskin up and down, over the glans. My jaw was clenching because of the E and I didn't have any spit to spare. I stood up. 'Hang on,' I said, my head spinning because I got up too fast. I went into the apartment and fetched a bottle of water from the kitchen. Standing over James, I tipped the bottle back and chugged almost half a pint. I felt it trickle down my chin and knew James would be watching it run down my white body. 'Wow,' I said, my head back, staring at the sky. It was so big. The things you think! The things you say! I lay back down next to James, only the other way this time, and held his dick for a moment, feeling the soft downy hairs at its base before slipping it into my mouth and pulling back his foreskin. It felt and tasted beautiful, rolling around inside my mouth, but my jaw kept clenching. James was moaning softly. I knew what he'd be doing: staring at the stars, thinking weird thoughts. He was still stroking my dick as I sucked his and it was real nice but at some point you gotta face up to the facts: we weren't going to get hard enough to do it. Maybe we didn't even want to fuck. I didn't want to do it to James. The thought of him doing it to me was kinda nice but I could live without it and after a while we found we were both just lying there again, staring up at the sky, our blood ebbing.

Later, I don't know when, much later, we got cold and made it in to the bedroom, where we crashed out. If I dreamt, I didn't remember anything.

When I woke, James was not around.

Ten minutes later, having checked the back yard, the bathroom, under the bed and inside one or two cupboards, I established that he had gone. This was strange. James isn't that kind of a person. He never just goes out. He needs a reason. He needs a good reason.

It was twenty before eleven. We'd slept late because of the E. Or I had, at least. I had no way of knowing how long James had been asleep. I felt pretty rough, my jaw still clenching and my limbs aching, although we'd neither of us been very energetic while we'd been up. Outside it was another hot day. When I stepped out the front door there was a hooting of klaxons from the Prinsengracht and a clatter of bicycles heading down Amstel. From a payphone I called the hotel where Ben and Matthew were staying. They hadn't seen James but Ben was able to give me Simon's address. Apparently he'd been handing out his business card after I'd stormed out of the bar the night before. I thanked Ben, who merely sniggered in reply, and I left the kiosk. Simon's street was close by the gallery and the bar, as he had said. I rang his bell then stepped back to look up at the front of the building. The windows were all closed and there was no clear sign of life. A cloud shaped like a snowman drifted over the top of the building. My neck began to ache from leaning back and looking up. I cursed Simon. And James – he'd fallen for a routine.

Just across the street from the apartment house was a coffee shop. The sweet, sickly miasma of dope overpowered even the smell of freshly ground beans. I got a large cappuccino and sat by the window, where I could watch the street door to Simon's building. I ordered a second cappuccino. A couple of tables away a woman wearing Oakley wraps sat reading a Dutch newspaper. There was a little direct light in the coffee shop but not too much. I guess she could have gotten along OK without the shades. I looked back across the street. *Kingyo no fun* is a Japanese expression meaning goldfish shit. The first time I heard it, the significance was not entirely clear to me. Matter of fact, it didn't mean a damn thing.

The Oakley woman's partner came back from the bathroom. He was wearing a slithery, artificial snakeskin shirt in some shiny yellow-and-green fabric, tight black jeans and beat-up Nike Airs a couple of years out of date. On anybody else the combination would have looked awful, but this guy wore it well. Real well. He had a kind of glamour. He almost shone. I figured he was a rock star on vacation or someone off the TV. He was casually toking on a spliff the size of a Californian Redwood, which again would have looked like an affectation if he'd been anybody else. But this guy was genuine. Just like James is genuine.

Something somewhere clicked. Not just somewhere. In my head somewhere.

I dropped a couple of crumpled colourful bills on the counter and left the coffee shop. So urgent was it that I reach Simon's door – I'd seen a guy go to enter while I was reaching for my stash of guilders – I didn't look, but just dashed across the street.

It was real close. I heard a jangling bell, a woman's voice, and I escaped with a knock on the back of my left heel. *Uh-huh, pretty fortunate*, I thought in a daze as faces stared down at me from the windows of the tram that groaned slowly by. Cyclists weaved lenticular patterns around me as I gawped open mouthed in the middle of the street, bells ringing, horns hooting, whistles blowing. The guy who'd been going to enter Simon's building was poised on the threshold, the door held open by his hand. Maybe, if I hadn't nearly been knocked down by the tram, he wouldn't have still been there and I would have been unable to enter. Everything happens for a reason.

I snapped back, dodging more bicycles as I hurried to catch the big blond-wood door. A blur of bell-pushes told me Simon's apartment number. The guy stood and watched as I mounted the stairs three at a time. I guess I didn't much care what he thought.

I stood outside the door to Simon's apartment. A big brass number seven on the door. I got my breath back. If I was right, though, there was no need to compose myself. I pushed the door with a finger and it swung open, creaking just a little for good measure. I went in.

I knew instantly that the place was not empty. At least not quite. Sure there was no sign of James, but then I hadn't expected there to be. Simon was good, real good. He was good *kingyo no fun*. There's good and bad, by which I mean how successful he got to be rather than what a good guy he was. Clearly, he was not a good guy. But then who is? Simon was a master of his craft. I knew that, within moments of entering his place, because I could sense that part of him was still there. I scouted round to look for it. I have experience. I knew what I was looking for. The traces take different forms. Sometimes you see stuff lying right there in the middle of the floor, like fresh slough, picking up the light and handing it straight back to you – like the shirt the rock-star guy in the coffee shop was wearing. It's like an old snakeskin or wings that an insect has no more use for.

There was nothing like that in Simon's apartment. He was more highly evolved.

I didn't want to waste valuable time looking for traces of Simon when I knew I should be out there hunting down 'James'. But you can't help it. And I guess I still had a little bit of my mind that needed convincing. I stared hard at the surfaces in the apartment, the things he'd got lying around like props. The magazines and newspapers, the novels in English and Dutch with realistically broken spines, a word-processor with the cursor blinking. An ashtray full of dead cigarettes – not Simon's – a stack of bland CDs: Prince, George Michael – Jesus Christ, even the Gypsy Kings. Hal Hartley videos, some French shit: Eric Rohmer, Robert Bresson, Maurice Pialat. I wasn't getting anything except further evidence that he was good at what he did. This cultural vacuum – it was no coincidence, no coincidence at all.

I stared harder and tried first to shorten my focus, then to extend it, to focus beyond the walls. It's like goofing around with a stereogram: it can take time, but if you get a glimpse, the rest comes easy. And there on the wall, or through the wall, between the poster for the Van Gogh Museum and the Arnolfini print, I got it. I managed to lose the basic building blocks of the poster, the frame, the bare wall, the print, and in the interstices I saw him, a trace of him. The sneer, the twisted lip, even the fleck in the eye. His signature on the wall. Like the shadow of the Hiroshima victim or the casts at Pompeii. I looked away then looked back and it was still there. He was still inhabiting this place even in his absence. Much as I now knew he was inhabiting 'James', also by his absence.

Trashing the place would do no good. Some things are eternal. And I had to find 'James'. It was an outside chance but worth a few minutes of my time to continue searching the apartment for any detail that might, in spite of his efforts, give me a real clue to the nature of him. Something that might tell me where to start looking. I swept the set dressings aside now, the CDs, the videos and the books, the cheap point-and-shoot camera, the bottles of liquor and the unwrapped packs of Camel Lites. Most of the cigarette butts in the ashtray were rouged with lipstick, but in a city like Amsterdam you couldn't take that as proof they had been smoked by women. Or by transvestites, or transsexuals – you could take nothing for granted here. It was one reason why James and I liked coming here and why we'd leapt eagerly on the gallery invitation when it arrived at the end of a dull month-long trail of book launches in private Soho drinking clubs, the Museum of the Moving Image and subterranean fetish joints in Spitalfields. Amsterdam was special, it was different. But it could make finding 'James' even harder.

The inverted commas. You want me to explain the inverted commas? Like I said, Simon is good *kingyo no fun*. He gets right inside, like all *kingyo no fun*, but then he stays there. He doesn't get shat out in a couple of days like the amateurs. He's there for keeps, or for as long as he wants to be.

Kingyo no fun try to get up their host's ass. They're shit trying to get back up the asses of bright shiny charismatic people – the goldfish of the world. Not the perch, the gudgeon or the minnows. The goldfish. They hang around, the *kingyo no fun*, just like goldfish shit – you ever sat and watched a fish tank, seen a goldfish take a crap and the long string of crap trails after it for as long as it takes to work loose. It can take minutes, hours, days. Some goldfish are never seen without *kingyo no fun*.

The world is divided into two groups of people. Those who are not *kingyo no fun* and those who are. Not all goldfish shine as brightly, however. James shone brightly. The guy in the coffee shop shone brightly but the woman with him kept her shades on pretty much the whole time, you can be sure of that; he shone so brightly, she'd have to.

At first they're just easing in, laying the groundwork. Later they'll strip naked, lose their clothes, their skin, their patina of ordinariness – leave it lying on the floor or fused into the fabric of the walls – and slowly, messily work their way in. Once inside, the less successful *kingyo no fun* stays there an hour or two. To the rest of the world they've just disappeared. But that's all the goldfish can bear, and the goldfish outgrows them, rejects them, and the *kingyo no fun* is back to being itself again, but strengthened, nourished.

That's the amateur, the part-timer.

The business – and Simon was the business, that was clear – stays up there.

It's not a gay thing, wanting to get up somebody's ass in this way. It's a people thing. A weak people thing. I know, I've seen it.

Further proof of that was to be found in Simon's bedroom. After his thoroughness in other respects I was astonished to find, nestling within the pages of a Jeffrey Archer novel – so far so good – a photograph. Just a little six-by-four glossy print, not very well taken, of a black hooker standing in a doorway in the red light district. It was the one thing in the whole apartment – with the exception of the stereogrammatical trace of the *kingyo no fun* himself, and the clothes I'd seen him wearing the night before dumped in the otherwise empty laundry basket – that was not entirely faux.

Apart from the girl herself, there was a clue in the picture. The rows and rows of doors in Amsterdam's red light district are pretty much homogeneous. Narrow doors that are almost entirely glass, with a brown or a red curtain on the inside that can be drawn across. Beyond the door a foreshortened passageway and another doorway, into the hooker's room. The girl stands in the street doorway, or sits on an elevated stool either in the doorway or in the room's picture window, which can also be curtained off. It all looks so artificial – a hurried though professional-looking construction of glass and alloy – and tacked on to whatever real buildings lie at the rear, you wonder whether behind the shallow little rooms with their air freshener and single washbasin there lurks a league of unscrupulous gentlemen who sneak in from the back when the curtains are drawn to help themselves to your billfold and plastic.

Bounded by Zeedijk to the north, Kloveniersburgwal to the east, Oude Hoogstraat, Oude Doelen and Damstraat to the south and Warmoesstraat to the west, the red light district is roughly heart shaped – a real, messy, asymmetrical human heart rather than its cartoon symbol. It rests, snug and reliable, in the oldest part of Amsterdam, functioning twenty-four hours a day on some streets. Men – and a steady stream of sightseers of both sexes – are drawn through its venous streets and capillary alleyways, past yards and yards of flesh that is stretched and pressed, twisted and uplifted.

James and I had spent an hour on our first day wandering round the district. We might not have wanted to buy, but that didn't mean we weren't interested in taking a look – it's something different, something you don't see in London, or New York for that matter.

Of course, most of the doorways face on to canals and the majority of those that don't are squeezed into narrow alleyways. The doorway in Simon's picture fell into neither of these two groups. His black hooker worked a street broader than the alleyways that connected Oudezijds Voorburgwal to Oudezijds Achterburgwal, and the angle of his shot revealed that a stone building rather than a canal was on the other side of it. When I applied my recollection of the area to close study of the map I found I was able to narrow down the possible locations. The girls worked in six-hour shifts, so I wouldn't necessarily see the black girl even if I found her street, but it was all I had to go on.

I needed James back, if only for confirmation. And he needed me. Now more than ever.

If I knew Simon half as well as I thought I did, I was on the right track.

*

There were fewer streets that fitted the bill than I had thought. In fact, I only had to tour the area once more before I was able to pin down the location. The strongest clue was the fraction of stonework visible on the far right of the picture, which formed part of whatever building faced the hooker's doorway. I soon realised, as I walked around the outside of the massive structure for the second time, that this was the Oude Kerk – the Old Church.

The street was in back of the Oude Kerk, little more than an alleyway connecting one of the canals, the Oudezijdsachterburgwal, to Warmoesstraat, and along it, opposite the church, a row of hookers' windows and doorways. I walked by once, then twice, trying to identify the doorway, but they all looked pretty much the same. The hookers themselves were more varied. There were a few Africans, a handful of Thai or Filipina girls and one or two Europeans. Several talked directly to me as I walked by; one black girl caught my hand and tried to drag me into her doorway. 'Fuckee, suckee,' she said, her painted lips and pneumatic breasts trembling. I held my ground and withdrew the photograph from the back pocket of my Levi's.

'Do you know this girl?' I asked her. She took hold of the picture with long-nailed glittery fingers and called out to a colleague two doors down. They spoke in French, which I did not understand, the second hooker looking at me appraisingly as I switched my gaze from one to the other. The first girl answered me. 'She is not there,' she said in halting but charming English.

'Where is she?'

'She is…later. Plus tard. *Plus tard elle sera là.*'

I understood that much.

'Where? Here?' I pointed to the doorway behind the girl who was talking to me.

'She is there,' the other girl said, pointing at a closed door twenty-five yards farther along towards the canal. 'Not now. Later.'

'Yeah, later,' I said. 'Like, when later?'

The girls both shrugged.

There was a beat. The three of us stood there in a triangle of silence broken only by the clicking of the first girl's nails on a long string of beads she wore around her neck.

'Fuckee, suckee?' she said hopefully.

I went back later and recognised her instantly. The slightly haughty angle she held her head at. The red earrings. And, frankly, the enormous breasts, thrust upwards and outwards in apparent defiance of the laws of nature. I hesitated for a moment before approaching her. In that moment everything could still change. I could leave undone what I was about to do. I could walk away and never see 'James' or 'Simon' ever again.

But then neither would I ever be able to look myself in the eye.

I took a different photograph from the pocket of my shirt and walked across to where she stood. As I accelerated to cross the street so did everything else. A train of events had been set in motion, even before I spoke to her, simply by my deciding to speak to her.

She told me her name was Stephanie and that she was from the Cameroon. I said that was cool but had she seen this guy. She told me she saw many, many guys. This one was special, I told her. Had she seen him? I slipped a twenty from my pocket. Yeah, she'd seen him. Did she expect to see him again?

Yeah, she nodded.

'What about you?' she suggested. 'You are a nice man.'

I warned her not to get her hopes up then took out my billfold and said we had business to discuss. As I watched her eyes greedily counting the notes, I knew she'd go for the deal. She sold her own body for hard cash, why not others' as well?

Crouching in a space no bigger than a closet, my breathing becoming wheezy, my knee joints seizing up, I plugged my eye to the tear in the curtain and watched and waited. Stephanie stood outside and touted for business. I had said for the money I was giving her she should simply wait for 'James' to show up, but she wouldn't buy that.

I said, 'What if he comes and you're busy and he goes with someone else?'

She told me he'd wait. He didn't just want to fuck. He wanted to fuck her. I winced. He'd paid already, she explained. Paid up front.

I wondered whose money it was. I wouldn't put it past the little bastard.

When she led her first john into the little room and drew the curtains at the front, I asked myself again whether I couldn't have waited in the street for 'James' to show up and tackled him there. But I knew I couldn't. I had to be a hundred per cent sure before I did anything, and for that I needed a close-up view. I fastened my eyes shut as Stephanie unclipped her sturdy brassiere and the john – a nervous-looking Scandinavian type – put a hand to his belt buckle. It seemed to go on for ever but can only have lasted five or ten miserable minutes.

Stephanie saw two more clients. I merely checked them out in the first instance then tried to switch off while she got on with it. I began to experience the absolute vertiginous depression that naturally accompanies the destruction – or imminent destruction – of everything you live for. At the same time I was tortured by flashes of hope. Even when fully convinced that you face total disaster, your mind is a wellspring of mad optimism. You never know…Even when you do.

I didn't even know what I would do when the time came. By not properly arming myself did I somehow think I was moulding the future, fixing the right conditions for a better outcome? I was a fool, had always been a fool. I should never have trusted James. With him it wasn't a matter of choice – he trusted everyone. And got fucked as a result.

Maybe I was a fool to think it had been a matter of choice in my case. I was, after all, no more a free agent than Simon was. Only he was better at it than me.

I heard conversation, half-recognised voices out on the street. I stuck my eye to the hole. There it was, he was, they were – James's tall, stooping figure was twisted into a gangling, distressing compromise. Standing by the doorway leering at Stephanie as if she were a glossy six-by-four in a skin mag rather than a human being. I hunched up a fraction, tried to flex my muscles, oil my joints. I heard a sound behind me but guessed it was an acoustical trick and dismissed it.

'James' was inside the air-freshened chamber now, his spine bent unnecessarily beneath the artificial ceiling, his body contorted, limbs abruptly snaking this way and that like power cables brought down in a storm. His face writhed with tics and spasms as two souls fought for its control. Stephanie rounded him neatly, interposing herself between him and me, so that I was spared the worst as he unbuckled his black Levi's, but I could still see his face – that once proud countenance become this battered canvas for a wrestling bout of light and shade. His eyes flashed once like a horse's – suffering but devoid of ordered intelligence. That look strengthened my resolve, but I found myself rooted to the spot, watching in horrified fascination as he started to thrust in and out of the still-standing Stephanie. His movements were ungainly but full of physical power, truly a case of mind over matter as Simon turned James's flesh into his servant. James's comments about fucking women came back to me and I don't think I imagined that lost, hurt look in his creased brow. If I squinted I could just make out in his left eye a small but distinct fleck of yellow.

This time behind me I did hear a noise, but I was too late to do much about it. There was a rush of air and a scuffling noise, then a sudden cold sensation in the small of my back. I twisted round and felt something scrape against my vertebrae. Something inside my body. The wiry African who had stabbed me then tried to bundle me over, but I thumped him hard and low, dug the knife out of my back with one twist and, when the man started to uncurl his winded body, opened him with it swiftly from groin to throat. I stepped right back to avoid the hot, slippery tumble of his intestines, and with a crash I brought down the curtain, rail and all.

'James' stumbled back, total confusion writ large across his crumpled face, and Stephanie spun round to face me. I quickly considered dispatching her for the double-cross but in a split-second decision – I am at least conversant with humanity – chose not to. She couldn't be blamed for not trusting me.

I looked at 'James', who tottered backwards unsteadily, and had a brief true vision of his own liver and lights slipping quietly out of a sewage outfall into the Herengracht and the soupy green water closing implacably over the still, small muscle of his heart. I knew that Simon's viscera were packed into the much-loved body of the man in front of me, just as his sick thoughts and wicked desires coiled in the scoured cranium I had for ten years stroked and kissed each night in our bed. In my hand was clutched the means to guarantee James's release into oblivion from this squalid and barbaric tenancy.

Proficient, cunning and ultimately successful, Simon would have believed himself eternal, but I was holding the gutting knife and he was in poor shape to resist. Some *kingyo no fun*, after all, are more eternal than others.

NINE YEARS

Jem's thinking: he said a rave. They went to a rave. Just up from King's Cross, they said, and Jem realises he's seen them, or others like them, spilling out on to York Way, pasty faced and wasted on Sunday afternoons. Jem wants to go to a rave but he doesn't know anyone and he thinks he's too old. Twenty-nine, too old. In fact he feels too old altogether with these people. He wants to be their age. What are they? Twenty-four, twenty-five?

But it's not just age. He's different. He doesn't want to be but he is. It's his upbringing, his professional status, all that stuff. Maybe it was a mistake getting back in touch with Dilly after nine years.

He's sitting there, Jem, in a basement room in North Kensington with these people he hardly knows. Dilly included. Nine years since he met her in a fringe play they were both doing. Dilly's still acting these days and so's Jem but just not on stage.

There's Dilly and Dilly's sister Joanne and a couple of guys – Johnny and Mr Fox – whose relationship to anyone else he hasn't figured out. And there's Joanne's six-year-old son Dean and Dilly's two dogs. German shepherds. Fuck, they gave him the fear. Not wanting to look a dick in front of Dilly, he's giving them extravagant hugs and stroking all the dirt off their coats on to his hands. It gives him something to do as well while the others all have a natter and he feels left out and unequipped to contribute. It's not as if they're being rude to him. They offer him the spliff as it goes round and, again for the sake of appearances, he takes it between forefinger and thumb and sucks it as if it's a straw. He hangs on to it for one more drag because he thinks he remembers that's how you do it. Then he passes it to Dilly.

It's Joanne's flat. Dean's sitting there wrestling with one of the dogs and Jem's shocked that they're smoking in front of him. The room's

a state. The whole flat's like a bomb site. Shit everywhere. Dean's toys
– toys that Jem reckons Dean only leaves lying around to make it
look to the DSS like he's still a kid – are scattered in every room.
Jem's been to the toilet and had a bit of a nose round. He's hoping
Dilly doesn't take after her sister and her flat's not like this. He knows
the dogs'll be there and they're bound to be pretty much in charge.
In any case he doesn't know for sure she's going to ask him back. He
walks back to the front room via the kitchen. There's a nappy on the
floor torn to cabbagey shreds by one of the dogs.

Dilly doesn't look up as he comes back in. They're talking
about the festival Mr Fox was at last weekend. Jem's wondering
whether it was the one in the West Country that was in the papers
with all the arrests and the local residents threatening to dig out
their shotguns.

He's thinking: these guys aren't dangerous. It's just a lifestyle. He
can fit in if he tries hard enough. Community's really important
to them, and family. Dilly's always doing stuff with her family.
Her old man plays R&B in rowdy nicotine-yellow pubs from the
shadow of the Westway to the Goldhawk Road and she goes along
when she can get someone to look after the dogs. He wouldn't
be able to cope with that long term, but perhaps he's not really
looking for long term. He wonders whether he's just after a fuck
but can't admit it to himself.

At the start of the evening, yes, maybe that's what it was about,
but pretty soon Dilly's making him laugh like she did nine years
ago. It wasn't just fancying her, then, it was liking her too.

Nine years ago after the play finished there was a cast party at
someone's mum's place on the Cally Road and he just talked to
Dilly. He wanted to sleep with her but lacked the confidence and
the right words to tell her. She knew he fancied her and she liked
him too but she was so lacking in confidence herself she couldn't
take the initiative. So they just wound each other up and by the
end of the party they knew that was it; their chance had gone.

Jem's been thinking they could have another chance tonight.
He's single. He thinks she is too. He can't ask her because it would
be like asking for a shag. But they've been out for a drink in the
Bush and had a plate of pasta and they've laughed and there's
some chemistry there like there was before. They're older now

so less prone to winding each other up. But deep down they're both as shy as they always were. I want to go now with Dilly, he's thinking. But Mr Fox has borrowed Dilly's car to go and get munchies and a pint of milk from the 7-11. It's ten minutes till he gets back. Jem's playing with the dogs and keeping an eye on the subtitles of the foreign film playing on the portable TV. The sound's down and Joanne's got Kiss FM coming out of the radio. Jem doesn't know any of the records. He wishes he did.

Mr Fox comes back and everyone's unwrapping a Mars Bar or a Toblerone. Dean's fallen asleep behind Dilly. No one goes to make the tea. They're all trying to make someone else do it. Jem says, I'll make it, knowing that'll make Dilly do it. But he jumps up and takes the teapot through into the kitchen, and Dilly follows him. He wants her to say something while they're alone but all she says is, Go and sit down, I'll do it.

He wants to put his hands on her, make her realise she doesn't need to be shy. But he hasn't got the nerve.

Jem goes back into the front room and no one speaks to him. He studies the TV screen and strokes one of the dogs. Dilly brings the tea in and he knows there's a chance they might get to go when the tea's been drunk. Johnny and Mr Fox gulp theirs down, thanking Jem for making it – as if his function has finally been made clear – and they're off. Dilly's is still near the top of the mug. Jem's not having one because Dilly got the number of cups wrong and he didn't really want one anyway.

Then they're outside saying goodbye to Joanne and climbing into Dilly's car. He's thinking maybe he should suggest she drop him off at a minicab place on Ladbroke Grove in case he's already made too many assumptions. But he's reluctant to throw the chance away so says nothing and Dilly drives to her flat the other side of the Westway. The dogs are in the rear sticking their moist noses into the back of Jem's neck. The roads are empty apart from occasional police vans. All the big white houses with their cracked, peeling façades are in darkness. It's late. Jem doesn't know this part of town. They're not really in an area, more sort of between areas, adrift between Maida Hill and Westbourne Park. Jem feels between states: excitement and anxiety. His stomach is fluttering like before going on stage and he's still scared of the dogs. It's as if they know him better than Dilly does, because they can smell the fear he's trying to hide.

She pulls up outside a huge converted Victorian terrace and they get out without a word. Jem feels as if he's walking on eggshells. He doesn't want to trespass where he doesn't belong. The dogs run up the stone steps ahead of them.

In a few minutes Jem's standing at the big sash window looking down over the railway line. He's comforted by the coloured signals and the clatter of a suburban passenger train being drawn towards Paddington. Its yellow windows judder unsteadily like frames of film in the gate of an old projector. Dilly's doing something with the dogs, getting them settled. She comes and stands behind Jem for a moment, watching him watching the train go by. Then she goes and turns down the bed and disappears into the bathroom.

Jem's inertia makes him miserable. He wants Dilly to say something or to touch him but he knows she's not going to. She wants him to make a decision. He doesn't know whether he can. He thinks about his own flat at the other end of the Bakerloo line: the warm bath, the comfy bed. Dilly's flat's OK though, not like her sister's.

When she comes back from the bathroom he's waiting in the bed. She doesn't seem surprised and opens the window before getting in as well. She's wearing a long T-shirt. He's kept his boxer shorts on. They don't speak. Jem can hear one of the dogs growling quietly in the other room.

He's making love to her slowly, listening to another train tap-dancing past the house, steps echoing off the walls. He opens his eyes to see that Dilly's are closed. Her mouth's open and he can hear her wheezing slightly. Two little shining lights point in his direction from the doorway and give him a fright. It's one of the dogs watching him.

He loses it and doesn't know what to say to Dilly because the dog's vanished.

They're lying side by side. Jem knows he shouldn't have tried to meld the past and the future because the present creates itself.

Soon he's out there in the night glancing up at her window to see one of the dogs watching him. A train rattles by. He follows the sound. The dog knows him better than he knows himself.

THE COMFORT OF STRANGLERS

Contracts or something. Release forms. Legal nonsense of some kind. 'Can't I sign them here?' he'd asked, flustered. The voice came back over the line: 'On site, Mr Campbell. On site. That's the stipulation. It's all written down. On site.' Still, there was something to be said for stealing a couple of days.

Paul Campbell sat back, enjoyed the brushed-velvet feel of the headrest against his scalp. The train skirted the sea, sharp shining cliffs soared arrogantly on the right side of the line. A row of white houses. Platforms. Dawlish. Gone in an instant. Paul wandered down to the end of the carriage, leant out of the window, salty side. It stung his tongue, hair whipping in the vanishing space, head clearing of tiredness as if it were mere foam.

Gina was fucking someone and it wasn't him. He couldn't remember the last time. One minute, the way Paul felt, the guy was welcome to her, the next he wanted to kill him. Or her. Or himself. Perhaps if they'd never got married. If he'd listened to the cautionary voice. If he wasn't living in Hampstead Garden Suburb and working for her father. Then it might be easier. He could just walk away. As it was, he had to make do with two days in Devon. She'd offered to come, he'd said no. It was midweek. She was still working, although she had no need to. She liked to keep her hand in, she said. She could have taken the rest of her life off without it making the slightest impact, but she liked to think the modelling industry would grind to a halt if she didn't turn up to jolly along a few hacks. Plus, she'd have two whole nights with Mr Man, whoever he was. Paul didn't really care. It wasn't anyone he knew. He didn't know anybody. Not up there.

The train peeled away from the sea, cut across water meadows, diving through copses, attacking agriculture. Paul went and sat down again, closed his eyes, dreamed of handing in his notice. I'm leaving. You want to know why, ask your daughter.

The ticket guy came round. Paul checked out the features under the cap, tried to feel something. Anything. A sense of coming home. He felt nothing. Nor had he expected to. This was no more his home than NW11. He came from nowhere and was heading the same place. He'd look up Tim, the kid whose folks kept a hotel. He had lived down here, after all, for, what, a few years. His teens. Early teens. Then what? These days he never had a chance to sit and think. Maybe that was a good thing. Fragmented memories of growing up all over the place. With this auntie and that uncle, a year or two with Nan and Eric up Southport way. He'd been sent a bag of Eric's silk cravats when the old guy copped it. Couldn't remember where he'd been at the time. They were good people, possibly the only ones he'd known, only ones he could remember, until he met Gina Graham. She was the kind of girl who had an abortion while still at school, then grew up over half-term, came back a young woman and left. Went out and got a job she didn't need – father tried to stop her, said she didn't need to work. Made of the stuff. Good commercial head on him, offered Paul a job, fool to turn it down, Gina said. He accepted it. Never looked back, didn't smile much either. Greyhound after the hare.

The train slowed gradually. Totnes. Pretty much as near as it dared get to Salcombe. No one there to meet him. The solicitor was coming down from Exeter, meeting him 'on site' at 2.30. Paul loped down the platform, saw the line of cabs waiting. Driver looked at him questioningly. Paul gave the name of a place outside Salcombe. Checked his watch. He wouldn't have to hang around long.

It was like another country. So far from the nearest railway line you had to go by cab. Not even Scotland was this bad. He scrutinised faces on the road – dog-walkers, cyclists, drivers – looking for signs. Nothing. They looked foreign. The cab driver grunted. Paul paid, got out in the middle of nowhere, started walking.

Grand from the outside, the cottage was a state, as far as Paul could tell peering through grimy windows. No sign of the solicitor. Over there between a dip in conflicting slopes you could see the sea. Just. A powder-compact mirror catching the sunlight. Sheep wandered desultorily over the cropped grass. The back door was open. Have a word with the solicitor about that. Anyone could walk in. Though it wasn't the sort of place you passed by chance. Nor was there any purpose here on this false promontory. The interior smelt of dust and old newspapers. Beams high in the black roof space, ceiling absent. Paul stood by the seaward window for a minute – the higher position revealing more blue – before climbing the open steps to the gallery where once there'd been a rough bedroom. He sat on the edge of the upper platform dangling his feet. Looking at the beams. Waiting.

Creeping green tendrils. Tough, wiry. White trumpets with no scent. The watery crunch of soft meadow grass underfoot, his own heavy breathing, pumping chest. Pain in his head, behind the eyes. Sudden sunlight, silhouettes, a blast of pain. Turning, features clear as day, then fade-out.

He came round with his head in his hands, perched on the edge. Swaying. He pulled back, gathered his knees to his chin, rocked, blocked the visions. His uncle had lived here alone, apart from the short time he'd fostered Paul. And during those years he'd remained isolated, cold, striking Paul on one occasion when the boy tried to shake him awake, thinking he was dead in his bed. Tim had been Paul's lifeline then. He looked at his watch. The solicitor was late.

Outside the air had freshened – tart, seaweed and diesel. Paul rounded the corner of the cottage, heard the scrunch of tyres before he saw the car. The solicitor had to park some distance away, the cottage having no clear access. He walked, briefcase in hand, towards Paul. Large black smudges where his eyes should be, dark snout for a nose. Pain flared up across Paul's skull, bent him double. A seagull screamed above, released him. Footsteps now. Paul straightened. The solicitor took off his aviator sunglasses, pocketed them, offered his free hand. Prickling with sweat, Paul shook it briefly, followed the man to the cottage.

You may only dream of death so many times before it becomes a reality.

Shoulders hunched over Paul's uncle's whittling bench, the

solicitor was laying out a number of papers on the only available surface. Paul scanned them, unpunctuated tracts of legalese, slight gaps where names had been typed by a different machine. His uncle's name, Hugh Orr, which Paul couldn't remember ever having seen written down before. Not even on a stone in the crematorium. Curious choice, to be burnt, considering the manner of his death. Individual, defiant, proud even. Then nothing. Smoke and a handful of ashes, could be anybody. Any *thing*. Paul hadn't gone. He was long gone himself. Up north. Somewhere. Anywhere. Away.

'…just sign here, here and here, and the cottage is yours,' the solicitor was saying.

'What if I don't want it?'

'It's yours now.'

No choice. Just like the old sod. Manipulative even from this distance. Paul signed. The place was his.

'What I want to know is why we couldn't have done this by post, or in your office,' Paul said, burning up.

'Your uncle's request,' said the solicitor, gathering his papers together. 'I'll have the deeds in the mail to you by the end of the week.'

He was already on his way out, fingers at his top pocket, turning at the door, his eyes black reflective pools once again. Paul stared after him as the door closed. Remained frozen to the spot as he heard footsteps receding, car door opening and closing, engine firing, wheels twisting on gravel. A silence descended on the dusty topography of the old cottage. A silence that revealed itself to be composed of the distant surf, a reedy wind and shrieking gulls. Paul didn't dare make a sound. He looked up at the beams. Smelt rubber, gas. The windows were streaked from past rainfall. He knew that in the far corner of the upper gallery was a big cardboard box the size of a fridge. He'd glimpsed it before the solicitor's visit. The south-facing window wouldn't open. Nailed shut. Paul ran for the door, tore it open, legs buckling as he careered down the slope towards the gully, the wind peeling tears from his eyes. He tumbled down the ravine, negotiated the awkward conjunction of soil and sand without care, ended up in a heap on the beach. Heart thumping in its bone cage, blood hammering in his temples. Sweat springing to the surface of his body. The terror. Inescapable terror. He beat a useless fist on the sand. Looked up through his blurry fringe at the line of marram grass and sea pinks at the top of the beach. Get it together. He had to.

Tim was glad to hear from him. 'Come and have dinner,' said the hotelier. His folks were away and he'd closed up for a couple of days. 'I've two friends staying, you'll like them. Come down.'

Paul threaded the antenna away, stowed the mobile in his inside pocket. Was there any point locking the cottage? Feeling of duty. Property owner, after all. It was no luxury villa, but it was his and neither Gina nor his father-in-law had anything to do with it. He wandered down the road hoping to pick up a lift into Salcombe, feeling more relaxed than he had since he'd boarded the train at Paddington.

A tractor overtook him, slowed down – there was room on the trailer – and took off again before Paul caught up. Bastard. He walked the rest of the way into town. Early in the season it wasn't very busy in the resort. A few hopefuls in brightly coloured shorts, carrying balloon-shaped buoyancy aids, stomped down the main hill towards the sea. The way to the hotel was a hidden memory that revealed itself corner by corner. A dog bounded downstairs on hearing his knock, pawed at the front door while Paul waited for Tim to flounce down and fling it wide open in his baggy shorts and sailor's smock. 'Paul. Come in, come in.' Tim shook his hand vigorously, clapped a hand on his shoulder.

Tim took him through to the bar, offered him whatever he wanted, spreading his arms. 'Beer, wine, cocktails.' There were dozens of bottles lined up of all shapes and colours.

'Give him a cocktail, Tim,' said a voice.

Paul swung round. Two women had entered the bar. One – bright eyed, wavy haired, mid-thirties – winked at Paul and giggled.

'Janet, Loulou, this is Paul.'

Paul stuck out his hand. Janet curtsied, winked again. Loulou took his hand, shook it with a man's strength, smiled grimly. She had a great mop of dark curls. Tim thrust a glass in his hand. Paul tried to keep up.

'Get that down you,' Janet said with another wink.

'What do you require, Janet?' Tim asked, wiping a fresh glass.

Janet winked at him, smiled a you-know-what grin.

The four of them gathered in a corner with drinks, laughing, talking easily, as if they'd all known each other for years. Tim kept folding his long body over the bar to refresh their drinks. 'Dinner time,' he announced with a flourish after an hour, maybe two. Loulou offered to help in the kitchen. Janet stayed and chatted furiously with Paul, winking, fluttering eyelashes, touching his arm. Half pissed, Paul stopped worrying and had another drink. 'You'll stay here tonight,' Tim said, smacking a plate of sun-dried tomatoes down on the table. Janet grinned, her eyes dancing this way and that. 'Ooh!'

Mountains of food, delicious. Paul ate and drank without restraint. Ten minutes before last orders they rolled out to the pub, stood shoulder to shoulder, shouted to make themselves heard. Something to say. Anything, dummy copy. When the lights went out for the last time and the warm, bright bar finally emptied, they laughed and joked their way noisily back across the road. 'Room seven,' Tim said to Paul. 'You don't need a key. Don't worry if Betsy visits you in the night.' Paul must have looked alarmed. Loulou said, 'Don't worry, love. Betsy's coming in with me.' And she grabbed the shaggy-haired bog terrier round the neck and rubbed noses with her. Janet threw her head on one side and giggled like a spring. Paul said a general goodnight and climbed up through the narrow building to room seven.

There was a tiny en-suite bathroom and Paul stripped down to his boxers, did the absolute minimum to his body. Killed the light, jumped into bed. The window was partly open, which was good. Reflected moonlight outlined a couple of items on the bedside table, the last things he saw before he dropped off like a stone – an old-fashioned dial telephone and, like a fat black figure eight, an insomniac's Batman mask.

When he woke, torn from the weight of his dreams like a ring-pull from a can, there were hands at his throat. A figure straddled him, naked except for a gas mask, restlessly struggling, hands closing off his windpipe. He flapped weak arms like fillets of veal, thrashed about. The hands slipped away, moved over his face, stroking hair out of his eyes, resting on his chest. Taking weight. The air being pushed out of him again. He panicked now, finding reserves of strength, bucking his attacker like a bronco with a cowboy. But the hands closed once more round his neck, squeezed, tenderly, some misdirected vestige of affection. Fuck it, he thought, why fight it? As his eyes bulged so did his cock and she rode him all the more energetically, her long wet hair whipping his face. Her eyes remained concealed behind huge black shadows but he knew who she was now. And then she was gone and he unable to stop himself rolling back into unconsciousness. Bumping and sliding into deep sleep, everything went black. Until the sun splashed his face with golden water and he woke to a pounding in his head. The black eye mask was on the floor. If he half sat up he could see in the wall mirror above the desk. There were faint purple bruises round his neck. Pack and go. Just get the fuck out.

He was halfway out of town before Tim caught up, fell into step beside him, panting. 'Look, Paul. Janet's terribly embarrassed. Apparently she walks in her sleep.'

'And some.'

'She stumbled into your room. Tripped over the foot of your bed…was how she put it to me anyhow.'

'Yes, well.'

Paul didn't stop walking but he had slowed down a little.

The two men fell silent as they reached a kink in the road. They both knew that down to the left, where the ground gave way to a scree slope threaded with bracken and thrift, was a tiny cove hidden from the road. As kids they'd played over every inch of the coastline round the promontory, negotiating sections of cliff at low tide that would be inaccessible later in the day. Approaching the little cove one hot August afternoon with the tide racing, Paul had been in front, clinging to the cliff edge some fifty yards ahead of Tim. Paul could still remember the bite of bitter, salty fear as he realised he could make it round to the cove and leave Tim behind, but only if he hurried. The faster he climbed, the slicker his palms became, the looser their grip on the shale. He stopped once and decided to go back. It wasn't worth the risk. They'd go together another time. Tim had got as far as he could and was shouting for Paul to come back. He looked down as a heavy wave slapped against the slippy green rock face only a few feet beneath his trainers. That got him moving, and not back, because within seconds it had become too late for that, but on towards the cove. They knew it was there because they'd seen it from the water, paddling in Tim's inflatable dinghy during a morning's mackerel feathering. The water splashed his bare legs and Paul swallowed what felt like a ball of dust and fibres. His legs turned rubbery and he had to rely on his hands, sweating now like a tightrope walker's. Just one more corner, one more ledge. And then he was there.

The cove stretched far enough back for there still to be a little sand uncovered by the sea, but it was wasting no time. There was a level path halfway up the slope. Paul trotted along it. Gulls hung like mobiles in the middle of the cove, on a level with Paul, rising and dipping according to the warm air. Then Paul's stomach turned itself inside out, the hairs on his arms and neck stood to attention. He shivered quickly. Blinked, but it hadn't gone away. On the far side of the cove. It was there. He'd seen it. On the far side of the cove, hanging by the neck, was the body of a man, his clothes seaweedy rags, his eyes pecked out. The black sockets transfixed the boy, their unblinking stare meeting his gaze across the width of the cove.

Tim got the police out to find Paul, who still hadn't returned by early evening. They found him sitting on the edge of the cliff staring out to sea, thumb stuck in his mouth. He wouldn't speak for a fortnight. The body, it was discovered, had been hung at such a height that the waves would cover it only at high tide. It had been there less than two weeks, they said. He was identified as a nobody, a drifter passing through. Suicide couldn't be ruled out, but the police were treating it as suspicious.

It was the curled lip that had Paul waking in the night, sweat standing out on his forehead like rain on a waxed car. The blackened eye sockets, of course, but also the mouth, the half-smile.

'You know, we probably saw him.' Paul looked beseechingly at Tim. 'We probably rowed right past in your dinghy and, if it was anything except high tide, we'd have seen him. Why didn't we do anything?'

Tim spread his hands. 'It's a long time ago.'

'Not as far as he's concerned. It's the very next second for him, just as it has been for the last twenty-odd years.' Paul stared at the banks of nettles at the side of the road, which had been laced with convolvulus bindweed like a girl's hair with daisies. 'That didn't use to be there.' He kicked one of the white flowers. 'I've got to get back, Tim. I'll give you a ring.'

He left his old friend still making faces and noises intending to convey that Janet had meant no harm. Whatever comfort the previous night's encounter had provided for her, it had done Paul no favours. He increased his walking pace until his breathing was normal again. When he looked up, the cottage had come into view.

He sat on the edge of the upper level, legs dangling. The big cardboard box was back there in the corner.

Then the box was in the middle of the gallery. In two minds over what to do, Paul found himself sifting through its dark slippery coils. Eels, angler fish, unknown creatures with huge black eyes. Mucoid lenses. He knelt before the box, arms thrust deep into its damp midst. The overpowering smell of rubber, the sour reek of crushed bindweed.

Paul closed the cottage door behind him. Walked to the road, crossed over, bundled his frame over the farmer's gate. The sun was still high, the sky like rice paper. If he moved his head too quickly in any direction a sharp little tear would appear. An angry confusion of lines scribbled by a lonely child with a 2H pencil. A black jigsaw blade just nosing through into the world. He tried to keep his head still.

He remembered the way from his childhood. It wasn't the kind of thing you forgot. The path unrolled under his feet, a brown carpet. The fence like a necklace, the copse lurching out of perspective like some E-head's huge black panther. The blackened greenery, starved of light, the tiny trumpets of the non-smelling convolvulus. The stars in his head, spinning. Punch drunk, reeling, he fell to his knees in front of the tough strands of weed that marked the edge of the land. He looked up, into the light, knew what he would see only moments before he saw it. Again.

He got up from the gallery floor, shuffled away from the cardboard box, its contents an oily blur. Stood looking over the edge, flirting with gravity. Giggled to himself. Out loud. Looked up at the beams, strong beams. Thick, solid. They'd have to be. Mainly they went the length of the cottage, others intersected them going the other way. Not so many of them. His uncle, a mathematician, would have enjoyed the geometries.

A chill brushed his arms. He almost overbalanced, drew back and sat down on the edge of the upper platform once more, his heart as leaden as his stomach.

The box cast a long shadow.

The white flowers of the bindweed, scattered like gems amidst the velvety undergrowth. He raised his head again. Blinded by the sun, he squinted to make out the approaching figures. Their silhouettes rippled, resisted definition, until they reached the gate in front of Paul. They loomed, laughing gaily, an image from an old poster. Mr and Mrs No-mark from Sussex, they use the train when it suits. Mr No-mark smokes a pipe. Mrs No-mark's cardigan buttons up the back. Their two children are never a nuisance.

Post-war fantasy figures, Britain getting back to her feet. Thanks to families like these. Mr No-mark's Fair Isle sleeveless sweater had been knitted by his good wife, who whetted those knife-edge creases in his trousers. Mr and Mrs No-mark both wore gas masks, the children also; their laughter was tinny but heartfelt. They swung the gate open, beckoned to Paul. His knees popped as he stood up, sweating at the temples, breathing in shallow draughts. They looked so contented, so free. *Join us*, everything about them seemed to say. Paul followed them into the field where a path soon materialised. The children skipped either side of it but never strayed far. Mr and Mrs occasionally held hands, looked back to reassure Paul. He was becoming

light headed, losing it, white flowers bursting silently in the air
in front of him. Tiny fairies coalesced out of the pollen, danced,
mingled with the grass ahead of the two children, who stamped
them into the earth.

The grass grew shorter, the flowers less frequent, until the
path was a pavement and the houses alongside were bay-window
semis. An Austin Seven in every drive. Catmint and red-hot
pokers in each herbaceous border. Ropes hanging from every
landing balustrade, dangling a noose in each darkened hallway.
The comfort of stranglers.

An open door, a swinging rope. The smells of rubber
and leather overpowering the mothballs and iodine. Not an
antimacassar out of place. Paul went in, fingered the coarse rope,
felt something somewhere tighten.

He tipped up the box, rummaged, mentally catalogued. The gas
mask, full-length leather coat, rubber salmon-fishing waders,
assorted rags and ties, the rope. They said it was suicide, whispered
it in the Devon pubs, the post office queue. No one knew. Even
normal sex was not spoken of here. Paul tried to picture his
uncle's face without the gas mask. It was blank. He slipped the
rubber strap round the back of his head, undid the buckle on
his trousers. Would this help exorcise the memories? Cause the
nightmares to disintegrate like smoke in a sudden breeze?

The coat might have been tailored for him. Would the
door open and his uncle walk in? Himself? It was too easy, as
if the beams had been nailed into place according to a set of
instructions, an auto-erotic's manual. Paul slipped the noose over
his head, gathered the slack.

Light filtered down through the dust-sparkly air between rope
and windows, a chance twist of angles illuminating a distant
corner of the mahogany hallway. Mr and Mrs standing stock still,
eyes like flies', snouts of undiscovered beasts. Children dead on
the floor at their feet, cold as January's turkey carcass, school caps
obscuring pecked sockets.

His legs protruded from behind the door. Paul closed it. The
fallen rope, the contorted legs, the wooden splinters under the

fingernails. His uncle in a gas mask, the rope an extravagant tie. The open coat revealing more than his physical nakedness. Paul bent down to pull the coat closed, opened it wider instead and crept underneath. His uncle was still warm. Had he come back earlier…With his cheek resting on the floor he saw his uncle's final message on the bare wooden boards only inches from his face. Its marble pallor spoke only to him and he answered it. The last drops of ink from his uncle's pen spelled a word too private for anyone to read. He ate it.

It was easier that way. By committing an act he would forget for decades he allowed the world to believe that a suicide note had simply been missing.

He was dimly aware of the scrunching of gravel as the rope tightened, comfortably. He felt hot, then very cold. He remembered the word. Imagined his head as a balloon being blown up almost to bursting point then tied with string. Saw a million flies hovering, their eyes pilots' goggles. The dead children. Goodbye, Gina, and fuck off. The blissful ease of resting the entire body in a hammock of lint, stained vermilion, flecked with petals and pearls. The salty splash of the sea over the sightless face. The greedy wheel of the gulls. Either he lost feeling in his feet or they slipped from the gallery floor. Swinging, his head a whirlpool of lights, a spinning galaxy, bloody feathers. Then a rush of strange sudden light, bitter seaweedy stench, a laying-on of hands. Something wet on his face. A dog barking. Soft hands at his throat.

BUXTON, TEXAS

Begin at the beginning.

Except it didn't, because although he met her for the first time on a wet January night in a cramped Paris studio she shared with her sister, it didn't really begin there. He was with a friend of the two sisters, a girl called Jess, who'd been a friend of his for some years, and he was in France only for a few days before returning to London. Jess introduced him to the two Russian girls and it was the younger one who made fewer remarks about his poor French.

But two days later when he met them again for lunch it was Ksusha, the older of the two, whom he found himself watching when she was talking and when she wasn't, and addressing whenever he had something to say. He wondered what her mahogany hair looked like let down. Maybe it began then, though he wouldn't necessarily have said so at the time.

Nor would he have said it began at the party in London when he saw her again and, like a released hostage being shown into a room containing a long, heavy buffet table, picked her straight out of the crowd. If it began anywhere, it was in two or three looks over dinner at Jess's house the following evening. Ksusha and her sister were staying there for a few months, taking English lessons at a private college in the West End.

When he arrived at Jess's, his jacket for some reason became the centre of attention. Ksusha said she liked it, which made him smile. He watched the light in her chestnut eyes, and over dinner, when she said she wanted to see a football match while she was in England, he smartly produced a Manchester City fixture list and suggested the away game at Tottenham with the easy confidence of a man who hasn't yet got anything to lose.

She said yes and he said he'd get tickets and he checked again before leaving that she meant it and she did.

Walking back from the match he found himself having to justify his passion for a team that clearly weren't destined for great things, at least not that season, and he talked a lot about what he called his imaginative life – the intoxicating punch of nostalgia, the healing power of personal mythology – but she seemed to pick up only on his use of the word 'fantasy' and he knew he had some way to go yet. He was actually pleased when three youths seemed to be following them down the unlit Tottenham streets because he instinctively took her hand and led her across the road to safety. Once the threat had gone he didn't let go and nor did she seem to want him to.

He asked her to stay the night, partly out of misplaced bravado and partly because he knew she'd say no, so it was safe to ask. She said no and he drove her back south of the river, headlights splashing off the white tunnel tiles like someone diving in at the deep end.

They met again at the weekend and walked in a park near Highgate.

'In Russia,' she said, speaking in French as usual, 'the parks are enormous and have forests in them.'

He watched the Canada geese on the ornamental pond and racked his brains for a way to touch her, kiss her, even turn and look at her, that wouldn't be clumsy and regrettable.

'A friend of mine is going out for a drink tonight. It's his birthday,' he said, looking at her in profile. 'People are meeting in a café. Do you want to go?'

'I don't know.'

Three dogs ran past and she brightened up suddenly, reeling off their Russian names.

'Aren't they wonderful?' she said.

He had to be honest. He was tired of pretending to be what people wanted.

People.

Well, girls. Women.

He told her he didn't like dogs and she said she was going to have two of her own one day.

'We don't have to go,' he said. 'If you don't want to, that's OK.'

She looked away. 'I don't want to enter into your life.'

The cold began to get to him and he pulled his leather jacket tighter round his body. How could he tell her she already had?

'In four months,' she was saying, as she watched a kite get stuck in the bare branches of an elm tree and a child start to cry, 'I go back to Moscow.'

Nevertheless they got back in his dirty black Mini and drove over to Westbourne Grove to look for the place where his friends were meeting. The fact that they couldn't find it seemed significant: he saw these friends less and less these days and that made him sad. Plus the fact that Ksusha hadn't wanted to go, but she'd said yes and so they'd tried to find the place.

Waiting in the red glow of traffic lights to return to north London she asked him what he wanted out of life. At times like this he was glad they communicated mainly in French because it meant he could say things that normally he would be too self-conscious to say.

'Someone to share my life with,' he said finally, after having mentioned his desire to see Manchester City return to the heights of '69, and listing a few ambitions concerning his work and professional life. He was surprised to hear the words come out but realised they were true. She was the first person he'd said it to.

They hit a squall on the North Circular and the car bucked a couple of times before expiring and rolling into the kerb.

'It's the rain,' he explained. 'All Minis have this problem.' But his chances of getting anywhere that night either in the car or otherwise seemed doomed to failure.

They sat and waited as the car was rocked in the wet night by passing vehicles.

'That's my car!' Ksusha cried as a BMW coupé creamed past.

She actually owned a Lada, which her father had given her, but the BMW was her dream car. He knew that even the Lada would have been a better bet than his Mini. It was the first time his choice of car had made him feel inadequate.

He was so pleased to see the tow truck arrive after only half an hour he leaned across, his hand already poised on the door handle, and kissed her. She took his hand from the door handle and said, 'Don't turn away when you kiss me,' before kissing him back, long and slow. The man from Britannia Rescue had to knock on the driver's window to get his attention.

She stayed the night but he suffered an attack of nerves. As paralysed as his little car in the rain, he tried desperately to get going, but the engine wouldn't even turn over for hours of trying. 'Wake me up if anything happens,' she said, and although she couldn't have been kinder, he prickled with embarrassment and frustration. Even sleep was a long time coming.

There was a choice of two films that evening and he was secretly delighted when she picked *Paris, Texas*. They started watching in bed and he leaned across to edit the adverts out of his video recording. But Ksusha was sleepy, so he switched the TV off and left the VCR to record the rest of the film, adverts included. He had thought he would kill the VCR as well, but then realised that, if he left the ad breaks in, when he watched the tape in a year or two's time, it would be the ads which would remind him of Ksusha. He knew he ought to live more in the present because he believed it to be the best way, but how often did he find himself thinking forward like this? Too often.

As they made love, and tiredness stole over him, the memory of the sinuous guitar music on the soundtrack wound its way into his head like a vine, tying knots behind his eyes and tickling the back of his neck where she was kissing him.

They watched the film the next day, to round off a slow, drizzly afternoon spent almost entirely on the sofa. He cried at the point where he always did – during Harry Dean Stanton's long speech in the booth – and again at the end of the film where the swollen, leaden sky had turned the same colour as outside his window. She turned and looked at him in silent amazement. He smiled a stupid smile and looked away, but she touched his cheek and wiped a tear, kissed him, and he tightened his arms around her as fat drops of rain began to explode against the window.

That night as they lay side by side in bed, her head resting in the crook of his shoulder, she talked about Moscow; how it would be at least five or ten years before things improved, how Gorbachev, a hero in the West, was perceived to have let the Russians down, how she joined friends dancing in Red Square after the putsch. She took him to Armenia, her mother's home, and Turkmenistan, where she waxed nostalgic for the vast USSR, to cemeteries full of young soldiers, not much older than her, who fell in the war. It was all a long way from Tottenham, and even further from Paris, Texas.

He listened silently, becoming sad as the night deepened around him. He didn't want her to go back. And she'd only just arrived. How was he going to feel when the day came? Assuming, of course, they were still seeing each other; but the way he'd begun to feel, he was unable to foresee any other outcome. Simply the way she smiled at him undid all the resolve not to get involved that in any case he never really mustered.

The last thing he heard her say before the waves of sleep closed over his head was her asking him whether he would tape the *Paris, Texas* soundtrack for her. He dimly wondered how she knew he'd even got the record.

The next day was Easter Saturday, and on Sunday they were driving up north to stay one night and be back late on Monday evening. City were playing Liverpool at home and he had thought they could see the game and tour round his old haunts. The idea seemed to attract her, especially a planned trip to his secret Crucian Pit, a tiny gravel pit hidden away next to the airport, where he'd spent so many happy afternoons as a boy that the place had become, as he said, part of his imaginative life. He recorded the soundtrack and stuck some more Ry Cooder and some Eric Clapton they'd been listening to on the end of the tape.

They went up the east side of the country using only A and B roads. They bounced up and down in the little car, laughing as they struggled to hear the tape over the sound of the engine. He'd spent the previous afternoon having the points changed so the car wouldn't give up and die every time they hit a puddle. The mechanic had asked him how long it took him to go so far north. 'I once got to Sheffield in two and a half hours,' he said with a little foolish pride.

'What's it do then?' the mechanic asked. 'Eighty, eighty-five?'
'A hundred.'

The mechanic shook his head, clucked what was either surprise or disapproval.

Every time they were overtaken by a Merc or a BMW, Ksusha would coo in excitement and tell him about this or that trip to Tbilisi or Baikal with friends of her father's, and he would step a little bit harder on the gas in quiet frustration. By the time they reached the A57 there were patches of mist, which thickened on the far side of Sheffield so that the Peak District's hills were as powerful and subtle as ideas behind the curtains of fog, and all Ksusha could see were a few white horses cantering across Ladybower Reservoir. They rolled down into Glossop and found a B&B where they shared a room with a dozen teddy bears.

'I don't want to complicate everything,' she said.

He'd brought up the conversation in the park because it had been niggling at him. They were in bed, the night soft as cotton pillows, but he'd been unable to make love.

'I know you've got to go back. I know that,' he said quietly, faltering over his choice of words. 'And although you said you didn't want to enter into my life, you already have done. And I'm glad you're there. Here.' He looked up at the black squares of the window and the flinty stars beyond. 'But we've got time. We've got four months. When do you go back? The beginning or the end of August?'

'The end.'

'Then we've got a month longer than I thought we had. I thought it was the beginning.' Aware that he might be making too many assumptions, that he could be putting his big foot in it as usual, he pressed on anyway. 'Live in the present. Be optimistic. You never know what might happen.' He bit his lip, having invited the instant response – 'One thing's for sure: I have to go back to Moscow' – but it didn't come. Instead, as if with an arrow out of the forest of possibilities, she cut him down.

'You're not an optimist,' she said with a half-smile that was just discernible in the darkness. The glass eyes of the bears glinted in the starlight. They knew she was right and he knew she was right.

It was like the equal opportunities statements some employers appended to job adverts: *striving* to be an equal opportunities employer. He was striving to be an optimist. His whole life was a fight, not against the terrible things that could happen, but against his fear that they might. He took the arrow in both hands and freed it from his chest. Yes, things could turn out bad, but he hoped they wouldn't.

How could her aim be so true when they'd known each other only such a short time?

She ran a hand through his cropped hair and he turned to smile at her. Even if her gaze sought out the chinks in his armour, it was good to know she was at least looking in his direction. And he appreciated her directness. He remembered the evening he'd driven over to pick her up, having gone home first to change into his suit, which he thought would be a good move because she'd previously said she liked his smart jacket. He waited for her to say something, then in the car asked her whether she liked it. She said no and he laughed and then she started laughing, too.

The nerves that had ruined their first night together had unravelled and were just about gone now.

The morning was bright and clear. They dawdled over breakfast and drove into Manchester. They were going to the match in the afternoon but first they drove down to the area where he'd been brought up, where he supposed he'd had the happiest times of his life, though he didn't say that out loud. They walked round the outside of his old house and he bared his teeth at the garish swimming pool the latest owners had stuck on the side of the house where his mother's vegetable garden had once been.

Ksusha was sitting on the bonnet of the car waiting for him. He took her hand and she jumped off. They kissed and then he saw over her shoulder two men walking across the bottom of the street – one about his age, the other a generation older – and he knew in a split second that it was his friend Neil and Neil's father. What was more, he knew that Neil had recognised him just as quickly. But he'd looked away, at Ksusha, and Neil had carried on his way and was gone.

His heart was beating fast and he took hold of Ksusha by the shoulders. 'That's amazing,' he said breathlessly. 'I haven't seen him in fifteen years, at least, and I recognised him just like that. They were fifty yards away. I couldn't even see their faces and yet I knew it was him.'

'And he recognised you,' she said.

How did she know? He hadn't even seen her turn round.

'How?' he asked.

'It's like a magnetic field,' she said. 'It's not just seeing the face. If you're close enough there's a field and you can feel things just as you would see them, better even. You were both in that field.' She smiled that smile. 'But why don't you go and say hello?' She jumped up and down. 'Go and say hello. Otherwise you'll regret it.'

He knew she was right so they got back in the car and caught up with them at the level crossing, where they were about to board a tram to go to the match. Ksusha waited for him in the car and he ran on to the platform and, sure enough, Neil wasn't at all surprised to see him. Even if his old friend hadn't physically recognised him from the end of the street, he'd known somewhere inside himself who had been standing there. Neil's dad pumped his hand for half a minute, looking more pleased to see him than even Neil was. The tram came and he said he'd look out for them at the ground. They waved and ran off.

The match was hard fought and both sides probably deserved the draw. Ksusha soaked up the atmosphere, becoming one with the Kippax for a couple of hours, though in her opinion the choruses of 'Fuck off Scousers' and 'You're the shit of Merseyside' were unkind and uncalled for. At the height of the excitement, after City had gone one up, she flung her arms round his neck and told him out of the blue how much she wanted to go to the FA Cup Final.

How to explain the complexities of ticket sales for such a game to someone who doesn't speak your language? Bond schemes, ticket registration members, club allocations and so on and so forth.

'You're never satisfied, are you?' he shouted in her ear over the gathering roar of the Kippax crowd.

'It's my nature,' she said with a big grin.

He knew it was at least partly true. And he'd learnt it was no good trying to change people.

Still, he knew he wouldn't be able to get tickets for the Cup Final.

'I may never get another chance,' she said, and that almost upset him. He wanted to say, 'You might. You could always come back,' but it seemed such a bad idea just to think such a thing, never mind say it, that he left it unsaid.

They left the ground, carried on a tide of slightly disgruntled blue and white, and soon after the walk back to the car they were heading south for the Crucian Pit.

'I know it's not always a good idea to go back,' he was saying, 'but this place has haunted me for years.' After being told about the place as a kid by an older, wiser fisherman, who must have felt it was time to impart the knowledge, he'd scrambled his way up the steep embankment one day with his rod holdall and fishing basket. The sun had beaten down on the Crucian Pit like on a sweet-smelling oasis and he'd spent long afternoons playing spirited Crucian carp to the net, never taking anyone else with him until one awkward fumbling evening when he left his fishing tackle at home and took his girlfriend instead. Since that summer the place had remained sacrosanct in his imagination, undefiled by human hand. The jets that took off every few minutes only a couple of hundred yards away seemed to guard it against trespassers.

Now he and Ksusha would reopen the secret of the place.

They parked down the lane opposite the embankment and walked down to cross the main road. Ksusha pointed out a series of steps worn into the muddy slope and his heart slowed. Had someone else been here? They scaled the slope and climbed between the barbed wire, and at the far side of the little paddock two bikes lay in the grass. They looked at each other. He began to feel like Harry Dean Stanton's Travis when he has to sit through the super-8 footage of his idyllic seaside holiday with Jane and Hunter, and Walt and Anne – the unbearable contrast between what was then and what is now.

They reached the edge of the open ground and looked through

the trees towards the pit. There were three young boys messing about at the water's edge, not fishing, but wading in. He felt like an old box of toys and precious belongings that had been tipped up and emptied out. Ksusha took his hand and squeezed it.

'You won't believe it now,' he said. 'That it was a secret place.'

Her look seemed to say she did. 'Let's go back to the car and find somewhere else.'

Reluctantly he turned his back on the pit and another jet tore open the sky on their left. The noise of the plane filled the emptiness inside him for a moment.

'Two years ago,' Ksusha was saying in a light chattery voice to cheer him up, 'we had to do agricultural work on a big complex outside of Moscow. It was next to a military airfield and every half an hour there would be supersonic jets taking off. You could feel it here.' She touched his hand to her chest. 'They started at five o'clock in the morning and for the first few days we couldn't sleep, but we soon got used to it.

'It was a way of getting students to do the farmer's work. They didn't force us to do it. You could always get off it by pretending to be sick.' She laughed.

They crossed the main road as a huge jet taxied along the runway.

'I wanted to make love there,' she said when they were back in the car. 'Let's find somewhere else.'

He doubted they would, but he put the car in gear, and they headed south. They went through Macclesfield and took the A537 over the hills. The *Paris, Texas* tape was playing and although there were rain clouds behind them, the sky in the east was still bright.

'It's so strange to see hills without trees,' she said. 'I can see why the English are obsessed with lawns in their gardens.'

He laughed and realised that if this corresponded to any part of his favourite movie, then it could only be the super-8 footage itself: the happy, carefree smiles, the shared jokes and throwaway remarks. The thought chilled him for a moment, but as they reached the highest point – the Cat and Fiddle pub – and cast their greedy eyes around before heading on down towards Buxton his spirits rose. The clouds were closing in and the slide guitar resounded in the little car. Now it was that shot through the windscreen of Walt's hire car twenty minutes in, of the road ahead and the windscreen wipers going, as Walt and Travis head for their first motel stop.

He drove slowly through Buxton so she could see all she wanted to see. She was a very appreciative and enthusiastic tourist, which made him feel like the local duke escorting her around his estate. He had known she would like Buxton and he'd chosen the A6 to head back on because he knew she'd like that as well, the lush green tunnel that was the Wye valley, the river skirting the road at several bends. The one good thing, as far as he was concerned, about her love of smart sports cars was that she liked it when he drove fast.

When the tape finished he rewound it and let it play again. They'd moved on a bit, in terms of the film, to the sequence where Travis and Hunter drive down to Texas looking for Jane: driving fast, having fun, sharing moments of affection, and just being on the road in search of something.

'There!' she shouted, but he'd already gone past the tiny side road, so when an escape lane popped up a quarter of a mile downhill he used it to turn around and then gunned the little car back up the incline.

They turned into the side road, marked only with a NO WAITING sign, and tacked up the side of the valley.

'I hope it goes nowhere,' she said, leaning forward in her seat. 'That's what we need. A road that goes nowhere.'

'No road goes nowhere,' he said.

'Who would use a road like this?'

'The farmer who lives at the end of it,' he predicted.

They rounded a bend and there was the farm, but the road seemed to go on past it, so he put the car back into gear. Immediately round the next corner was a gate. He stopped the car, considered going on regardless, but reversed instead. They got back on the A6 and only a few miles farther down the valley nipped into another side road. He drove hard uphill on the straight sections, braked gently for the sharp bends, pipped the horn and accelerated out of the turns. At a junction, where the right turn was signposted for the village, he went straight on, not looking at

Ksusha, though he was aware of her watching him. He wanted to find somewhere but was nervous in case they did. Suddenly on the right a track popped up between two fields. The loose surface and piles of pale stones suggested an unfinished road. It looked good and Ksusha smiled as he guided the Mini into it and pulled up on the left-hand side by the wall behind the biggest pile of stones. He killed the engine and sat back, breathing deeply. She leaned right across and took his face in her soft, strong hands and kissed him.

The tape of the soundtrack had reached Travis's long speech: 'He was kind of raggedy and wild, and she was very beautiful, you know...'

'That's me and you,' he said, switching off the tape.

'When I saw you in Paris,' she said, 'you looked so strange, so different to all the Parisian men, with your two jackets and your earring.'

'It was quite fashionable for a while to wear two jackets, a denim jacket under a leather jacket,' he replied, fingering the steering wheel. 'For a couple of weeks anyway.'

He fidgeted, worried about the farmhouse he could see across the field on the right-hand side, and about the two roads at the top and bottom of the track. He could hear a car going by. But she soothed him.

'Look at the lambs,' she said, brushing her thick hair out of her face. She said 'lambs' in English and sounded the 'b' in an innocent, childlike way that made him smile and feel slightly less nervous. The fields on both sides were full of toy-like black-and-white lambs, all tufty little coats and stage-drunk knees. She got him to move into the passenger seat and sat facing him on his lap. When he held her close he saw the clouds drawing in over the fields.

It started to rain while they were making love, a tinny tattoo like on the taut roof of a tent, and Ksusha squirmed in delight, her hair in his face.

Evening came on quickly as the clouds battened the sky down for an early night. She opened the window – curiously just as he'd been intending to – and the cool air caressed their exposed arms and legs and the lambs cried and cried in the lengthening patches of shadow. What remained of the clear sky in the south-west was a wash of royal blue. He knew it was a moment he would remember for the rest of his life, a moment when everything gelled, when life was so much more than the sum of its parts and became close to what some people would expect heaven to be. And now she was looking into his eyes, smiling the smile that dispelled his fear that to her he was just someone to sleep with for a few months. He held her tightly and looked at the rain stippling the windscreen because he didn't believe she would want to see him cry.

She didn't like it when he was serious, he knew, because it made her afraid. But making love brought him closer to her, and with the lambs crying and the rain falling he felt himself slide deeper into the secret place they'd created between the two of them. It was a place no one would ever trespass upon, whether it remained open land to them both for ever or became fenced off and hidden away when she went back at the end of the summer.

They got out of the car on shaky lambs' legs and watched the night come whispering across the fields. It was a while before the cold and the rain sent them running back for cover. He turned the key in the ignition and the encroaching night chased the little black car out of the track and sealed it up after them.

The rain grew heavier but the road was kind, cradling the Mini round fast corners, unrolling its wide straights like great carpets before them. They glowed, warm and happy but hungry, and he knew exactly what he was looking for: a friendly country pub right by the side of the road with good food, English ales and some special undefinable quality that he wouldn't know until he felt it.

'I'm really hungry,' she said.

'I know,' he replied, touching her hand as she squeezed his leg. 'We'll find somewhere.'

He drove past the fast-food dives in Belper, still believing the magical road would throw something into their path before Derby and the motorway home. And when it did, right by a bridge over the river, he saw it only at the last minute, and had to turn and brake sharply straight into a parking space outside what looked indeed like the perfect place.

They stepped into a warm den and were immediately cloaked by a sense of well-being, safety and reassurance. The place was perfect. Looking around, like a child in a Christmas toy department, he couldn't believe it. Home-made steak-and-wine pie, steak and kidney, real ales, smartly turned-out murmuring locals, and a bright smiling barman with a ring twinkling in one ear. They sat at a table by the fire and the barman changed the tape that was playing. He put on an Eric Clapton track that had been on the end of the *Paris, Texas* tape and they looked at each other, disbelieving, their hands clutching across the table, smiles that were too big for their faces. He had to look away but could sense her still looking at him. It was almost too much, but the barman arrived at just the right time with two steaming plates of bright peas and carrots and huge fresh pies. The barman smiled before he went away.

'I could die now,' she said quietly, and he was suddenly caught in a falling lift, his eyes wide in the firelight. 'I'm so happy I wouldn't mind if I died now.' He dug his nails into her hand.

The barman said they had rooms if they wanted to stay. He described them in loving detail but they explained that they had to get back.

Outside, the rain had settled in for the night. They crossed the river and the tyres hissed through the rain into Derby and on to the motorway. She took a cushion from the back seat and rested it against the window, turning to smile at him before closing her eyes. He took the speed up steadily, overtaking, eventually staying in the outside lane as the returning Easter traffic failed to get any lighter the nearer they got to London. He slipped the tape into the stereo. It was on the last track of the album, 'Dark Was the Night', the one when Travis drives away. There's a three-quarter profile shot of him just driving and you can see him blinking. You don't see his tears, just the blinking.

She woke up and jumped when she saw the world rushing by the window so fast. He'd taken the little car right to the top, past whatever the needle could show, to a hundred. It had gone past the shaking, rattling stage and all you got was a steady airy thrum, but one that went right through the body and made you feel one with the car. She turned and looked at him, smiled at him, and he pointed at the speedometer.

'We're flying,' he said.

She nodded her head, still smiling. 'Just as long as we don't land,' she said.

It was around the sharp bend after Toddington services that they finally took off.

And no one saw them land.

CITY OF FUSION

This girl, this stylist. This girl – 'Sometimes I just assist' – this girl scatters the earth then joins the dots. Unhappy with distinctions, she wants earth and sky to be one. Style and content the same thing. This girl, this...*girl*.

She's in, at last she's in. She floats up to the reception desk. More flight deck than reception desk, all frosted glass, underlighting and height. All bullshit. You've practically to stand on tiptoes. She loses the book, stands it on the floor, leaning against her leg. *Book*. Some book. Some stories it tells with its *pictures*.

She flicks her hair behind her ear, then does it again before it could possibly have fallen back. She knows. She knows she's doing it, she knows how it looks. No one's watching. She glances round: the only creature with manners to raise an eye in her direction is the camera for the CCTV.

'I've come to see Jim Cover. I've got an appointment,' she says. Like that's his name, his real name. Some name for an art director. Just like that guy she saw last week at *Dazed & Confused* was really called Jefferson Hack. A journalist, an editor. Yeah, sure. And Nigel Draper runs the curtains franchise at Harrods.

She hears someone ask her for her name. She looks down, meets the girl's eye, tells her what it is. 'Eleven o'clock,' she adds. 'And I have got other meetings.' Just a little white lie. It had taken months to get this one, to get this far. Months of phone calls, disappointing shoots, more phone calls. Months of joining the dots. Literally months.

The girl gives her a badge saying VISITOR. Yeah, right.

'Take the lift to the eighth floor,' she says. 'He'll meet you there.'

She turns, viscose slip dress catching on her arse. She likes that, likes knowing the girl at reception is still watching her, wishing she had an arse like that. Or a dress like that.

The lift doors close. She checks out the mirror. Eight floors of mirror time – what a treat, a rare treat. But it's got a kind of tacky bronze sheen to it. Like the mirrors in the Ladies at Singapore airport, they had something on them, or in the lights. They did something, performed some kind of sorcery. Only in Singapore they did it to flatter you, make you look tanned. Here the intention is the opposite. Do they use the stairs or what, these people? Thinking about Singapore brought back the spectral image of André. The twat. Yeah, right.

She'd told André about the mirrors, tried to drag him into the Ladies. For a self-confessed rebel he was terrified of overstepping the mark. Wouldn't go in with her. Told her it was the same in the Gents. Probably was. He was still a twat. He'd wandered round the airport with his hand shading his mouth and chin because he'd heard they didn't allow beards in Singapore. What did he think they were going to do, come and give him a shave? Yeah, right.

When the lift doors open there's a guy waiting for her. He's holding a can of Coke.

'Yeah, hi,' he says to her shoulder. 'Through here. You've brought your book.'

She follows him. He stops by the newspaper-strewn table to grab a cigarette from someone else's pack. Flicks open a Zippo lighter. Imitation (like André's). She lugs her great book after him to the couches. There are three huge couches, set in an unfinished square. He sits down on the edge of a cushion, spreads his legs. His cigarette winks out, he didn't light it very well. As he lifts the faux Zippo again she hears the conversation of three women sitting round the table behind her. Their disembodied voices are punctuated by cigarette sucks and newspaper flicks.

'You know, he's sort of small and Woody Allenish, if you like that sort of thing,' one of them is saying.

'For fuck's sake,' says another.

He's waiting for her, chugging his Coke. She lifts the book up off the floor, slides it across her slippery lap into his. He supports it on his knees, undoes the zip, opens it. Doesn't speak as he turns the huge, plastic pages. The photos are good, she knows they are. They're very good. No worries there.

'I, like, you know...' she says.

'Yeah.'

He turns over, takes a drag on his Camel, swallows some Coke. There's some sort of colourless substance running out of his nose like snail slime. He's turning the pages quite quickly, his eyes sliding across the images: the shimmering silks on Canvey Island, the Oakley sunglasses in Subterania (she knows someone who knows someone who supplies crap doves to the girl who sleeps with the guy on the door), the hooded tops in St George's Gardens. Is he looking properly?

'Here, you know...I don't know...' Her hand slews across the image, pointing at something that she knows signifies nothing. It's all a game, only this guy always gets to roll twice.

'Yeah, right...Interesting.' He nods, sucks on his fag, turns the page.

She can see sunlight shafting through the bristles stuck on the end of his chin like surviving spines on an ancient hairbrush. This fashion for goatees that aren't even goatees, this fashion, this...pitiful sheep mentality. Fuck 'em.

'Sometimes I just assist.'

Why? Why did she say it?

Right at the nadir she gives in, exactly when she's at her most vulnerable she lies down and says come and fuck me. And fuck her they do, invariably.

Like when she met André: she was down, very down, after a drug thing with those two boys from Latimer Road. They were dropping tabs of acid like they were Shreddies. Whole fucking bowlfuls. And then they went up on to the Hammersmith & City line at Goldhawk Road. Yeah, right. Good idea. Get down on to the track and take a walk. Nice one. Fine until you've got trains coming from both directions. The two boys had it all timed and they ducked out, escaped into the BBC somehow. She heard later they were arrested in the middle of the pitch at Loftus Road like the end of some disappointing 1960s movie. Carrying? The filth, in a rare shaft of constabulary wit, said they were surprised they could stand up they were carrying so much stuff. Pockets crammed with narcotics. Acid, Es, powder, barbs – some German stuff the Shepherd's Bush bobbies said they'd never even seen before. And these guys patrol the White City Estate.

Maybe she was lucky that night, although it was hard to see it that way at the time. After narrowly missing point-blank impact with several trains (funny how when you want one you can wait for fucking ages, but when you're wandering down the middle of the track off your face on LSD there's one every two minutes), she thought it would be a neat idea to lie down on the ballast between the tracks with her right leg an inch from one of the live rails. Yeah, right. She was just lucky the next driver to come along was awake and already applying the brakes for Ladbroke Grove.

Somehow she got off virtually scot free on that occasion, unless you counted André. She went to some kind of rehab clinic – not her idea but her parole officer's. And there he was, just the kind of boy she liked. Short and Israeli-looking with army fatigues and scrag end of beard. Like he'd been planted there by whoever was in charge of Ironic Twists of Fate. And when he asked her what her name was and she heard herself saying 'Lilith' after a Ramsey Campbell story she'd read as a little girl, she saw his dark little eyes light up. For whatever reason, that sealed it. 'Lilith,' he whispered, and that did it for her.

As soon as she makes the comment about assisting, even the low level of interest Cover has been evincing vanishes altogether. He flips through the remaining pages. She makes a half-hearted attempt to puff up her dawn shoot on the Thames foreshore by Bankside Power Station, but the moment, if it has ever been within her grasp, has gone. Gone like all the others. Cover is just another art director, just another bored coke-head manipulative bastard looking for an excuse to tell her to fuck off. Like he needed one.

She realises he's saying something as he zips up the book and passes it back to her. Something that doesn't quite fit.

'I'd be interested to see more,' he's saying and she doesn't know whether to believe him or rub ash in his beard. There's an ashtray on the table but he's been flicking on to the floor, constantly, as they speak.

'You wanna see some more?' she hears herself asking.

'Yeah.' He sucks on a burning filter. 'I'd be interested to see more.'

It's just shit to get rid of her. Surely. But he doesn't need to. He could just tell her to go away and never come back. They do, don't they?

No, they don't. They say they'd be interested to see more. Because they know that one day, in the far future, these young no-hopers will be discovered by someone else and become Young Turks, and *they'll* be the old farts who never took them seriously. It all comes back to number one.

She stands up, takes the weight of her book.

'Yeah, right,' she says.

He drops his filter on the floor, prods it unnecessarily with his toe. It's a gesture. He doesn't miss a trick. But neither does she. He grunts, looks towards the lift.

'I can manage,' she says, and is away. She only has to wait a second or two before the lift arrives. When she glances back before stepping in, he's back at the table where the three women are, helping himself to another cigarette. One of the women shakes her head as if to get hair out of her face, but her hair's cropped to the bone. Fag in hand, elbow on the table, put-down on her painted lips.

She gets into the lift, goes down through the building, past all those minor copies of Jim Cover, those insincere, miserable shadows of their own pathetic and unrealisable ambition. Fuck 'em.

Yeah. Right.

Every year around mid-June, at least since she met André, she – this girl, this stylist, this *Lilith* – gets jittery. In fact, it's been happening for years, since before the André episode. Which was why, when he explained everything to her, it all made such perfect sense. It had always seemed, or so it *now* seemed with the benefit of hindsight, some sort of big, grown-up version of PMT. Jittery she'd get but also full of excitement and anxiety. Unformed anxiety. Until André. Anxiety without a nucleus around which to coalesce. Like water vapour without dust motes about which to condense. So there could be no rain, no release of tension. Until, one day, she'd realise the tension had gone. She'd get up in the morning and maybe it had rained in the night. Summer rain. Midsummer rain. Big fat blotches on the pavement flags. A smell in the air like no other. Summer rain. Midsummer rain.

André told her about midsummer. She wanted to know how midsummer could arrive so early on in what we perceive as being summer, but he told her not to be so 'fucking dense'.

'From this moment on,' he told her as they climbed up Primrose Hill on a rare tranquil evening, 'the forces of light wane and continue to do so until the sun starts to wax again.'

She can still remember that night. André was more considerate and solicitous to her that night than at any other point in their relationship. He told her as she leant through the gradually darkening air towards the summit that she resembled a swan. She was wearing her viscose slip dress with spaghetti straps from Koh Samui – the same dress she wears now as she lugs her portfolio from magazine to magazine – which she'd acquired only days before. She'd got it to use in a shoot and liked it so much she hung on to it. Never in fact used it. She did something with papery soft jerkins from Errol Peake instead. The model, an androgynous black girl from North Kensington recommended by a friend of a friend, tried hitting on her, which she found kind of weird but flattering. She pretended she hadn't understood but let the girl keep the jerkin – 120 quid's worth. (Saw her again at a party in Kensal Rise and the girl, still wearing the jerkin and hanging on the arm of Andrea Dworkin's stunt double, stiffed her.)

She still thinks about the swan thing, the single remaining shred of evidence that André wasn't a complete prick.

Two days after her humiliation at the hands of Jim Cover, she's at a party in Soho. Some production company. They call them films, the rest of the world calls them adverts, puffs, promos. The nearest they get to real movie production is product placement. The nearest they get to being broadcast is when Channel 4 does a documentary on the industry. And even then they hit the cutting-room floor.

Not Lilith's kind of place. Nevertheless, she finds herself swinging from a fire ladder high above the Soho roofscape at three in the morning, softly intoning harmonies from early Cocteau

Twins songs, and she has to admit it has something going for it. Someone two flights below is yelling at her to come down, which is taking the piss a bit since he gave her the drugs in the first place. She's watching the procession of faces in the clouds, waiting for André's. She knows it'll come because it does every time. Not a night has passed on E without his face appearing to her, whether out of the clouds, the trees or just the air itself. She knows all she has to do is touch it once and he will be banished for good.

She takes another step up the ladder. There's another wall about fifteen feet up, another bit of roof. Renewed shouting from down below. Rising levels of hysteria sweeping up from the well of sound that is the party. Strange 1980s disco tracks have replaced the hip hop and scratch beats since the DJ fucked off home a couple of hours ago.

All she has to do, to create the geomancer's 'city of fusion' and harmonise the landscape, is bring together the energies of earth and sky. She reaches for the clouds. That would do it.

Then she'd be free of him for ever.

Yeah.

Right.

Soho at five in the morning rivals pre-revolution Bucharest as the most charmless place on the planet. Forget all this crap about café society, post-club cappuccino at Bar Italia – if Soho at dawn is a hub of anything, it's a hub of quiet despair. Taxis prowl like black panthers and all the poor, lost gazelle dreams of is to be eaten up by one. Money or no money. Every cabbie knows if he picks up a fare at first light in Soho he'll either be trekking round Forest Hill half an hour later looking for a cashpoint, some hopeless drunk in the back slurring the name of his bank, or sitting with the engine running, the *Sun* resting on the steering wheel and the meter ticking over outside some desolate East Finchley conversion, a young girl crashed out on an unmade bed two flights up.

Lilith flagged one down on Oxford Street. It looped around a traffic island, yellow bollards viciously bright in the limpid, post-dawn fumes. 'Shepherd's Bush,' she says as she climbs in the back, careful, even in the state she's in, not to give the driver the option. The number of times she's been stiffed trying to get back to Tottenham…Shepherd's Bush is closer but the thing to remember is that eight out of ten black cab drivers are bastards.

She passes out, coming to miraculously just as they hit Holland Park roundabout – she likes its giant barometer, filled with gushing blue like a hypodermic, always has to give it the once-over whenever she comes this way. To ignore it would be to court disaster.

'Abdale Road,' she says once, distinctly, through the glass partition when he asks. 'Opposite the end of Ellerslie Road, you know.'

He grunts.

Yeah. Ignorant fuck.

The look he gives her when she counts out the right money and smiles her sweet smile, she can use that look. Store its malevolence and use it against him in the future. Him and his kind.

She waits till he's gone before pushing open the gate and dragging herself up the path to the front door. No point making it easy for him. Upstairs, she stands at the window staring up Ellerslie Road. Nothing. The sky holds no clues. Overcast as far as she can see.

She collapses on to the mattress without taking her things off.

If she dreams she remembers nothing when she wakes at midday, her legs aching. As she fights to untie her Caterpillars she notices light blue scuff marks all over the toes and heels. She wets her finger and rubs at one or two but they won't budge. She pushes her hair out of her face and thinks about the night before – vague memories of tearing up fire escapes, climbing up to the sky. Did she perhaps reach it? Is that it?

The flat is quiet, the other tenants out at work. She won this room on the toss of a coin. It's the biggest and has the best view – the break in the houses opposite to allow for Ellerslie Road gives good sunsets – but she can't shake off its few ghosts. Something or someone still pollutes the atmosphere. The rancid smell of ancient couplings occasionally wakes her in the night. Not just one couple either. The room is a psychic bulletin board covered with old notices. As soon as she hits the mark with one or two decent magazines she'll be out of there and heading south of the Uxbridge Road. Not necessarily Brackenbury fucking Village, but definitely out of flame-throwing distance of the White City Estate.

In the pocket of her Helmut Lang jacket there's a handful of earth. She fishes it out and carries it to the kitchen, where the floor is cleanest. Standing in the centre of the room, she opens her fist and allows the loose soil to tumble on to the off-white lino. Then she's down on her hands and knees looking for the lines. The lines that join the dots. She's looking for the pattern of the days. She's heard it called prophecy. This girl, this stylist, this…geomancer.

This time she doesn't look any of them in the eye. Not until she gets upstairs. Once again eight floors to check out her reflection. As if she doesn't already know it inside out.

'Hi,' she says to Jim Cover as she sashays – there's no other word for it – out of the lift.

He's already got a fag in his mouth this time. Does he recognise her? She can't tell.

'I came a couple of weeks ago,' she says, without losing any ground. 'You said you wanted to see some more.' She's really going for it. He's nodding, going, 'Yeah, yeah.' They sit. She slides the book across to him, sits back this time, crosses her legs. She's confident. Never been more so.

He starts quickly and has to go back, or slow down at least. She watches his thumb drift to the corner of the plastified page, ready to turn it, then drop back: he keeps finding more stuff to look at – and he's looking at it *properly*. He's nodding now, making little grunting noises somewhere inside his oesophagus – he likes this stuff. Engrossed, he forgets that his cigarette is Bogarting between his fingers. Ash topples to the floor. He drops the butt absent-mindedly, nodding again. Reaches for another fag, lights it on autopilot.

'This is good,' he mumbles through constrained lips. 'You've, I dunno…you've got…'

She doesn't need him to say it. She's knows she's got it this time. He's going to commission her to do something. He's not going to buy *these* pix – that's not the way it works – but he's going to buy some new stuff off her. And he's going to pay her for it up front.

And it was all from the lines. The dots and lines. The random dots of earth and the lines drawn between them.

She thinks back to her themed shoots. And everyone else's themed shoots. Desert islands, villas on the outskirts of Havana, unshaven guys with greasy hair and drooping braces, *Batman* pastiches, *Blade Runner* rip-offs, fake 1940s post-war chic, stuff, stuff – stuff, stuff, stuff. She's left all that behind. Themes are out – the randomly scattered earth on the kitchen floor told her – and randomness is in.

With this shoot she's gone against all fashion's received wisdom. She's used a thin, wasted-looking girl – so far so traditional – that she found loitering outside Boss Models in Berners Mews hoping to get spotted, and she's dressed her in a wild mish-mash of clashing styles. She's got her in a lilac suede shirt-dress by Scooter, wedge-heeled black satin shoes from Prada, chain belt by Sally Gissing from Harvey Nichols and a black visor from Fabris Lane Etalia Sport. All of that lot photographed down a meagre cobbled alley off the Whitechapel Road.

Then she's taken her over to the DLR at Westferry and thrown at her a Nic Janik rayon-mix dress, brown-tinted goggles by Killer Loop and a pair of Christian Louboutin's fuchsia satin slingbacks. Wonderful disorder, horrible carnage. And Jim Cover's shaking his head, transported – as far as someone like him can be.

'This is…you know…'

She knows.

She smiles, crosses her legs like a man, catches sight of her boots – the blue scuff marks still there from the other night. The sign that she was going to make it sooner rather than later.

Little bits of sky.

Yeah, right.

AVENUE E

Two days after my son and daughter-in-law took off on holiday from Cape Canaveral, my grandson paid me an unexpected visit.

James's expression on the video entryphone looked pained when I asked him, in the nicest possible way, what on earth he was doing here.

'I was just passing, Pops, and thought I'd see how you're doing.'

No one ever just passes any more. Not these days. Everything is pre-arranged, everyone forewarned. I'm not saying it wasn't a pleasure to see my grandson, just that I could also see what was going on.

'Have you heard from your dad?' I asked James as I buzzed him into the building.

The conversation continued as James made his way up in the elevator.

'Er, yeah,' he said. I watched on the screen as he gazed out through the glass wall at the shimmering surface of the Millennium Pool. 'Why did they do that?' he asked, referring to the decision taken by Ken Livingstone's office in 2010 to flip the Dome and fill it with koi carp.

'Don't change the subject,' I told him as he stepped out of the elevator on the forty-third floor and rode the gliding walkway to my apartment.

'Dad's fine,' he said once we were sitting out on the balcony with drinks.

'I know he is. He's scarcely been off the line since he left.'

'I guess he just thought since he was going such a long way...'

It was Alfie's first trip into space; he and Emily had been saving up for it for years. He'd called as soon as they'd docked. The rooms in the orbital resort, of course, had virtual gravity, but WAT&G, realising correctly that space tourists would want to cavort like astronauts when they called home, had installed video links in the zero-G hub of the resort. I could see the earth rotating over his left shoulder as he asked me for the nth time if I would be all right while he was off the planet.

'Anyway, James, what about you? You look like you're off somewhere. Don't tell me you're joining your mum and dad in orbit.'

He brandished his flight ticket.

'LHR – SHANGRI-LA,' I read.

'I'm going on one of the new triple-deckers,' he announced. 'The Airbus XXX480.'

'Let me guess,' I ventured. 'You'll be staying at the Hilton.'

'You've been?' he asked in astonishment. 'They've only just started direct flights.'

'I've read the book,' I explained.

James looked blank, but I could hardly have expected him to have read James Hilton's 1933 novel *Lost Horizon*, for which the author had dreamed up Shangri-La.

I knew how his holiday would pan out. The ten-hour flight would touch down at Shangri-La International Airport. On his way through immigration, his passport would be stamped 'Shangri-La – Great Lost Valley of the Himalayas'. Every official would wear a little crest bearing the name of his destination. James and his fellow independent travellers would fail to discern the tiny TM, but only because they chose to. That way they remained in on the joke.

Shangri-La was just the latest in a long line of bogus resorts opened around the world by FantasyTravel Inc., Dreamflights International and getaway.com among other offshoots of the entertainment giants. The conglomerates had guessed correctly which way to jump when MP3 and other Net effects had decimated CD sales in the new century. The submarine hotel complex Atlantis had been such a hit when it opened in 2013, complete with glass-sided sleeping capsules and restaurant menus boasting 'actual Atlantean seaweed', it had been followed, with indecent haste, by the Bermuda Triangle Experience and the Recovered City of Dunwich. Making out it was built on piles driven into the actual remains of sunken Dunwich, in the twelfth century the biggest port in Britain, the Recovered City was a complete sham, but that wasn't the point. The bells of the sunken churches, which according to legend could be heard from forty fathoms on stormy nights, were piped into every mock-medieval bedroom.

Visitors to the Bermuda Triangle Experience would hear the captain's voice drift cheerily over the PA as they flew into the space defined by its hallowed coordinates: 'We are now entering the Bermuda Triangle. The instruments on the flight deck are all over the place. It's crazy up here. Good luck, folks.' Pure theatre, but it pulled in the punters and share prices rocketed.

I looked at James's open, expectant face. He was my flesh and blood, my own son's offspring, and I loved him. His ticket cannot have come cheap. What right did I have to puncture his dream of exotic travel? He was bright. It was only partly his fault the world worked the way it did. Six months prior to Shangri-La's opening to international travellers, DreamWorks SKG had released Todd Zapiek's *Shangri-La*, the most heavily hyped product in the history of digital film. Paying scant heed to Hilton's novel and ignoring two previous film versions, Zapiek's film whetted the appetite of the world's youth for travel to completely imaginary destinations, which were then variously 'discovered', 'opened' or 'reconstructed'.

'I've seen it five times,' he told me. 'It's just so cool that the place lay hidden for so long. They've restored it pretty much as it was.'

'What do you hope to see?' I asked him.

'What life was like so long ago – and so far away.'

'You imagine you're going to a real place,' I said, 'but in reality you're travelling to an imaginary destination.'

'Look at the ticket, Pops.' He waved it in front of me. 'Looks pretty real to me.'

'The price looks real enough,' I agreed.

'You can get a week in Shangri-La for half the price of a long weekend in Oz, or a day trip to Xanadu.'

'James, they're theme parks, fairground rides – nothing more, nothing less. You're being taken for a ride.'

As night fell, we moved inside and settled in beaten-up armchairs in my den, surrounded by memorabilia from my own travels.

'I'm sorry, James.' My cynicism having upset his delicate balance of irony and enthusiasm, I wished I'd kept my mouth shut. 'I'm a selfish old man.'

He shrugged.

'Hope Mum and Dad are all right,' he said.

'They'll be fine. You and your dad are both looking for the same thing. It's the same anybody wants – to go somewhere new, somewhere different. It's what I was looking for when I was your age.'

'Dad told me about New York.'

'That was before your dad was born. Before I met your grandmother.'

I'd always lived in London, and when I'd been James's age London had been considered the coolest, most exciting city on the planet. I couldn't wait to leave it, however, wanting to be in another, even more exciting city. I flew to New York and walked around Manhattan. It was all I did for days – walk. I walked from one end of the island to the other. I criss-crossed it on foot. I stayed in cheap hotels, moving on, travelling light, slowly formulating a plan, an insane plan perhaps, to walk every street in the city.

No man is an island, except Fred Madagascar. It was one of my favourite gags, credited to a northern comedian who ended up on a religious TV programme. But every man is an island. And every woman and child. We're all islands. We may be joined by bridges and tunnels, but each of us is still essentially an island, and it's a mistake to believe, as I discovered, that being stuck on an island in any way restricts your freedom.

'Once I'd walked every street on the map,' I told James, 'I started looking for ones that weren't on it.'

'Yeah, right. Did the drugs work, Pops, or what?'

Yes, the drugs worked. The drug was the same one James was on; Alfie too. It was stronger than wanderlust, had fewer side effects than itchy feet. It was the adrenalin rush of discovery, the desire to leave a footprint where no one had made their mark. It was the suspicion – later the conviction – that the map didn't tell the whole story.

Time and again I fetched up in Alphabet City, heading down one of the four lettered avenues, recrossing Tompkins Square so many times I sliced it into quarters. The City Fathers, naming this tiny grid-within-a-grid, appeared to have exhausted the ordinal series, which you might reasonably expect to be infinite, and embarked on a new series of alphabetically ordered avenues – so why stop at D?

I started dreaming of Avenue E. I woke with images of it in my head, but they faded before I reached the bathroom. My breakfast on those freezing December mornings was coffee and doughnuts from street vendors. As I raised the paper cup to my lips and blew, steam rose in a cloud around my head. In it I would catch a glimpse of Avenue E, its used bookstores, grungy cafes and six-floor walk-ups archetypes of those scattered throughout Alphabet City.

'You obviously found it in the end,' James said, raising his own coffee mug to his mouth. He pointed to the street sign hanging on my wall: AVE E.

My search for clues was not confined to the East Village. I listened in on conversations at the Empire Diner at Tenth Avenue and 22nd Street, snatching the briefest impression of Avenue E as I wiped the condensation from the window with the back of my hand, before the real view re-established itself in a ziggurat of yellow cabs and cross-town buses. I peered over browsers' shoulders in the Strand Book Store on Broadway; the musty atmosphere would be the same in Avenue E's smaller bookstores, but no one was reading the out-of-print guide to hidden New York that I needed. In the Modern, I stared at Edward Hopper's blank-faced ciphers, convinced that whichever bar they were drinking in, whatever gloomy rooming house was currently acting as their prison, each was dreaming of Avenue E.

I started taking cabs, not convinced the drivers' unpron-ounceable, unvowelled names weren't some kind of code. The last cab I took, I asked the driver to take me to Avenue E. We drove around for hours as the meter climbed and I kept on insisting that my destination did exist. The part of my mind that knew I couldn't afford the fare before we'd covered even ten blocks shut down after fifteen, and I ended up battered and shivering, huddled up on the floor of a derelict meat market on the West Side. I limped across to the East Village by way of 14th Street, my search over.

'I had that made for me,' I told James, looking at the sign on the wall.

'Neat job,' he acknowledged.

'But I did find what I was looking for.'

'You did?'

'I found it, but it wasn't where I'd expected it to be. It wasn't on the ground, but in my head, where it had been all along. It was nothing more – and nothing less – than my search for it and my inability to find it.'

James let this sink in, then commented, non-committally: 'Cool.'

After he had gone, to get the Cross-rail link to Heathrow, and we had both talked some more about my son and his mum and how he would be just fine (reassuringly, no shuttle had failed to complete its mission since the *Challenger* disaster), I took the Avenue E street sign down from the wall and held it in my hands.

As I looked out at the glittering lights of London, I moved my fingers slowly over the sign's weathered surface, feeling the microscopic striations that could only have been caused by decades of wind-borne grit. My thumb caught on the jagged edge at one end of the sign, the kind of jagged edge a craftsman would have been unable – or unlikely – to reproduce. The kind of jagged edge that would make you think it had been torn from a post somewhere in the real world.

SKIN DEEP

Henderson agreed to go on the expedition only because he thought Elizabeth was going along, so when he turned up at Washington services on the A1(M) and found only Bloor waiting to meet him he felt like a child with an empty Christmas box. It was important, however, not to show too much disappointment, given that Elizabeth was Graham Bloor's wife. Bloor waited for Henderson to ask, then explained.

'Elizabeth wasn't feeling up to it at the last minute,' he said, flicking ash from his cigarette into the little foil tray that sat on the plastic table top between the two men. 'Women's things, you know.' He placed the cigarette between his lips with his forefinger and thumb. Henderson wasn't sure whether he mistrusted *all* men who held their cigarettes in this particular way, or just Bloor.

'So it's just the two of us, then,' Henderson said, eyes sliding across Bloor's heavy, jowly features to the other tables in the cafeteria. Apart from a couple of thickset lorry drivers sipping scalding tea from greasy mugs and a rep in a grey double-breasted suit taking dainty bites round the edge of a white bread sandwich, they were the only customers. It was still early, not long after eight. The only two kitchen staff – women in their forties with tight curly perms and pink housecoats – were leaning against opposite sides of a doorway chattering in low voices.

'Looks like it, doesn't it?' Bloor said, picking his cigarette out from between his lips for the last time before grinding it out in the ashtray.

The plan was for Henderson to leave his car in the car park and go with Bloor. The idea had appealed to him when it had included

Elizabeth sitting in the passenger seat. He had imagined sitting in the back and watching the soft spring of hairs on the back of her neck. She would have put her hair up in a grip especially, because she was no slouch when it came to understanding her own appeal. But with Elizabeth left at home – she and Bloor shared a sizeable detached house in Gosforth – it was sadly inevitable that Henderson should take the seat alongside Bloor. He drove the Mercedes the way Elizabeth said he made love – fast, undeviating and without a backward glance. The way he dangled his arm out of the window was telling.

As Bloor put more miles between them and the services car park Henderson became increasingly miserable. Not even the bleak splendour of the Borders cheered him up, unable as he was to think of anything other than Elizabeth arching her back cat-like in bed.

She complained unceasingly about Bloor, his habits and the way he treated her; the oily manner he adopted with female shop assistants and waitresses, the unshakable confidence that she was his and would never leave him. And in that, at least, he appeared to be right, not that Henderson felt able to criticise her for staying: Bloor's success in various businesses had provided comforts aplenty; they wanted for nothing on the material side, and Elizabeth was a material girl. Henderson knew this – she would pick at the cloth of his lapel disdainfully and frown at his chain-store shoes – but it in no way coloured his feelings for her. She was a deeply attractive woman and Henderson knew he had to be doing a lot better than he was as a business studies lecturer to lure her away from her Gosforth lair for more than a night at a time. He didn't blame her, because he would have done the same in her position.

'So where are we heading?' Henderson asked to break the silence.

'The Highlands, of course.' Bloor pressed the cigar lighter home.

'I know, but whereabouts?'

'Oh, I forget the name. Some place. We'll leave the car and go on foot. Find somewhere to pitch the tent when it gets dark. And hopefully get lucky either tonight or tomorrow.'

'But there's no guarantee, is there? That we'll find one.' Henderson's heart was sinking still further at the prospect of more than a single night spent with Bloor.

'No guarantee, that's right, but plenty of incentive. Curtin's offering two grand. His client must be offering double that.'

'Christ,' said Henderson. 'Why would anybody pay four grand for a stuffed cat?' He looked out of the window at the passing outposts of Scots pine, wondering again about the ethics of the job.

'It's not just any old cat. The wild cat's as rare as rocking-horse droppings. Two grand, though, eh? Not bad for a couple of days' work. And it's like I said: fifty–fifty.'

'What about Elizabeth's share?' Henderson asked.

'What share? Would you expect to get paid if you'd stayed at home?'

Henderson bristled with righteous anger. Elizabeth was entitled to her share, and he'd no doubt she'd still be expecting it. She'd helped with the research, after all, picked the most likely spot to yield a wild cat. He'd offer her part of his share when they got back, assuming of course they found one of the damn things and managed to catch it and kill it without damaging the pelt. Curtin had made it quite clear to Bloor that if the cat was disfigured he wouldn't pay them a penny. Quite why he was being so fussy was a mystery to Henderson, who never would have expected taxidermists to adhere so strictly to whatever moral code prevented the man substituting a swatch of tabby fur. Maybe his client was enough of an expert to be able to tell the difference: why else would he offer such silly money? The wild cat's basic colour was yellowish grey and while five out of ten domestic strays could match that, they wouldn't have the wild cat's strong black vertical bars and dorsal stripe, nor its broad, bushy tail, which the textbooks – and Elizabeth – had taught them was the surest means of identification. The last thing they wanted to do was turn up at Curtin's with a feral moggy.

Henderson, though, had had grave doubts about the expedition's viability since it had been mooted. Indeed, he had needed to be convinced the wild cat actually existed, having grown up with the idea that the British Isles were devoid of any genuine wildlife. And then the books Elizabeth had trucked back from Newcastle Library all said how elusive the wild cat was and how the closest encounter you could reasonably hope for was a set of paw prints in fresh snow, or twin mirrors startled in car headlamps. Systematic tracking, the naturalists wrote, would very rarely produce a result.

So when Bloor swung the wheel of the Merc in a wide arc and scrunched to a halt in pine cones and dirt at the edge of the unmetalled road in the Middle of Nowhere, Highland region, Henderson felt their chances were minimal.

'Got everything?' Bloor asked before centrally locking the boot and doors.

Henderson nodded, hefting his rucksack and peering up the track. Bloor bent down and tucked the keys under a rear wheel arch.

'No point carrying anything we don't have to,' he said, 'and who's going to nick it out here? Let's go. We have to move as quietly as we can. They're very shy.'

'Do you really think we'll find one?' Henderson asked.

'I'm not going home without one.' And with that he immediately got into his stride. Henderson followed him into the semi-gloom of the forest. Once he'd got used to the sound of their passage, Henderson listened out for other noises, but the forest remained silent: no clouds of flies buzzing in stray patches of sunlight, no tiny creatures scratching through the undergrowth, and, most surprising of all, no birds clattering through the tops of the trees. He didn't get too close to Bloor but was careful not to lose sight of his broad shoulders rising and falling twenty yards in front.

'It's getting dark,' he shouted forward when he realised the trees had started to close in around them.

'Ssh.' Bloor flapped a hand in the air. 'Wild cats are nocturnal,' he said, catching his breath when Henderson had drawn level. 'The darker it gets the better our chances, but we've got to be quiet.'

They set off again, Henderson bringing up the rear, thinking about Elizabeth. They'd met two years previously holidaying on Paxos. Henderson had been struck by the unmistakable look of a bored wife when he'd happened to take breakfast on a couple of occasions at the same time as her and Bloor. He followed them one evening to a taverna that was well off the tourist trail and sat in a dim corner with a bowl of olives and a bottle of white wine. Bloor tucked into course after course while Elizabeth looked over his shoulder and once or twice crossed sightlines with Henderson. Walking to the hotel she looked back a couple of times and he was there at the edge of the surf, trousers rolled up, jacket slung over his shoulder with calculated nonchalance. So when she came downstairs half an hour after going up with Bloor to find Henderson drinking alone in the bar, neither of them was really surprised.

Henderson ordered another bottle of wine and they shared it with a round of conversational hide-and-seek.

'You do the shopping together every Thursday evening,' Henderson guessed. 'You push the trolly and load in all the basic stuff while he marches in front picking up vacuum packs of Continental sausages and firelighters for the barbecues you never get round to having.'

'You ring programmes in the *Radio Times*,' she said, raising her glass to her painted lips, 'then forget to watch them, sitting there listening to music instead and nursing a bottle of beer. Old jazz stuff probably or movie soundtracks. Comfort music.'

'And then when I do remember to set the video for something,' he continued, 'I never watch it but record the next thing over the top of it instead. I have tapes filled with the ends of shows I wanted to watch.'

'You don't go to singles bars,' she crossed her legs, dress riding up, 'but you do watch women in pubs, always married women. You try to catch their eye when their husband goes to the toilet.'

'You take long, long showers after he's gone to work, loving the feel of the water on your body. Then you might stretch out on that extravagant sheepskin rug in the living room.'

'Like a cat,' she added, draining her glass. And so they wandered down to the sea, talked some nonsense about the stars and returned to the hotel, to Henderson's single room. She showered and slipped back to her own room before dawn with Bloor none the wiser.

In the week that remained it was inevitable that Henderson

should get drawn into the group; it was the only way to escape suspicion. Henderson cultivated the other man's friendship at the same time as screwing his wife, who suddenly developed a taste for long solitary walks, usually to deserted stretches of coastline but occasionally just up to Henderson's room on the top floor. Bloor, though already a successful businessman, was attracted to the older, unflashy lecturer, and would sit for hours fascinated by his theories, the names he dropped so casually: dinner with the head of the CBI, invitations to the wedding of the ICI chief executive's daughter.

'How much of it is true?' Elizabeth asked on one of their walks.

'Enough,' he said. 'The rest is just confidence.'

Henderson played him like a fish, paying out line when he praised Bloor's acumen, comparing his strategies to those of top-flight Germans and Japanese, tactfully offering advice like a speechwriter deferring to a senior minister. Bloor glowed and bubbled for the remainder of the Greek holiday, persistently cracking terrible jokes about the name of the island: 'Do you know this is where they make the stuffing?' he would grin and splutter from the dregs of yet another bottle of ouzo. 'Paxos,' he'd repeat time after time, 'Paxos, Paxos,' and trail off in incomprehensible mutterings, Elizabeth's hand on his arm (her other under the table on Henderson's linen trousers) and a smile on Henderson's lips.

They were booked back on the same charter and Bloor actually suggested to Elizabeth that she sit with Henderson rather than suffer the smoking section. At Gatwick they made plans for Henderson to come up to Newcastle as soon as his teaching schedule would allow. In fact, he was to make many more trips up the A1 than the ones Bloor would know about. After a weekend as their guest in Gosforth he'd come up again on the Wednesday night, every other week, his Thursday being completely free, and get a room at the St Mary's in Whitley Bay where Elizabeth would join him once Bloor was out of the way at work. They'd walk along the windswept beach as far as Cullercoats and make jokes about how it compared to Paxos. Neither of them spoke of love – except Elizabeth when talking about Bloor ('He does love me, you know') – and yet there was clearly a need of some kind on both sides. She would get on the phone to Henderson when Bloor was called away at short notice, as he was with increasing frequency, to Copenhagen and Brussels, and Henderson's car would find itself pressed into more and more demanding service.

They snatched a weekend together in Alnwick when Bloor was in London. He left long, whining messages on the answerphone, which they heard when Henderson accompanied Elizabeth back to the house before driving home to Leicester. Where was she? Why hadn't she called him back? Then he'd wheedle: 'Don't worry, darling. I just hope you're having a nice time. I'll see you when I get back.' It gave Henderson no little grim pleasure as he motored south to think that at some point Bloor would pass him going north on the opposite carriageway. He had begun to feel jealous of the man and started inventing excuses to avoid coming up for weekends at their house; no longer could he easily bear seeing them together. He didn't know whether Bloor had put on weight or whether he just *saw* him as fatter, slower and more complacent. For all her abandon in bed at Whitley Bay, Elizabeth was still married to the man.

The expedition had been on the cards for a few weeks, ever since Bloor had bumped into his old friend Curtin at a Rotarians dinner and the taxidermist had raised the subject of wild cats. Elizabeth did her research and suddenly the trip was on, but minus one person.

Bloor had come to a halt and Henderson caught up with him.

'Isn't it getting too dark to see one now even if there are any?' Henderson asked, wiping sweat from his forehead.

'Not if you're looking.' Bloor hitched his rucksack up his back. Heavier than Henderson's, it contained the tent, a Primus stove and some provisions. 'We're more likely to see evidence of a cat before we see the cat itself. The carcass of a hare or a buzzard. Try and keep an eye out.'

There was a note of sarcasm in his voice that Henderson had not heard before and didn't much care for. It occurred to him that apart from moments when Elizabeth had slipped to the loo, it was the first time he'd been in the company of Bloor without the man's wife also being present.

Around 11.30 p.m., still having seen no trace of their quarry, they found a tiny clearing and set up camp, Bloor pitching the tent while Henderson got the Primus going. The sky above the pines was an indigo velvet pincushion.

'I envy you sometimes,' Bloor said as they sat back after eating, 'being single.'

'Oh?' Henderson said neutrally.

'Well, you know, the freedom. You can do what you like.' Bloor leered, waggling his eyebrows.

Henderson thought about his response. 'I suppose so, although I don't really have much time for any of that.'

Bloor said, 'Is that right?' and for the first time Henderson wondered whether he might possibly suspect. 'I thought with your job there would be a lot of free time, and what with all those nubile young students hanging around you could be, you know, making the most of it while you still can.' He took a cigarette from his pack of Bensons and continued: 'Only I'm beginning to wonder if I'm past it. You know. I'm forty-six, not as fit as I was. I don't know if I still satisfy Elizabeth.' He stared at Henderson, then placed the cigarette between his lips and spun the wheel on his Bic lighter. 'She's still a young woman.'

'I don't think age comes into it,' Henderson said.

'No, I don't suppose it does.' Bloor flicked ash over the Primus. 'I mean, look at you. You're older than both of us.'

'Put together.' Henderson laughed, but it was a nervous laugh.

For a few minutes the only sound in the night, apart from the occasional hoot of an owl, was the hiss of Bloor dragging on his cigarette. Then he spoke again. 'I've got something I want to ask you,' he said, and Henderson's stomach muscles clenched. 'Would you – and tell me if you think I shouldn't even have asked – but would you sleep with Elizabeth, if she wanted you to?'

Henderson was speechless.

Bloor stubbed out his cigarette.

'OK, look, I shouldn't have asked. Forget I said anything, OK?'

Henderson still couldn't find the right words.

'It's been a long day,' Bloor was saying. 'I think we both need some sleep. We've got to find that damn cat tomorrow and the earlier we get up the more chance we'll have.' So saying, he crawled into the tiny two-man tent.

'I'm going to sit up for a while,' Henderson said. 'I won't be long.'

Henderson woke at dawn, shivering and hungry, to discover that Bloor was already up. His sleeping bag had been rolled and folded into a tiny pouch and his rucksack stood ready to go. Henderson dragged himself out of his own sleeping bag and took a swig from a bottle of mineral water he kept tucked away. He pulled on some clothes and half-heartedly performed a couple of press-ups. Bloor appeared while he was taking a leak at the edge of the clearing and they set off soon after without either of them having spoken.

Mid-morning they came across a rabbit, or more precisely its skin. Something had eaten all the meat – odd bones lay scattered around – and tossed the skin aside, expertly turned inside out. Bloor took it in his hand and held it up so that the skin fell back over itself like a glove puppet.

'Wild cat,' he said.

'Really?'

'They can be vicious,' he added, turning the rabbit skin so that the head, which was still intact, flopped this way and that. 'Mind you, a domestic cat can do this just as easily.'

They pressed on deeper into the forest. Bloor stayed in front and Henderson stared as hard as he could into the soft light between the boles of tall pines, because the sooner they found the cat the sooner they could get back home. Surprisingly it bothered him that he couldn't get to a phone to ask her how she was feeling. Her periods were generally over fairly quickly, two or three days at most, and although she suffered a little, she, and Henderson, always celebrated their arrival as proof that they'd got away with it for another month. They took precautions, but, because of the circumstances, they worried a little when it got to three weeks.

It was just before they were going to stop for food, around 6 p.m., that they came across the weasel. It had been skinned as cleanly as the rabbit. Bloor held it up triumphantly, appearing to scent success.

'Curtin couldn't have done a better job himself,' he said as he turned the skin over in his hands.

'What do you mean?'

'This is what he does. He skins the animal – dead, obviously – and then uses the carcass to make a mould, usually in fibreglass, unless it's something this small.'

During their reconstituted meal Bloor continued.

'He invited me to spend a day at his workshop when he was mounting a puma he got from the zoo. The puma died of old age and he was commissioned to mount it for a museum somewhere in Wales.'

'Mount it?'

'That's what they call it. Mounting or stuffing. It takes weeks to do a big cat apparently, but I was there on the day he skinned it.'

Bloor pushed his paper plate away and lit a cigarette. The shadows around the clearing were thickening as the sky was gradually leached of daylight.

'He hung the carcass upside down from a chain fixed to a beam and it's amazing how easily the skin comes away. He'd pull a bit and it would unravel a further inch or so, then he'd take the scalpel and delicately free it from the fat and gristle. It's bizarre when you see the skinned carcass with its bug eyes and exposed muscle and tendons. It's beautiful in a way.'

Henderson rigged up the little kettle on the Primus to have an excuse to look away from Bloor, whose face had taken on a look of mixed revulsion and fascination.

'What does he do with the carcass?' Henderson asked.

'Takes a mould in fibreglass then calls up the knacker's yard who come along and take it away. Unless it's something small like a bird, or that weasel, in which case he slings it into the field. Apparently there's a lot of fat foxes round where he has his workshop.'

'So the stuffed animal you see in a museum isn't an animal at all. It's just the skin with some kind of cast inside?'

'Exactly. He generally uses expanding foam. You could pick up a tiger with one hand, they're so light.'

'It's a bit disappointing, isn't it?'

'Not really. It depends where you think the essence of the animal really is: in the carcass or in the skin. Because once you've skinned an animal all you've got on the one hand is a lump of meat, and on the other you've got the skin, which was all you saw while it was alive, after all.'

'But it's only skin deep.'

'Aren't we all, though?' Bloor said with a grimace, plucking his cigarette from between his lips. 'What would you rather see in a museum, or in your front room for that matter, a bloody carcass or a stuffed skin? I know which I find more attractive.'

Henderson wasn't entirely convinced by Bloor's logic. Obviously, the carefully prepared, titivated thing in the glass case was more attractive, but if you'd slung the beast's beating heart in the bin and scraped all trace of its brains from its skull, how could you still call it an animal, albeit a stuffed one?

'What about my wife?' Bloor asked suddenly from out of the darkness. 'Don't you find her attractive?'

Henderson cast around for a way to answer but ended up spluttering: 'I don't know. I haven't, you know, I don't see her in that light. She's your wife.'

'But she's a beautiful woman. Surely you find her attractive?'

'Well, yes, she's attractive, of course. But I don't see how it's relevant.'

'Just making a point,' Bloor said, sucking on his cigarette and causing the end to glow as it crept further towards his lips. 'We only see the surface of things, you see.'

The blue flame on the Primus sputtered and died.

'Shit,' said Henderson. The water hadn't yet boiled. 'Have you got another gas canister?'

'Over there.' Bloor pointed towards his rucksack. 'Side pocket.'

Henderson got the wrong side, fiddled around in one of the pockets and found nothing.

'Chuck me a torch, will you.'

Bloor lobbed him the thin pencil torch he kept in his jacket and Henderson peered into the rucksack.

He saw the canister but also noticed something else. Stuffed into a zip-up compartment that had not been fastened were several screwed-up tissues, all spotted and streaked with dried blood.

Bloor's disembodied voice made him jump: 'Can't you find it?'

'Got it,' he said, twisting round to the little stove and fixing the new canister in place as Bloor dampened his cigarette butt and flicked it into the darkness. 'Call of nature,' Henderson said, getting up and disappearing into the trees.

He needed to get away for a moment. Clearly, the most likely explanation was that Bloor had had a nose bleed and had kept the tissues in his rucksack rather than litter the countryside (despite his tendency to drop cigarette ends). But something was nagging at Henderson, plucking at his brain: hadn't Bloor seemed just a little bit too knowledgeable in the business of skinning animals, and where for that matter had he been to so early in the morning?

'Something wrong?' said Bloor softly.

Henderson started.

'Can't seem to go,' he said, miming zipping up his fly. Bloor grunted, lit a cigarette and turned to look into the forest. It was very dark by now, like an old house, the tree trunks like table legs. The whole place was deathly silent apart from the occasional floorboard creak as an owl alighted on a high branch.

'It's out there somewhere,' Bloor said.

Something is, certainly, thought Henderson. Even if it was only the hidden animal in Bloor, the dark side of his character that enjoyed tearing small creatures apart. Though, presumably, if he was responsible, he was doing it either to frighten Henderson or convince him that the wild cat was within their grasp and thereby persuade him to go deeper with him into the forest, and into the night.

The two men stood staring into the gloom. Bloor spat on his spent cigarette and flicked it into the forest, where it was accepted silently by the carpet of needles.

When they'd packed up and were heading off again Henderson followed close behind Bloor, extremely tense, wondering what he would say next. He felt like a small boy with an angry, unpredictable father, and, like a child, he didn't seem to possess the courage either to run away or talk straight. As they walked,

Henderson even started thinking that the whole premise for the jaunt could have been fabricated: there was no deal with Curtin and they were as likely to find a tiger as a wild cat in this God-forsaken corner of the Highlands. He felt a strong urge to call off the search and return home: Bloor was no more the country boy than he was, but the other man at least had the advantage of knowing where they were going. Henderson started watching his surroundings with greater interest – the way the hills on his left seemed to rise to three distinct peaks; the change from pure pine forest to a mixture of larch and Scots pine – so that he felt a little less dependent on Bloor.

'What's next then, Graham?' he heard himself asking, as if to convince himself that they were actually hunting wild cat.

'Black panthers,' Bloor replied without a moment's hesitation. 'They've been seen just outside Worcester.'

'That's ridiculous. There are no big cats in England.'

'What do you know about it?' Bloor spun round and glared at Henderson. 'Hmm?' His dimpled chin jutted forward. 'What do you know?'

Henderson stared into the black holes of Bloor's eyes.

'Curtin knows a woman called Meech, a photographer, who lives down there and she saw one. OK?'

Bloor's sarcastic tone tipped the scales a fraction and Henderson felt some power flow his way; just a drop but he lapped it up. 'A black panther?' he said.

'Well, it was black, it was a cat and it was the size of an Alsatian, so what do you suggest?' Bloor took out a cigarette and bathed his face in a cup of orange fire.

'She could have been mistaken.'

'She's a wildlife photographer.'

'Did she get a picture of it?'

Bloor dragged on his cigarette and blew a column of smoke directly into Henderson's face. 'She wasn't quick enough.'

'Shame,' said Henderson, stepping around Bloor and taking the lead for the first time. There was no path but he marched off in what had been a straight line for the last twenty minutes. After a moment he heard Bloor mutter something and start following. Henderson hid his growing unease with a confident stride, but he knew he didn't possess the bluff to carry it off for very long. If Bloor was lying about the black panther he'd done so convincingly.

They marched for another half-hour. There could have been dozens of wild cats watching them from the trees for all Henderson was aware. His mind was focused exclusively on Bloor, and he didn't slow his pace until the shout came: 'We'll stop here.' In the renewed quiet Bloor's breath chugged like an idling locomotive. 'We need some rest,' he added, as if he now needed to justify his orders. 'It's mental as well as physical. If we're not alert we don't stand a chance.'

He had echoed Henderson's own conviction but the older man was unable to prevent himself falling asleep next to Bloor in the two-man tent, and when he awoke Bloor was gone. The power shift, if it had happened at all, had been reversed. Bloor was out there somewhere either tracking rabbits and rodents and gutting them with his bare hands, or watching Henderson from behind a tree. Maybe he was genuinely searching for the wild cat, but there were too many maybes: Henderson had had enough. If he was right and Bloor knew about them, then Elizabeth needed to know, otherwise she'd be at a disadvantage when Bloor got back to Gosforth.

There wouldn't be a phone for miles. The only thing for it was for Henderson to retrace their steps to the car and get the hell out. It wouldn't take more than a couple of hours to bomb it down to Newcastle. He could be with her – a quick glance at his watch – by 7 a.m. He was sure enough of Bloor's knowledge now to take the not inconsiderable risk of stealing his car.

Henderson started packing his rucksack, suddenly terrified that Bloor would return and catch him in the act, but he had a thought and scribbled a quick note telling Bloor he'd woken up early and gone looking for him. He took from his own bag only the essentials and slipped out of the tent. The note could buy him an extra hour or two, enough time for Elizabeth to pack a bag and leave with him if she wanted to. It wouldn't be ideal, but at least she'd have a choice.

He crept through the trees for the first hundred yards in case Bloor was close by, then broke into a steady run, ducking and darting between the trunks. It was still dark but he was surprised by the clear tracks they'd left the day before: the path was easy to follow. Cresting a rise he stopped dead, blood hammering in his chest, sweat trickling down from his scalp. Twenty yards away, crouched down between the lines of trees, ears flattened against its skull and broad tail beating on the soft forest floor, was a cat. A wild cat. It bared its bone-white teeth in Henderson's direction, then, with a twitch, was gone, swallowed up by the darkness. Henderson started breathing again, exhilarated and feeling privileged to have been allowed those two seconds' intimacy. He suddenly felt overwhelmingly grateful that they had not found a wild cat: *he* couldn't have killed it and he would have been unable to prevent himself staying Bloor's arm.

The wild cat had gone and Henderson was free to do the same. He slipped between the thin trunks like a wraith, glancing up at the three hills on his right, the sky beginning to glow with the soft breath of dawn. He ran, just ran, and whether he possessed a keener sense of direction than he realised, or did it simply because he had to, he covered the distance in good time and tumbled out of the forest, which seemed to snap shut behind him. The Mercedes gleamed in the early light. Henderson bent down and reached under the wheel arch for the keys, found them, almost dropped them, flung the door open, started the engine and spat gravel at the dark line of trees already receding in the rear-view mirror. Somewhere in that lot was Bloor, hopefully now sitting by the tent waiting for Henderson to come back.

The house was quiet. Set back from the road and protected by high hedges – you couldn't even hear the traffic unless you made an effort. Getting no response ringing the bell, Henderson went round to the back – vaulting a high white wooden gate – and found the kitchen door open. He called Elizabeth's name but could hear only the blood rushing in his ears. The kitchen was clean, devoid of signs of breakfast, and the wall clock read 9.25. The return trip had taken only a little longer than expected. She would normally be up and have had breakfast, although Bloor's absence would obviously allow for a change in routine should she wish it.

Henderson made his way into the hallway, fingering the banister rail as if it were made of china.

'Elizabeth,' he called once more, and was disturbed to hear his voice break. He felt his face burning red and a little knot in his stomach tightening.

He stood silently on the landing for a moment. The house was still. An impossible draught brushed the back of his neck and a ripple ran over his scalp, pulling the smallest hairs erect. He took another step towards Elizabeth's bedroom, pushed open the door and stood on the threshold.

Amid a jumble of mad thoughts and a nauseous sinking sensation, he wondered how long he'd known at the back of his mind that this was what he would find. He approached the bed, determined to retain enough strength in his legs to stay standing.

He took her in his arms and was careful not to hold her too tight in case the stitching broke. As he sat on the bed rocking gently forward and back, forward and back, he thought with infinite sadness that here was a woman he could have loved, if he didn't already. Flooding through came the realisation that subconsciously he had strongly desired her separation from Bloor. Each time he looked at her – the puckered skin round the eyes, the lopsided mouth – he pictured Bloor at work. He relaxed his hold.

Later, outside by the white gate he'd vaulted to gain entrance to the grounds, he found a large bundle of sacking material. It was damp and sticky to the touch but gently he peeled the layers away to get at what lay inside, which he then lifted out and cradled in his arms, unmoved by the powerful stench and seeping fluids. After a time he laid it down again and drew the covers over.

The sun crossed the sky slowly, passing the zenith, burning only dully through the gathering scraps of cloud. The house remained silent apart from the creak of Henderson, upstairs once more, rocking to and fro on the bed, sheets sliding, slats groaning.

A creak on the stairs announced the new arrival.

'Curtin told me that's how he started,' said Bloor.

Henderson tensed but didn't let go. He turned his head enough to see Bloor in the doorway hugging the slippery carcass to his chest, tears tumbling from his ravaged, poisoned eyes.

'Mounting the things he loved – his dog and his cats – because he couldn't bear it when they went away. It must be different with pets,' he added blankly. 'Which one of us has her now, do you think?'

Henderson traced his finger over her skin, stretched tight across the mere shape of her shoulder. He didn't know what to say.

AUTEUR

My folks called me Trevor. To get back at them I dropped out of
college and became an actor. And changed my name to Ginger.
It seemed a good choice, given my dyed black ponytail. Actors
never work – common knowledge – so I got a job as a waiter in
Pizza Express on Upper Street.

'They're the only chain makes half-decent pizzas in this
country,' I heard one studiedly unkempt punter say to his date,
trying to impress her.

'I like Pizza Hut,' she said.

They didn't stand a chance.

Or leave a tip.

I continued to look for acting jobs but they were a bit thin on
the ground. Or at least they were in 1995. Despite John Major's
best efforts with the 'heritage industry'. Frankly, I'd rather eat my
own foot than ponce around in period costume showing families
from the West Midlands round the Museum of the Moving Image.
I'm much happier serving Four Seasons with extra pepperoni to
pissed-up life assurance salesmen in shitty suits.

'Do you want any garlic bread or a side salad with that?'

'If I wanted garlic bread I'd fucking ask for it,' said a guy in a
stripy shirt who placed his mobile on the table next to his bottle
of Asti. He was about my age, but loaded, and resented having to
engage in conversation with a waiter. Some people's eyes simply
don't swivel that far up.

To get back at him I crushed up a dead roach with a pestle
and mortar and sprinkled it on his pizza along with the extra
pepperoni. Watched him wash it down with several bottles of
Peroni from behind the cappuccino machine. If I'd wanted him to

stop for a moment and frown at a forkful I'd've been disappointed. But I guess I didn't, so I wasn't.

At table sixteen, a guy with a Florida tan and three packs of Camel Lites on the table before him ordered a Marinara. His companion, a short guy with little round glasses and a number-one back-and-sides, wanted an American Hot with extra onions and peas.

'You know, if you get an American and help yourself to some chilli oil you could save yourself 80p,' I said, not exactly Salesman of the Year. 'It has the same effect.'

He thought about it – for a nanosecond – but stayed with the order he'd given me. At least he thought about it.

I was on my break when they came in.

'Ginger, you've got three on table twelve,' Paola told me. She was a nice girl, Spanish, but was going out with a hard Northern bastard called Con. I'd seen him once and decided never to step out of line with Paola. There's a whole section of my imagination dedicated to picturing what guys like Con would do to me if they caught me at it with their significant other. But not everyone looks like Con. Nor does everyone look like Paola, which is more to the point, but never mind.

I was working upstairs that night and anyone sat by the window – which meant tables nine to nineteen – got a good view of the Screen on the Green, which was showing Hal Hartley's *Amateur*. I'd already seen it at the Metro and had a right job keeping awake. My friend Ian, who'd insisted I accompany him despite my clear antipathy to crap American 'art house' movies, thought it was 'excellent'. To get back at him I urged him to rent *Top Gun* on video – 'It's not shit,' I told him. 'It's really, really not shit. You expect it to be shit and it isn't.' He rented it and a couple of days later asked me cautiously in what way did I think it was not shit. I referred him to *Amateur* – and indeed to *Simple Men*, the previous piece of Hal Hartley's shit Ian had dragged me to – and told him if I ever went to the pictures with him again it would be after a full investigation had been carried out to make sure Hal Hartley had never been allowed anywhere near the film in question. If he'd so much as been invited to the preview or goosed the best boy it was a no-no.

Hal Hartley could offer me the deal of the year, ten million up front, and a phalanx of buxom beauties to fellate me between takes, and I'd still tell him to take a hike. Yeah, I wanted to be an actor, but there was one thing I was not prepared to do. I'd do most things: nudity, violence, IV drugs. I'd quite happily do the M in SM. I'd let them drive right over me with a three-wagon road-train in the Western Australian desert. I'd even eat shit if it furthered the plot. But I would never, ever work for Hal Hartley.

What I really wanted was a part in *Jacob's Ladder*. But it had already been made so I couldn't have one. I wanted to go mental on psychoactive drugs, rolling around on the deck doing that vibrating thing with my arms and legs.

I stood by table twelve for a full minute while they finished a conversation. *Oh, I've got all night.* Well, yeah, I did have, actually. There were, as Paola had told me, three of them. A girl with cropped dark hair and werewolf-pale eyes, another girl with long blonde hair, blonde except for the roots, that is, and an Indian-looking boy with a fashionably floppy fringe and bum fluff.

'Can I have a Veneziana, please?' asked the first girl – the one with the cropped hair. I tried to guess what she did – I always try to guess what punters do – but all I got was the fact that she was nervous. Every time she spoke, at least to me, she raised her hand and lightly touched the side of her face, almost as if checking it was still there. The dyed-blonde sparked up a Marlboro and muttered something about extra cheese, and then I noticed that the Indian boy had a light meter dangling round his neck, which was either a total pose or suggested these people might be worth getting to know. Even if it was a total pose, they might repay a minute or two's chat.

Plus, the dark-haired girl was quite cute, for all her nervousness.

I was over at the dumb waiter, sending the order down to the kitchen, when I noticed her doing that thing that film directors do with their hands – making a letterbox-type viewfinder with her two hands, thumbs splayed at right angles. She was doing it at Paola, who suddenly dropped one of the pizzas she was carrying. I say suddenly – actually it seemed to happen in slow motion and I seemed to view it simultaneously from a number of different angles, like the wooden beam that falls on Donald Sutherland's

ceiling-restorer's cradle in the church in *Don't Look Now*. There
was a brief sense of unreality, but then the crash of the plate on
the tiled floor and the disintegration of the pizza itself – La Reine
with extra olives, I couldn't help noticing – brought me back to
my senses.

When I looked back at the three film student types they were
laughing and the director-girl was no longer looking at Paola.

I weighed up the relative advantages of helping Paola and
delivering the film students' drinks order.

'Peroni,' I announced while Paola cleaned up somewhere
behind me. The director-girl – she was called Elaine, as I would
find out later – nodded, almost imperceptibly, and her eyes
seemed to flicker as they crossed sightlines with mine. The
blonde girl, Sand, and the boy, Jay, were sharing a bottle of the
house white. Not a great wine, but they didn't look that well off.
I'd considered slipping them the Frascati but didn't in case they
took offence. No point playing against yourself. The odds were
stacked as it was.

Sand was speaking. 'Yeah, but we've only got the camera for
a day and we can't switch it. You know that. If we don't do it
tomorrow we don't do it at all. You know?'

Elaine was nodding. Jay looked pretty spaced out. I distributed
the drinks slowly, hoping to catch more.

'I'll fucking kill that tosser if I get my hands on him,' Jay said.

So: not all that spaced out, then.

'One swallow does not make a summer,' said Elaine,
bizarrely.

'Where are we going to find a replacement at this stage?' Jay
again, sweeping his long hair out of his doleful eyes.

'Are you making a film?' I asked.

Jay turned to gaze out of the window while Sand looked at me
appraisingly and Elaine took a nervous sip of her beer.

'Someone let you down?' I persevered. 'I might be able to
help.'

'We're doing a road movie,' Elaine said, catching my eye for a
split second, but that was OK, she was nervous. 'Only we're doing
it in London. Strange place for a road movie, right? But it's gonna
be kind of post-ironic, you know?'

'Post-ironic?' I scratched my head.

'Well, you know, the received wisdom is you can't make a road movie in Britain at all, never mind in London.'

'*Butterfly Kiss*,' I said, unhelpfully.

'Yeah, but it was shit,' said Sand.

Since I couldn't argue with that, I asked: 'Where's it set?'

'On the Westway. It's kind of like…' This was Elaine, but she was struggling a little.

'Like *Radio On*?' I ventured.

Elaine sort of ummed and aahed.

'Someone just made a short film. I think it might even have been called *Westway*,' I offered, vaguely wondering how my other tables were doing.

Jay finally acknowledged me. 'Fuck off,' he said, and rearranged his knife and fork.

I'd get him back for that one day, I decided. Somehow.

'We know,' said Sand. 'But we only found out after we'd written ours. But it's different. That was very British, you know, very kind of gloomy and miserable.'

'Yeah,' Elaine chipped in. 'It was a *miserablist classic*.' And for some reason they fell about, Jay collapsing in an implosion of scoffs and snuffles. Elaine looked at me. I had a feeling they were sharing a joke at my expense, though I couldn't see how. 'Ours is, er…kind of going to acknowledge the fact that the road movie *is* an American phenomenon, you know? That's why we had to have an American lead. It's kind of Stephen Frears meets Hal Hartley.'

Oh my God. 'Oh really?' I said, heading straight for the dumb waiter.

We'd talked for so long, their pizzas were ready. I dished them out, then, kneeling down to impart a degree of intimacy, said: 'I know just the man for the job.'

Jay immediately said: 'Oh yeah? Who?'

'You need an actor capable of doing a convincing American accent. Someone who can drive a car and can handle a meaningful pause.'

'Yeah.' Elaine was nodding. 'That's right. Ideally he'd be American, though.'

'But you'd take someone who could do the voice.'

'At this stage we might have to,' said Sand. 'He doesn't have much to say.'

Jay sniggered at this for some reason.

Elaine was nodding as she sawed at her Veneziana; Jay's expression had reverted to a scowl. I didn't know what his problem was. Maybe he was after a shag, though with whom I couldn't tell. He certainly wasn't getting one off me.

I arranged a meet with them for the following morning. Eight o'clock at some sports centre under the Westway. They must have been quite desperate, having exhausted all possible avenues – friends of friends and so on – to go for my offer. I played him up, my actor friend: lots of experience, bumming around doing ads at the moment – lots of dosh, no respect. He wanted to do something real. Something with balls. I suggested they let me have a script and I'd pass it on after my shift – as luck would have it, I explained, I was meeting up with Ginger later.

'Ginger?' Jay exploded.

'That's the guy's name,' I said. I don't know why. I didn't think they'd go for me as I was. Maybe it was the red shirt, the dirty plates I was carrying, the serviettes I picked up off the floor as I went.

They didn't leave a tip.

I got back at them by turning up half an hour late the following morning. Which was stretching it a bit if I was hoping to win them over. But I figured they were desperate enough to go for what I'd got. I reckoned it was a lot.

'So where's Ginger?' Elaine said. She was wearing a neat-looking leather jacket with big pockets and turned-up tartan cuffs. Her hair had been washed that morning. It glinted in the wintry sun.

'You're looking right at him.' I could have been Dennis Hopper. Or Jack Nicholson. The accent. Spot on. 'I can act. I can drive. What more do you want?'

Elaine looked round at her colleagues.

Jay was just licking the gum on a roll-up. It was probably a spliff, he was so fucking cool.

'You're a waiter,' said Sand, not unkindly, just sort of matter-of-fact.

'And you didn't leave a tip. We're none of us perfect. I've read your script. I've even learnt my *line*. I can make your film. What do you say? You've only got the gear for one day.'

Jay cupped his hands about a match then cast it vaguely in my direction, plucking his roll-up from between his pouting lips. He was wearing a red baseball cap. Back to front, natch. 'You've got a right fucking nerve,' he said, and stalked off.

I looked at Sand and Elaine. Sand was non-committal; Elaine I sensed I'd got. In which case Sand would follow. 'What does he do anyway?' I asked, tilting my head in the direction of the disappearing Jay.

'Sound,' Elaine said. The fact she answered me at all signified she'd accepted the situation.

'So we do need him back,' I said.

Elaine looked at Sand, who sighed and undid the clasp holding her crinkly, damaged hair in place. She shook her head back and grasped her hair in two hands, reaffixing the device. Without a word but with a quick look at both of us, she went in pursuit of Jay.

'The car's down there,' Elaine explained.

'What is it?'

'It's a Beemer.'

I raised my eyebrows, impressed.

'An old model. A 2002ti or something. You've read the script.'

I had. A couple of times in the cab on the way home from the restaurant. It sucked, but it was a film. Even if only a short film. With one good line. But at least it was mine.

I craned my neck to see whether there was any sign of Jay or Sand.

'He'll come round,' Elaine said. She'd cocked her head on one side. 'That was pretty confident of you.'

'I knew I could do it but I didn't think you'd give me a chance. It was a perfect opportunity.'

'You haven't actually got any acting experience at all, have you?'

I smiled at her. She wasn't stupid.

'The thing is,' she said, 'the part's changed. A little.'

And somehow I knew what she was going to say.

'He's got a shaved head.' She looked for my reaction. I was too canny – and prepared – to let it slip. 'At least at first. It's part of the whole non-causative approach we're adopting in the narrative.' She punched her hands deep into the pockets of her leather jacket. 'Really he should shave it at the end. Sackcloth and ashes. For his crime. But in a way he kind of anticipates it. A stitch in time, after all.'

What the fuck was she on about? What the fuck was she *on*?

Despite the fact this was nothing but a crummy fifteen-minute short about a guy who drives his clapped-out old Beemer up and down the Westway and finishes with his girlfriend, I went along with the change. Almost before I knew what was happening, Elaine was leading me from the macadamed football pitch towards the Harrow Road.

'We've got to get you a haircut,' she was saying, and I didn't know why, but I wasn't protesting. I didn't even seem to think it was a bad idea. As we reached the pavement I looked right and saw Sand and Jay bent over a padlocked bicycle discussing something in earnest. I could read the stencilled letters on the bike's crossbar: GRAVLAX. I didn't find this strange.

Although it was still early, there was a barber's that was open in the adjacent parade of shops. My Mini was parked up outside. Elaine seemed to know the guy. 'Number one all over,' she told him, the words seeming to wriggle out of the corner of her mouth. I sat in the chair without a fuss and found myself enjoying the buzz of the clippers as they worked at my scalp. I was aware at one point of a line of men waiting against the back wall for their turn. They wore a mixture of flat caps and peaked affairs and some of them puckered moist lips around a series of slender, sizzling roll-ups. The ceiling was Dulux Nicotine. I noticed the barber, who was lame, coming towards me with a cut-throat razor. The hand that held the blade landed on my shoulder for support. Elaine's hand appeared on my other arm, a comforting gesture I found unnecessary. The mirror was crowded with ghosts, but when I next looked in it I saw an empty wall behind me. The old men had disappeared. Just an orange plastic chair, a fan heater and a pile of well-thumbed copies of *Club International* and *Forum*.

We were leaving the hairdresser's before I even realised Elaine had paid the man. I watched him take his razor to a long strap of leather. I caught my reflection in the glass of the door and winced.

I got her back by dragging my feet on the way to the five-a-side pitch. Jay and Sand were back, prepared to go with the situation. I ran my hand over my shorn head, enjoying the sensation. Tiny bits of hair fell on my Gap flannel shirt.

'Untuck the shirt,' said Sand.

Jay: 'Yeah, and do something with the pendant.'

'Are we going to get started or just fuck about all day?' I said, pulling my crystal pendant from inside my T-shirt. I didn't know where it had come from but I knew I liked it. I didn't want to lose it.

'You play Elaine's boyfriend,' Sand explained.

'I've read the script,' I said. 'I go out with her, she's mad, I drive her home and I dump her.'

'That's not the way we see it, Ginger,' Jay said. He was fingering a sound boom that had appeared from somewhere.

'No, well, I wouldn't expect you to.'

'If you can't handle it, you know,' he jeered, 'maybe we could get you a stunt cock.'

'The way I see it, Jay, you're the only one's gonna need a body double.' I didn't elaborate and I sensed Elaine had had enough of our bickering. She had a film to shoot. Sand was messing about with a hand-held light, switching it on and off.

'The car's just over here,' Elaine said, linking arms with me as we moved in a group back towards the Harrow Road once more. I felt her body warm and firm next to mine. I sensed there were things inside it, but didn't think about them too hard. She reminded me of an old girlfriend whom I'd loved intensely and eventually scared off: she'd gone off with a mate of mine called John, or Johnny. I felt as if I'd shot forward a long way into the future.

'You'll need these,' Sand said, handing me a set of keys to the BMW. The fob was imprinted with a highly intricate design that I recognised though I didn't know where from. Elaine held me closer.

I didn't know whether it was method acting or whether she just reminded me increasingly of Clio, the girl I'd loved too much, but I found that I was attracted to Elaine. It wouldn't be difficult to play the part of her boyfriend. As we all piled into the car I wondered whether the film had started. Jay and Sand were sitting in the back with their equipment. It seemed very bright to me with the lights on but I kept quiet. I only had one line and that didn't come until later. As well as playing my girlfriend, Elaine was directing. I glanced round at her as I pulled away from the kerb, unnecessarily stripping rubber from the old tyres. She was doing that thing with her hands, zooming in on the side of my face as I drove.

I got straight into the part without waiting for direction. They could edit later, I figured. I worked on a little tic under my left eye, nearest Elaine. She was still doing the business with her hands but reeling off her lines at the same time. It occurred to me that there was no camera, but for some reason this didn't seem to matter. My perspective shifted about wildly. When I was aware of driving I was also aware of Jay and Sand behind us doing their stuff with the lights and the sound, but now and again I would get a view from outside the car and there'd just be the two of us. Me and Elaine. Or Clio. My hand on her leg, her right leg. She was wearing a skirt, a short leather skirt. I didn't remember it from before. She stretched her leg out a little, as far as it would go. I worked my hand up under the skirt. The soft yield of her knickers was warm against my fingers. She leaned across and flicked her tongue in my ear just like Clio had done the night I'd got off with her for the first time at some dumb party in Heaton Mersey. Her hand snaked round my leg and she grabbed my cock through my jeans. I gasped, swerved, regained control – didn't lose it. My hard-on *or* the car. She was whispering something. I couldn't tell what it was. Then she took her hand away and her other hand appeared from nowhere and she was zooming in on my crotch. A quick wipe-pan and we were looking out the front of the car. All this at sixty, sixty-five, heading towards Shepherd's Bush on the Westway. Ladbroke Grove Tube slid past on the left. One frustrated passenger murdering another on the platform. Your next eastbound service has just departed Goldhawk Road.

And when I next looked at my lap I saw that someone had got my cock out. I didn't know whether it was me or Elaine or Clio. Or Sand, on Elaine's direction, reaching over my shoulder from the back seat. Or – God forbid – Jay. And yeah, I was *on*, obviously I was *on*. Elaine was giving it some with her free hand. Her other hand, I noticed, had somehow acquired Jay's light meter and she was checking out the lowering sky over the West Cross Route. 'Stay on the Westway,' she commanded, suddenly unhanding me. I was close, I'll say that. But suddenly somehow the camera was on Elaine and she was spouting lines from the script, stuff about the cinema, the dimensions of the screen and the windscreen of a car. '...late twentieth-century perspective that's impossible to get away from. Being in a car allows you to star in your own movie. The rear-view mirror represents the impossibility of going back. There's no rewind button in real life...' It was pretentious shite. Second-hand Ballard. Self without the wit; without the irony, the distance. Without the ideas. But Christ, I fancied her. I downshifted as we rolled off the elevated section, mindful of the speed cameras – the signs were everywhere, the automatic flashes popping at anyone hitting forty or above. I was still turned on but my cock had somehow been put back inside my jeans. I had no recollection of having done it myself. But someone had. We had it on film. I thought about audiences at the ICA sitting through it – guys with goatees and girls with absurdly tiny silver rucksacks – and thinking it *meant* something. Stroking those goatees in the bar afterwards, reaching inside those little bags for packets of fags that could barely fit inside. Discussing 'it', the film, and what 'it' meant. Whatever 'it' was. Bunch of cunts. Bag o' shite. We turned left into Bloemfontein Road and glided past the White City Estate.

We dropped Sand off at the junction with Uxbridge Road and somehow made it back to where my car was parked in five minutes flat. I was driving but I wasn't really aware of any resistance, whether from traffic lights or language. I was reading all the road signs and shop names but the words all seemed to be on our side. For once. The bike must have been Jay's. I may have been wrong but I think I saw him dump the sound boom in a dustbin on his way to unlock it from the railings. Elaine and I left the BMW without locking it – she looked at me and raised her eyebrows but I said, quick as a flash, 'It doesn't matter, we won't be needing it again.' She followed me to my car. An orange Mini with a blue driver's door where it had once been knocked by a gate on a level crossing. Lucky escape that one. It was unlocked. What was the point? 'Get in,' I said, gruffly, aware that she could edit me out later. I peeled away from the side of the road and U-turned at twenty-five, thirty, accelerating fast. We'd soon caught up with Jay, who was cycling slowly uphill, making heavy weather of it and wearing a helmet. He'd be needing that, I thought, and nudged his back wheel with the front nearside wing. He went straight down without a sound, and when I looked in the mirror he wasn't moving. That was for telling me to fuck off in the restaurant.

I took Elaine up to Kensal Green Cemetery and, although I'd thought you couldn't do so, drove right in through the main gate. I bounced the old Mini along the path and veered left for the canal. In the shadow of the gas-holders I pulled on the handbrake and we moved into the back seat.

I asked her whether this was still in the film and she laughed. The branches of horse chestnut trees scraped against the windows of the car as I rolled her sweater up over her tits and enjoyed their feel against my cold hands. She was wrestling with my belt buckle. The next thing I knew she'd taken hold of my left hand and was peering closely at it.

'What are you doing?' I asked her.

'Reading your palm. You've got a very interesting lifeline.'

I pulled my hand away sharply, feeling angry and hurt and afraid.

'What's the matter?' she said, grabbing for my hand.

'Don't,' I shouted. 'I don't like that stuff.'

'Why not?'

'I don't want to know what's going to happen. That's why I never watch trailers. I have to leave the cinema when a trailer comes on for a film I want to see.'

We found ourselves outside the car, walking by the canal, even though there wasn't meant to be a towpath on the north side.

'They tell you the whole story. There's no point going to see the film if you watch the trailer carefully enough. Soon we'll all only watch trailers. They won't make films any more. Only trailers.' We passed a brightly painted barge. 'We won't be able to go to the pictures together. You'll be sitting there whispering to me you know what's going to happen. My mum used to do that. She'd sit there and say look at him, he did it, you just watch. And she was right every time. Even if she wasn't, she spoilt it for you because it changed the way you watched. You should watch the film at the speed the director wants you to watch it at, not try and second-guess him. Or her.'

Elaine didn't say anything but tried to grab my hand again instead. I just laughed and chased her up the bank.

The next thing I knew we were back at her place, although still outside in the street by my car.

'Trailers are the palm-reading of the cinema,' I was saying. 'You should know that, you're a director. And a palm-reader.'

'I'm in control,' she said. 'I have to be in control. That's why I'm making this film.'

For a moment she looked as if she was about to do that thing with her hands, but she didn't.

I delivered my line: 'I've had enough of mad people,' I said, becoming aware only at that moment that I was going to finish with her. I'd always been convinced that palm-reading and being mad went hand in hand.

'Oh, that's it, then. You're dumping me,' she said, hands on hips, not taking any shit.

I shrugged and nodded.

She said: 'Well, at least let me get my coat, then you can run me home,' which puzzled me because I understood we were at her home, but then I realised this was where she worked. I watched her go up the steps into the building. She started going up the stairs that I could see through the glass doors. How could I have thought it was her home? It looked nothing like where someone would live. I dived into the Mini and made off up the high street, looking back in the rear-view mirror to see whether I could make her out in the first-floor windows. I saw her as I approached the point where the road bent. She'd pulled on a shiny red coat and was bending down, squinting out of the window after me. She knew exactly what I was doing. Then, as she mimed a sudden progressive, stage-by-stage zoom, I saw what *she* was doing: I understood as I hurtled round the corner and straight into the war memorial.

In the next scene, the last scene, the scene no one's expecting, she's back at her place with a new boyfriend – I think it's Jay. They're arguing over something. She's going to come into her bedroom sooner or later. I pull the covers up around me, moving carefully against the skirt of broken windscreen glass. I'm wearing the Mini like a duvet. She'll come in and see me. That'll get her back.

TRUSSED

1

It was Caroline who told me that once past thirty-five, there's no way you will meet any more people who could come to mean something to you. Thirty-five is arbitrary, of course: just because it was thirty-five for Caroline doesn't mean it'll be thirty-five for you or me. It might be thirty-six or forty, but it's around that age. The reason Caroline formulated this theory was she'd just (barely) survived a run of disastrous relationships and really thought she'd found the right guy in Graham, whom she met at a dinner party in the week following her thirty-sixth birthday. Pleasant, considerate, he was even talented and apparently trustworthy, but he turned out to be worse for her than any of them and she ditched him. The mutual friend who had invited them both to his dinner party forwarded an e-mail that allowed Caroline to discover that Graham had done a bulk mailing to all his friends saying that Caroline had got rid of him because 'he didn't go with her furniture'. Underneath which he'd added: 'Fuck the middle classes.'

'He's more middle class than I am,' Caroline said to me. 'And to think I trusted him.'

Just before Christmas, something happened that made me wonder about Caroline's theory.

Since I work only part of the week, I have plenty of spare time to myself. When it comes around to Christmas and I have a sack-load of cards to post, rather than spend a small fortune on stamps, I hand-deliver any that are within reach of my Tube pass. Being a part-time worker, I welcome the saving this represents.

Judging by some of the cards I receive year after year from names that become increasingly hard to decipher (or do they just mean less to me with the passing of time?), everyone operates the same rules as I do with regard to Christmas cards. Which is this: I continue to send cards to certain people year in year out, whether or not I've heard from them in the intervening twelve months. They may not have sent me a card in recent memory. They may never have sent me a card. But it becomes a point of honour. I imagine them opening their card from me and smiling a sly little smile, thinking to themselves: So he's still out there, still sending cards.

One of the people I always send a card to is Chloë. I make a point of including the diaeresis on her card because I remember how she was always a stickler for it. Chloë lives in an art deco block of flats on a busy road in WC1. I arrived there on a chill, bright afternoon in the first week of December. I looked down the ranks of names by the bell-pushes and found Chloë's. I pressed the buzzer and waited for a reply, but none came. I pressed again, then waited a couple of minutes before trying a third time. There was still no answer. This was not especially surprising; no doubt she was at work.

There was no general letter box for the building, and the glass doors could not be opened from the outside. Nor could a card be slipped through the gap between the doors, as a brass plate covered the join from the top to the bottom. I stepped back on to the pavement, the traffic roaring by just inches behind me. I wondered how agreeable it might be to live so close to such a large volume of cars, buses, lorries and motorcycle couriers. This is the price you pay for living in town.

Possibly at this point I should have withdrawn and added Chloë's card to the pile that required posting, but it seemed silly to be this close and not be able to find a way to gain entrance. I noticed an elderly man in a thick overcoat and knotted scarf approaching the doors from the inside. I quickly ran up the steps and smiled at the man as he crossed the threshold. He didn't return the smile but he did hold the door open for me. Once inside, I pulled back the concertina doors to the lift. I rode the antique elevator to the top floor and walked down the shiny linoleumed corridor to the door to Chloë's flat.

I hesitated, unsure whether to knock or simply slip the card through the letter box. There was a small brass plaque affixed to the door bearing Chloë's name, which I found quite charming. An indication of a strong personality. Chloë Thomson lives here, whether you like it or not. She's even got her name on the door.

I first got to know Chloë when we were students living in the same halls of residence. Most of the male students considered her unapproachable simply because she was so beautiful. There was something about her manner as well that discouraged close contact. But that was fine with me, since I wasn't immediately sexually attracted to her and the slight distance allowed us to get on as friends.

Instead of either knocking or posting the card, I squatted, bending my legs at the knees, and gently pushed open the flap. I was suddenly glad I had neither knocked nor roughly pushed the card through.

Chloë was trussed up in a sheet or a straitjacket and was hanging upside down from the ceiling by a rope attached to a substantial-looking hook. She was in the main room, which was located at the end of a narrow hallway. Other doors stood half open off the hallway. Chloë's body swung lightly from side to side. All I could hear was the faint creaking of the rope as it swung against the hook. I laid Chloë's card on the mat for a moment as I contorted my body to try to read the expression on her face.

I heard a sound from behind me. With care I swiftly reinverted my body so that I was crouching on my toes on the doormat.

One of the doors behind me, on the opposite side of the corridor, was being unlocked from the inside. Tumblers retracting, bolts rumbling through their housings, chain rattling back. I didn't wait. Only at the end of the corridor did I remember, flushed with adrenalin and feelings of guilt, the card that I had left lying on the mat. It was too late now. I saw a figure emerge from the flat opposite Chloë's and turn to lock the door. I could have hid and waited then gone back to have another look, but I don't mind admitting the whole episode had spooked me. I didn't know whether what I had witnessed was sex or torture or both, whether Chloë was alone or accompanied by someone I had not been able to see, and until I knew that, I didn't know how to feel about it.

That evening the telephone rang.

'Hello. Guess who this is.' It was Chloë, sounding eerily bright and cheerful.

'Well, well,' I stalled. 'Long time no hear. How are you?'

'Great.' I remembered then, she always said things were 'great' when I'd first known her. She said they were 'great' when they clearly weren't. When they were anything but. And she always said it in that automatic, falsely cheerful manner. 'Great.'

'Good,' I said.

'Thank you for your card.'

'You got it, then?'

'Of course.' She didn't make any reference to where she had presumably found it, though I'd worked out what I would say if necessary: that I had given the card to someone who was entering the building, asking them whether they wouldn't mind delivering it. 'Of course I got it,' she added. There was a moment's silence and suddenly I felt certain she knew I had been there and had seen her. I didn't know what to say.

'So how's life?' Chloë asked, which I hadn't been expecting.

'Fine. OK. How about yourself?' I added.

'Oh, this and that.'

I sensed another pause. Pauses in conversations with women like Chloë worry me. I sought to head the pause off at the pass by babbling. 'You must be terribly busy. We all are, these days, aren't we? Seems impossible ever to stop for breath, never mind find the time to get together, have a drink, talk about old times. You know...'

I was appalled at myself.

'I'll get my diary,' Chloë said.

What had I done? Before my visit to Chloë's building, I might have quite fancied meeting up for a drink. Now, I felt anxious. I didn't want to get mixed up in anything unpleasant.

We agreed on a lunchtime the following week.

I got to wondering why I had continued to send Chloë a card, and was forced to admit the possibility that it was because I saw her as a potential partner, as long as she and I both remained single. There was nothing to be gained by jumping to conclusions: either Chloë was a would-be Houdini getting in some training, or I could be about to find myself needing an escape route of my own.

2

I suppose I should have known better than to accept an ivitation to go out for a drink with a man who downloads pictures from alt.sex.fetish.amputee. And who admits it to a female colleague just as he's opening the refrigerator to get the milk to make her a cup of tea.

Patrick opened the giant fridge door and took out a TetraPak pint of milk that had already been opened. I tried not to think about the other contents of the fridge, though I had presumably seen some of them on previous visits to the mortuary. He poured the milk into the china mug – his concession to delicacy – and because of the inexpertly opened carton, a trickle of milk ran down the outside of the mug on to the stainless-steel table. It was funny that Patrick spent his working hours cutting open bodies, yet was no more skilled than the rest of us when it came to opening a pint of milk. I watched him squeeze the teabag with an unidentified instrument, then remove it and pass me the mug with the handle pointing towards me. He was polite: I'd give him that. Some men didn't even get above zero on politeness. In which case, they would never get above zero with me.

Of course, I was assuming Patrick was interested in me. That he fancied me. I never make such assumptions rashly. The cups of tea, the shy little smiles, the bouquets he gave me to take home on the Tube. The looks other people gave me when they saw the purple ribbon. Flowers were flowers to me then: my flat needed brightening up. I'm on the top floor of an art deco block facing front, with the gardens at the rear, so if I want flowers I have to fetch them myself.

To be honest, I could have done without the trips to the morgue, but the ash cash came in handy. Some doctors choose not to do it. Others, in the case of our hospital, lack enthusiasm for the subterranean corridors, the dripping pipes, the condensation on the distempered walls. You just have to check the body, make sure there's nothing suspicious and sign a form. There's not much to it. But on my first visit, the combined effects of the hike through the sweaty underground corridors and the sudden chill in the morgue itself made me feel slightly faint. Plus the sight of Patrick surrounded by several gurneyed bodies and one lying right there on the table, chest splayed.

He offered me a hot drink and suggested I sit down. It became a feature of subsequent visits: we'd sit and chat while the body I'd come down to check lay waiting. Patrick seemed completely unaffected by the banal juxtaposition of life and death and I contrived to appear blasé in order not to give offence. He asked me about life on the wards, questioned me about internal affairs, so that I formed an impression of him leading a hermetic existence down here in the bowels of the hospital. I wondered whether he was frightened to come up and mingle with the rest of the staff and the patients. Did he worry that he would somehow taint them by his mere presence? I doubt it.

In his late thirties or early forties with thin sandy hair and somewhat old-fashioned imitation hornrims, Patrick wore a grey coat not unlike a village grocer's. There were unpleasant stains on it. I tried not to think of Patrick as a lower form of life just because he worked in the morgue; there is a tendency among doctors to think like this. The mortuary attendants are rarely great socialisers, not known for their interpersonal skills, and you can understand why. Patrick was also an only child. Our conversations covered some diverse areas after a while. I examined my motives for continuing to go down there after it became clear that Patrick was attracted to me.

I was not short of the attentions of men. There were one or two half-hearted suitors stumbling about the foothills of possible courtships. Had I been especially interested in either of them, I would have given some encouragement where appropriate. At the hospital there was another doctor, a senior registrar like me although in a completely different department, who had asked me out a couple of times. Had he pressed just a little harder, showed a tiny bit more resolve, we could have been a few months into some kind of relationship. But he, like the fellow outside work, seemed weak. Possibly they were even a little frightened of me, which is silly really, when you know me. I'm a pussy cat. I rather like to be dominated.

Patrick, too, was shy. Some of his shyness I put down to the difference in our status and Patrick's acute sense of that. Some of it was natural reserve, not unexpected in a man with his social contacts. He wasn't the sort of man who needed an address book. Lots of cards with names on, not many telephone numbers. But his very persistence in the face of such odds charmed me. I could see him trying to reach me, slowly over a period of months. The sound of his voice on the phone – 'Would you like to come down and do a part two?' – brightened up the odd afternoon. As I said, I could use the ash cash, and at £33 for a once-over and a signature, it was easy money.

Even his gaffe, when he boasted about downloading pictures of double amputees, failed to put me off. Mainly because it came only a couple of minutes after I saw his eyes blaze with life for the first time since I had been going down there. Just as I was preparing to sit down, my heel slipped in something wet on the floor, causing me to teeter spectacularly for a moment, bent double in front of Patrick. I know from seeing myself in the mirror how much of my cleavage would have been revealed to him at that moment. In fact, I knew from the look on his face just how much was revealed. Pretty much everything. My life used to be punctuated with promises to myself that I would visit Rigby & Peller and get measured up for a fitted bra, but I never quite got round to it, and most of my bras had been ill fitting since I put on a bit of weight after giving up smoking to celebrate getting my first house job.

Patrick looked away, but I had seen the flare of excitement in his eyes, confirming my suspicions. The body I had gone down to check was that of an amputee and I think Patrick was only searching for a way out of his embarrassment when he joked about my balance being worse than hers, and then sought to make amends by talking about the pictures you could download from the Internet.

It was just a couple of days later, when I was next down in the morgue doing a part two, that Patrick asked me whether I would go for a drink with him after work – a real drink out in the real world. Yes, I said, why not.

In the pub we sat in a far corner away from other drinkers. Patrick had never told me anything about his domestic situation, past or present, and I never asked. Looking down at my hands, which were folded on the table in front of me, he told me I was a beautiful woman. A very beautiful woman. In an attempt to cover his nerves, he immediately raised his pint glass. I took his other hand in mine and squeezed it. Awkwardly he swallowed a mouthful of beer, spilling a thin trickle out of the corner of his mouth, and set his glass down. I caught his left knee between my two legs beneath the table and pressed them together. Then I released his leg, swept a beer mat on to the floor and bent down to pick it up. I did this as slowly as I could, even checking for myself that he had a good view, and when I returned to an upright position he was flushed and smiling.

We took a cab to my flat and, for the next seven hours, had sex, made love, whatever – virtually non-stop. In the early hours of the morning, returning from a visit to the kitchen for more orange juice, I teased him about his references to the amputee pictures and clasped my hands behind my back, dropping to my knees on the bedside rug. He leapt out of bed, his engorged cock bouncing comically, and fucked me right there on the rug. I played along by not using my hands. My faked helplessness clearly excited him more than anything.

It was not long before we were experimenting with bondage – ties and dressing-gown cords and leather belts. Patrick was curious about the hook in the living-room ceiling. The flat's previous owner had had it inserted into the steel joist when he needed to get his piano in through the window, so the estate agent had told me. For the next three weeks we slept together four or five nights a week, invariably at my flat. We were always either having sex or going to work shortly after having had sex; half the time I was light headed and completely scatty. I wasn't in love, I knew that, but I was in lust. I caught myself wondering once or twice whether what we were doing was wise, given… well, everything. But I swept these thoughts aside. Looking back now, I realise there was an undercurrent of anxiety, which I wouldn't acknowledge at the time. I gently resisted Patrick's moves to tie me more and more tightly each time, but I never resisted them firmly enough. I gave off all the wrong signals and he perceived nothing but encouragement.

When he produced a length of sturdy rope I grew agitated.

'I don't think so,' I said when he pointed to the hook in the ceiling.

He dropped the rope and unzipped his fly, taking out his cock, and began to masturbate. I could never watch him doing this without wanting to do it for him, so I knelt down in front of him and took him in my mouth. He bent down and pulled my top up over my head then slipped the straps of my bra off my shoulders. I reached back and undid the catch. He placed his warm palm over my left breast and gently squeezed the nipple. I continued with long strokes up and down, up and down. Reaching around with one arm – Patrick had developed some muscles down in the morgue – he picked me up and laid me on the bed.

After we had both come, we lay side by side, looking out of the bedroom, across the landing, at the hook in the living-room ceiling.

'Please,' he urged one final time, and I just shrugged.

The boyish excitement he displayed as he trussed me up was endearing.

'Trust me,' he said.

He was careful tying the rope to the hook and let go of me only once he was sure it was going to take my weight.

Maybe it was being upside down that completed the change in the way I saw things. Patrick sat in the corner of the room masturbating while I swung gently from side to side unable to move my arms or legs, a double amputee. He just watched and wanked, which I decided was not on. I wasn't happy. I no longer did trust him.

So later, after Patrick had let me down and I had said I wanted to spend the night alone, and I found the Christmas card on the mat in the corridor, I called Ben and we chatted. He asked me out for a drink and I thought I could probably do with a reality check, so I accepted.

3

The incident with the hook changed everything. Chloë told me she didn't want me to come to the flat any more. She sounded as if she meant it. I thought she might cry, but she didn't. At least, not on the phone.

Nor did she want to do any more part twos, she said.

I tried to talk to her, but she wouldn't discuss it.

Most of the ash cash now went to a senior reg in A&E, a rosy-cheeked rugger type called Bryan Demeter. I didn't offer to make him any tea and the part twos were ticked off and signed for as fast as the undertakers could wheel them away.

I took up smoking. I heard that Chloë applied for a consultant's job in Aberdeen. I tried to contact her but she was always in a meeting. I could have gone upstairs to look for her myself, but I didn't. The nearest I got was the first staircase. There was a door at the foot of the stairs to which I had a key. It led out to the bottom of an interior well in the great old building, with blue sky at the top. I went there for a cigarette, as smoking was forbidden in the mortuary. I craned my neck and stared at the upper floors. Somewhere up there was Chloë. I wondered sometimes whether I would ever see her again.

About sixty feet up was a swath of safety netting stretching right across the well. I noticed a bird that had got its feet entangled in the netting and been unable to escape. It had died there, starved of food and water, hanging upside down by its feet.

I dropped my cigarette on the ground and extinguished it with my toe, then locked the door behind me and went back down to my bodies. Among them was a young woman who had been brought down from A&E that morning. Bryan Demeter had done the part one and told me about her; I don't know what made him think I would be interested. Her name was Caroline and she had been viciously beaten about the head with one of her own Philippe Starck dining chairs. Scrawled across her dressing-table mirror in red lipstick were the words 'Fuck the middle classes'. Detectives found the lipstick at the rented flat of her boyfriend, Graham. He went quietly, apparently.

THE PERFORMANCE

You could do as much or as little as you liked. That was the appeal of the place. Activities were laid on for those who wished to join in, but there was no pressure on those who did not. Thus, a stressed-out pharmaceuticals executive who wanted to spend his week's holiday reading trash novels could do so while his wife attended aerobics classes and perhaps took out a small boat when the wind freshened after lunch. Their children, meanwhile, would be looked after by a fleet of highly qualified nannies and nursery workers.

The set-up suited comfortably-off hard-working couples who needed time to unwind and found the rigours of childcare incompatible with relaxation. But the resort was also popular with childless couples, who appreciated the fact that other people's kids were kept out of the way. Whether you've been unable to reproduce, or simply chosen not to, other people's children are rarely ideal company.

The day of the performance began like any other.

The sun rose around 6.30 a.m, although most residents didn't become aware of it until a couple of hours later. Breakfast was taken outside. A hundred tables in a grid, all laid with starched white linen, filling the space between kitchens and pool. There was a canopy that could be pulled across when it rained, which it did infrequently but spectacularly, accompanied by an electrical storm. The first meal of the day was a leisurely business for all except those intent on waterskiing, which kicked off early.

My wife and I chose a table close to the pool and Eleanor watched the peaceful undulations of the water's surface while a beautiful young waitress brought us coffee, croissants and fruit.

I sat with my back to the pool and observed the steady influx. I saw the Television Actor and his wife pick a table in the shade. I had lost count of how many days we had been at the resort – we had entered that phase of any holiday when time becomes meaningless – but it was long enough to have put names to a lot of faces. Fictitious ones, of course, since we hadn't actually met and spoken to anybody apart from exchanging the briefest of pleasantries. The Television Actor bore a resemblance to a rising small-screen star married to a slightly more famous film actress. He enjoyed the same kind of prematurely greying good looks and gently expressive features, defaulting to an amused half-smile. His wife was not particularly attractive and compounded the misfortune by wearing garishly mismatched combinations – a floaty dress over home-made cut-offs, a Hawaiian shirt with floral-print shorts – but husband and wife seemed comfortable in each other's company.

At the table next to our own, the Reading Man and his wife sat down. The Reading Man had started the holiday promisingly with a fêted literary thriller by a young Scottish woman writer, but as the week had progressed, his books had become progressively trashier and correspondingly thicker. Still, though, he appeared with a different one each morning. I read the name on the cover. A successful British crime writer, if not one I had ever read. The Reading Man was already a good thirty pages in. His wife stared beyond the pool at the haze over the mirror-smooth turquoise sea. The slightest of muscular spasms betrayed her impatience, which failed to register with her husband. Printed on the sleeve of the Reading Man's T-shirt was the web address of a pharmaceuticals business, almost certainly his own.

The resort was exclusive, prohibitively expensive, and it was safe to assume the logos and URLs on the polo shirts and baseball caps of most of the middle-aged male residents were advertising their own companies. Any labels on their wives' clothes bore the names of top designers.

The Queen Bee ('B for bitch,' Eleanor had said on the first evening) entered with her three daughters, their father tagging along behind. The Queen Bee was a statuesque blonde in her mid-forties who always dressed and made herself up with extreme care. Her daughters ranged between fourteen and eighteen. She smiled rarely, presumably to discourage the development of facial lines, yet every day she occupied a sunlounger by the pool from the moment breakfast was finished until either the sky clouded over or lunchtime arrived, whichever came sooner. Her daughters arranged their long, lithe bodies around her, similarly stretchered under the fierce sun, while their father sat at a table in the bar area, smoking cigarettes and studying the pictures in a magazine devoted to walking shoes and climbing boots.

We had noticed the Queen Bee leaving the plane on landing at the nearby international airport surrounded by her family, and then again on the evening of our arrival at the resort. Once we had unpacked, we had come down to the bar and ordered cocktails. Like everyone else, we turned our chairs to face the sea, as if awaiting the start of some kind of spectacle. The Queen Bee appeared with her youngest daughter. They passed swiftly through the bar on their way to the hotel reception, mother's brisk stride requiring daughter to trot alongside. Her face a mask of annoyance, the Queen Bee was berating her daughter, too angry to lower her voice for propriety's sake. The snatch we heard was Dopplered like a police siren: '...ruined my holiday before it's even begun...'

Once breakfast was over, my wife took a beach bag over towards the lines of loungers and sun umbrellas that ran parallel with the water's edge and what passed for a high-tide mark. I was intending to go for a walk as far as the perimeter fence at the far end of the beach. First I helped myself to a second cup of coffee and watched as Eleanor made her way slowly across the beach, looking around her at residents who were staking out their territory for the morning. The light poured through the sarong she wore wrapped around her waist allowing me – and anyone else who might be looking – to appreciate the length and deceptive youthfulness of her legs.

When Eleanor had passed out of sight, I drained my coffee cup and collected my baseball cap and key. I would go back up to the room before heading out. Walking between the tables, I was surprised to see the Crossword Man sitting alone on the edge of the grid and altered my route to pass directly by him. Head down, silver pen gripped in meaty right hand, he was solving a big puzzle in a paperback book full of them.

The Crossword Man was another, like the Queen Bee, whom we had noticed before the holiday had even begun. At Heathrow Airport, he had been ahead of us in the queue to check in. The flight was delayed, we had read from the monitors, but the Crossword Man – then, of course, we had not yet given him the name – appeared neither to speak nor read English, and he was trying to make sense of the check-in clerk, who merely turned up the volume and slowed down her delivery as she repeated herself: 'The flight is delayed by two hours. If you take this voucher to any of the restaurants in the departure lounge, you can get a complimentary breakfast.'

The Crossword Man was drawing attention to himself. First by his stubborn refusal to leave the check-in desk until he understood what was being said, and second by his dress. In spite of the early start and the somewhat chilly temperatures for late April, he had elected to travel in his holiday clothes, an orange-and-white Hawaiian shirt and beige shorts that were a size too small. Snorting and shrugging in typically Gallic fashion, he kept saying, '*Je comprends pas, je comprends rien*,' looking around for support.

In schoolboy French, I did my best to put him in the picture. Placated, he wandered off to claim his complimentary *petit déjeuner*.

I was surprised to see him still working at his crossword, because usually by this time he was to be seen walking in the sea. Twice a day, straight after breakfast and just before dinner, he would walk, chest deep, in the sea in a straight line parallel to the shore. He would start at one end of the resort and make his way to the other, a distance of about half a mile, and then come back.

As I passed by his table on the edge of the grid, I took a sly look at a creased manilla envelope that lay on the table next to his crossword book. It seemed that he may have been using the envelope to protect the book. Perhaps it was the very envelope in which the volume had been sent to him. I was able to read the name and part of the address: M. Jean-Daniel Lang, 1020 Bruxelles.

Upstairs in our room, I stripped off and took a shower. I stood in front of the full-length mirror inspecting my body with a critical eye. The hair on my chest was turning a little grey. I was thickening around the middle. Some of the male residents with whom I had played beach volleyball were completely relaxed about removing their T-shirts and exposing the evidence of their high living. I wasn't doing too badly myself, but I would remain covered up. Wrapping a towel around me, I walked through the bedroom to the balcony overlooking the sea. Because of the trees in the foreground, I couldn't see Eleanor, but I did spot the Crossword Man – or Jean-Daniel Lang, as I would now have to call him – pushing his bulk through the water. Because he walked where it was deep, right on the edge of the shelf just before it fell away into the dark, he encountered a considerable amount of resistance. His habitual activity provided him with vigorous exercise.

I didn't see Eleanor until lunch. She had dozed in the morning, she told me. I told her I hoped she had used the sun cream.

'Where did you get to?' she asked me.

'I walked down the beach,' I said, pointing. 'There are some rooms down there, as you know, but beyond that there's a patch of scrub and then a chain-link fence. I followed that down to the beach where you climb up a rocky incline, and guess what you see when you get to the top?'

'What do you see?' asked Eleanor, as she signalled to a waiter that he should bring us a bottle of wine.

'There's a little inlet, with a small boat tied up, and then the beach continues for a mile or so until those mountains you can see at the end of the bay. On the beach in the distance I saw some locals.'

'So real people do live here, then?'

We had seen little sign of them on the bus ride from the airport.

'They were too far away for me to see them in any detail. It was very strange. It reminded me of eastern Europe, seeing people going about their lives on the other side of the frontier, as if…as if…'

'As if what?'

'I don't know. As if they lived normal lives just like us.'

Eleanor gave a sharp laugh as she poured two glasses of wine.

'The Reading Man,' she said, as she stood the bottle, streaming with condensation, in the middle of the table.

I turned around slowly. The Reading Man and his wife were three tables away. She was staring at a point over his head, while he remained oblivious, his nose buried in his book, which he was now more than a third of the way through.

'I saw the Queen Bee,' said Eleanor. 'She and her daughters occupied the umbrella next to mine this morning.'

'I thought you were asleep,' I reminded her.

'Not all the time.'

We went and got our starters from the buffet, our plates piled high with cold meats and chunky beetroot. The food was all paid for in advance and we would leave at least half of it. As we returned to our table we passed Jean-Daniel Lang, whose book was folded open at a new puzzle next to his plate.

'Why does a single Frenchman come here?' Eleanor asked once we were sitting down. 'He doesn't seeem to know anyone, or make any effort to get to know anyone. I mean, why doesn't he go to a resort run by a French company?'

'He's Belgian, darling,' I said. 'Not that that answers your question, but he is Belgian and his name is Jean-Daniel Lang. He lives in Brussels.'

'I see.' Eleanor's smile told me she believed I was still playing the game, inventing an identity for the Crossword Man.

'He's a widower,' I went on. 'He used to come here with his wife, who was English. They lived in Crawley. After she died he moved back to Brussels, but carried on coming here. He solves crosswords because…well, because he can.'

'So he's not a paedophile, then, come to ogle the adolescents?'

'Absolutely not. The only time he looks up from his crossword book is when he's walking in the sea.'

'Darling, if he had been married to an Englishwoman and living in Crawley,' Eleanor argued after a few moments' pause, 'wouldn't he be able to speak pretty good English? Especially given his love of language.'

'His English is quite good actually,' I said. 'He was just pretending at Heathrow. Winding the woman up. He understood perfectly well what was going on.'

Eleanor didn't bother to reply. I could see that she was bored. I was bored as well. Everyone was bored. Perhaps that was the point. She pushed her plate away and poured herself another glass of wine. I waited for a moment after she had put the bottle down before picking it up and filling my own glass. If she noticed, she gave no sign.

'What will you do this afternoon, darling?' I asked.

'I don't know, darling. Doze? Read?'

At home, if we called each other 'darling', the word would be loaded, the delivery making it clear that irony was in play. Here, it became reflexive. Part of the routine. As much a function of habit as wearing flip-flops around the pool, or dressing up for dinner.

At the front of the resort, away from the sea, there was a court for *boules* or *pétanque*. On my way back to our room after lunch, I heard a metallic click followed by a deep, theatrical groan, and turned to look out of the open window. Two floors below, Jean-Daniel Lang was playing *boules* with Michel, the lone Frenchman on the resort staff, a student on his gap year. Michel's ball appeared to have struck one of Jean-Daniel's, knocking it aside and sidling up to the *cochonnet*. Jean-Daniel protested good-naturedly as he threw a decent final ball, then ambled up the side of the court to inspect his position. I watched Michel take aim, then dispatch his own last ball with a wayward flick of the wrist, sending it right to the end of the court. Jean-Daniel seemed pleased and stepped inside the court to measure the relative distances of his own nearest ball and that of Michel's.

The distances were similar, although it was clear from my vantage point that Michel's was very slightly closer, but I noticed Jean-Daniel shrug as he compared them on the ground. Michel pointed to his own ball and shook his head, kicking it away with his deck shoe. Jean-Daniel looked satisfied as he rounded up his *boules*.

Michel explained that he was on beach duty and Jean-Daniel nodded. The two shook hands and parted. I went to our room, where I changed into my swimming shorts, thinking that I would divide the afternoon between the pool and the beach.

Residents began taking their seats in the bar area soon after six. Eleanor and I had not seen each other since lunch, despite my having spent half the afternoon on the beach. Our paths had not crossed. Having been up to the room to change into a linen suit and open-neck shirt, I chose a chair in the bar and pulled up another one next to it. Both were facing the beach. I angled mine so that I could watch the bar as well as enjoying the view. When Eleanor finally appeared – long after the Reading Man and his wife, the Television Actor and a new character, the Emeritus Professor, who affected a straw panama and smoked thin cigars – I watched her looking around the bar, her gaze skating over me three times before she spotted me.

'Didn't you recognise me?' I asked as she settled into the chair alongside mine.

'After a while everyone begins to look the same,' she said.

'Good afternoon?' I asked.

'Relaxing. You?'

'I swam.'

'All afternoon?'

'Not all afternoon.'

'Did you read?' she asked.

'No, I feel somehow let off the hook by the Reading Man. As if he's reading for all of us.'

'How's he getting on?'

'He's just there.'

He was sitting a few chairs along, reading a surprisingly thin book, about the size of a theatre programme. His wife sat straight backed, staring out to sea and cooling herself with a fan improvised from two or three postcards that she must have bought from the hotel shop.

'Maybe he finished his book for today and didn't want to start another big one until tomorrow?' I suggested.

'The Queen Bee has surpassed even her own high standards,'

Eleanor said, looking over at the bar, where the blonde mother-of-three was leaning on one leg to pick up a drinks order from the bar, accentuating the transparency of her dress, which was pulled revealingly taut over her impressive behind.

'Now that's how to wear a thong,' remarked Eleanor.

The Queen Bee carried her tray of cocktails towards the lines of chairs facing the beach. Her husband, who I now knew was called Stewart since we had shared a beach volleyball court in the afternoon, put down a pair of binoculars with which he had been scanning the horizon, and took the tray. The girls helped themselves to their drinks, smiling over the little umbrellas and pieces of spiked fruit.

I looked beyond them towards the beach. Some clouds had formed, running across the top of the sky where they gathered the deep velvet oranges and russet pinks of the impending sunset, and trailing faint skirts either side of the main part of the beach. Following one of these wispy drapes of cloud down to the sea, I saw Jean-Daniel Lang already chest deep in the water, walking in a straight line parallel with the shore.

His chest angled slightly one way, then the other, he forced his bulk step by step through the deep water. A hush fell across the rows of hotel guests sitting facing the sea. I watched the Television Actor lean over to accept a nut from the outstretched hand of his wife, without either of them taking their eyes off the Crossword Man. The remaining free seats were quickly taken as residents stepped away from the bar, drinks in hand. The distance between the line he was walking and the rows of seats in which we were all sitting was perhaps as much as fifty metres, so I wasn't sure whether I could make out the expression on his face. I wasn't even sure whether there was one. I would have said that he looked the same as usual: impassive, unselfconscious, even self-involved. He must have been concentrating on the mechanics of his sea walk, taking care over the placing of his feet.

He was just over halfway past the main part of the beach, where small waves lapped on to a slight rise in the level of the sand, creating the impression of a proscenium, when he stumbled. Aware of a collective intake of breath, I waited for Jean-Daniel to right himself and continue, but he had lost his footing and obviously failed to make contact with the sandy bottom. He began slowly to topple, his arms wheeling, grasping at air, then to subside. He was falling seawards. Maybe at first his left foot had still been touching bottom, but he seemed now to have lost even that tenuous contact.

'Can't he swim?' whispered a voice in the row behind me.

'Apparently not,' came a hissed reply. 'That's why he walks in the sea. He likes going in the water, but he can't swim.'

Lang's head disappeared under the water and I sensed the audience around me sit up even straighter in their seats. The Queen Bee reached out and took her husband's binoculars, which she trained on Lang. His head appeared above the surface, and, despite the distance, we could now all see the look on his face. It was one of surprise. And then it was gone again. A gentle swell washed over him and this time he didn't come bobbing back up.

We waited. And waited. But the sea had closed over his head and was not about to give him up. He had gone.

There was a moment of absolute silence, then the first clap was heard. A woman in the second row stood up as she applauded. Within a few seconds, the people around her started to join in, clapping and, in some cases, getting to their feet. I saw the Television Actor and his wife stand up together, clapping furiously, their faces wreathed in smiles.

'Bravo! Bravo!' shouted the Emeritus Professor as he, too, rose to his feet.

The Reading Man, his books forgotten for once, was showing his appreciation. Even his wife was standing and contributing to the applause, the tension flowing out of her facial muscles, allowing her to grin.

I turned to look at Eleanor, and found myself looking at her waist, because she too had jumped up to applaud.

Slowly, I rose and followed suit. I glanced at Eleanor, who smiled at me with unrestrained joy.

ACKNOWLEDGEMENTS

Dan Crowe published 'The Rainbow' in *Butterfly* (he now edits *Zembla*). 'Dotted Line' was published on the website of Manchester band Performance after Joe Stretch, the band's lead singer and lyricist, suggested I write a story under the same title as their first single. David Pringle, when he was editor of *Interzone*, published 'The Cast', 'Flying into Naples' and 'Negatives'. 'Christmas Bonus' was commissioned by *Time Out* when Christopher Hemblade was acting editor. Joel Lane and Steve Bishop published 'The Inland Waterways Association' in the Tindal Street Press anthology *Birmingham Noir*. Thanks to Charlotte Mullins, former editor of *Art Review*.

Samantha Hardingham introduced me to David Rosen and asked me to write a story about him and his work; 'The Space–Time Discontinuum' appeared in *Experiments in Architecture* (August Projects). Thanks to Sveva Ricciardi and Flavia Allongi for 'Flying into Naples'. Chris Newman and Julie Royle helped directly with the research for 'The Churring', which was written specially for this collection, while Michael Marshall Smith and Brian Howell helped indirectly on 'Negatives', in that they also worked in the office featured in the story (and both subsequently wrote stories set there). 'The Madwoman' was written for the third and final Barrington Books anthology, *The Science of Sadness*, edited by Christopher Kenworthy, who ran the influential imprint for three years in the early 1990s. 'Kingyo no fun' was published in *Love in Vein II* (HarperPrism), edited by Poppy Z. Brite. Thanks to Fanny Blake, Feico Deutekom, Liz Jensen and Will Self. 'Nine Years' was published online, in *Circuit Traces*, in 1995.

'The Comfort of Stranglers' was published in *Dark*

Terrors 2 (Victor Gollancz) edited by Stephen Jones and David Sutton. Special thanks to Chris Kenworthy, Conrad Williams and Tim Nickels. Thanks to Susannah Hickling and Alice Egorova for 'Buxton, Texas', which was published in *AbeSea* magazine, a large-format 'visual paper' edited and published by the artist Sebastian Boyle. Elaine Palmer published 'City of Fusion' in *Technopagan*, one of a series of anthologies published by Pulp Faction. 'Avenue E' was commissioned by Boyd Tonkin for the *Independent*, to run as the opening piece in their travel section on 1 January 2000. 'Skin Deep' was first published by Ellen Datlow in *Twists of the Tale* (Dell). Thanks to Ian Cunningham. 'Auteur' was published in *Ambit*, which is edited by Martin Bax, assisted by Kate Pemberton.

Serpent's Tail have been great supporters of the short story. 'Trussed' was published in one of their anthologies, *Sex, Drugs, Rock 'n' Roll*, edited by Sarah LeFanu. 'The Performance' appeared in issue four of *Matter*, edited by Em Brett and Lily Dunn.

Grateful acknowledgements are due to Stephen Jones, Ramsey Campbell, Karl Edward Wagner, Ellen Datlow, Terri Windling, Jill Adams, Helene Nowell, Maxim Jakubowski, Keith Brooke and Rick Cadger, the editors of certain anthologies, magazines and websites where some of these stories were reprinted.

Thanks to Pete Ayrton, John Williams, Lisa Gooding, Martin Worthington, Rebecca Gray, Ruthie Petrie, Alastair Mucklow and Jenny Boyce at Serpent's Tail. Thanks also to John Saddler, Peter Crowther and Kealan Patrick Burke, and to Mike Harrison, Gareth Evans, Joel Lane, Mark Morris and Rhonda Carrier. Special thanks to Kate, Mum, Julie, Jo, Simon, Charlie and Bella.